Praise for *Kissing in America*

An ALA *Booklist* Best Fiction for Young Adults Book
An Amazon Best Book of the Month
A Junior Library Guild Selection
An Amelia Bloomer Book List Selection
A New York Public Library Best Book for Teens
A Chicago Public Library Best Teen Fiction Book
An *O Magazine* Summer Reading List Selection
A TAYSHAS High School Reading List Selection

"Margo Rabb writes with compassion and clarity about lives that are worth telling, journeys that need to be taken, peace that needs to be reached. I loved it." —ELIZABETH GILBERT,
New York Times bestselling author of *Eat, Pray, Love*

"Wonderful. Margo Rabb has created nothing less than a women's map of American mythologies." —E. LOCKHART,
New York Times bestselling author of *We Were Liars*

"That Margo Rabb can write a story so gorgeous, funny, and joyous that is also unsentimental and honest is a testament to her skill and to her heart." —SARA ZARR,
author of *Story of a Girl*, a National Book Award finalist

"It is a marvel and I love every word of it. Funny, sad, wistful, wise, and altogether memorable." —MICHAEL CART,
past president of YALSA

"Rabb's funny and big-hearted second novel is bursting with resonant themes of love, death, family, art, and identity, fully embodied in a diverse cast of wonderfully fallible and entertaining characters."
—*NEW YORK TIMES BOOK REVIEW*

"This feminist rom-com reminds us it's never about the boy but the joyride." —*O Magazine*

"Wise, inspiring, and ultimately uplifting—not to be missed." —*Kirkus Reviews* (starred review)

"Rabb knows the perfect point to interject humor to diffuse a potentially devastating situation—a leavening of sorts to the reality that death and love inexplicitly alter the landscape of a person's life." —ALA *Booklist* (starred review)

"This story makes for a hilarious, thought-provoking, wrenching, and joyful quest." —*Publishers Weekly* (starred review)

"A well-balanced read that exposes readers to weighty ideas and difficult feelings while keeping them entertained and emotionally invested." —*BCCB* (starred review)

Praise for *Cures for Heartbreak*

A *Kirkus Reviews* Best Book for Young Adults
An ALA *Booklist* Editors' Choice
A Book Sense Children's Pick
An Association of Jewish Libraries Notable Book
A New York Public Library Book for the Teen Age
A TAYSHAS High School Reading List Selection
A Capitol Choices Noteworthy Book

"A sad, funny, smart, endlessly poignant novel. It made me feel grateful for my life, for my family, and above all for the world that brings us gifts like the gift of Margo Rabb."

—MICHAEL CHABON,
Pulitzer Prize–winning author of *The Amazing Adventures of Kavalier & Clay*

"Margo Rabb's story beautifully brings together the intensely personal and the historical, and rings with the authenticity of a bitter yet illuminating truth."   —JOYCE CAROL OATES

"*Cures for Heartbreak* is full of sadness, humor, and quirky details that ring completely true. I thoroughly enjoyed it."

—CURTIS SITTENFELD,
New York Times bestselling author of *Prep* and *American Wife*

"Black humor, pitch-perfect detail, and compelling characters make this a terrific read."   —*SLJ* (starred review)

"Rabb leavens impossible heartbreak with surprising humor, delivered with a comedian's timing and dark absurdity. Readers will cherish this powerful debut."   —ALA *BOOKLIST* (starred review)

"A compelling as well as tearful read."   —*BCCB* (starred review)

"When the last page turns, four new and fascinating people have been born into the reader's consciousness."   —*KLIATT* (starred review)

ALSO BY MARGO RABB

Kissing in America

Cures for Heartbreak

Lucy Clark Will Not Apologize

Margo Rabb

Quill Tree Books
An Imprint of HarperCollins Publishers

Quill Tree Books is an imprint of HarperCollins Publishers.

Brief excerpts of this novel were originally published in the *New York Times* in different form under the title "Garden of Solace" in October 2019.

Library of Congress Control Number: 2020952903
ISBN 978-0-06-232240-1

Typography by Laura Mock
21 22 23 24 25   PC/LSCH   10 9 8 7 6 5 4 3 2 1
❖
First Edition

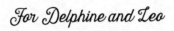

For Delphine and Leo

There are always flowers for those who want to see them.

—HENRI MATISSE

LUCY CLARK WILL NOT APOLOGIZE

part i

NOT IN WONDERLAND

These pains that you feel are messengers.
Listen to them.
—Rumi

one

PANCAKES FROM HELL

Once upon a time, in a girls' boarding school in Texas—long before I needed to stop a murder—it was Pancake Day.

On Pancake Day, everyone lost their freaking minds.

At Thornton Academy, a pancake-like object existed on the regular menu, but it wasn't actually a pancake. It tasted like glue sticks mixed with cinder blocks. Flo, our school chef, had to follow strict rules from our headmistress on what and how to cook; once a year, when the headmistress left for her Stars of Educational Leadership conference, Flo made whatever she liked.

RECIPE: Non-Pancakes
(Official version approved by headmistress)
Serves 150

8 pounds oat flour
2 pounds bulgur
5 cups egg substitute
Ineffectual amount of baking soda
75 squirts butter-flavored cooking spray
Heaping cup of despair

RECIPE: Once-a-Year-on-Pancake-Day-Real-Pancakes
(Courtesy of Flo's mother)
Serves 150

10 pounds white flour
4 beautiful cups white sugar
1 cup baking powder
Shocking amount of real butter, eggs, salt, and buttermilk
Large sprinkle of hope

My kitchen duty job today was to deliver the pancakes to the inmates.

I dropped off a stack at the closest table, where the first years sat. They were known as the Ducklings; they were fuzzy and innocent and gobbled their pancakes with endless glasses of creamy milk. I was a grizzled fifth year, a junior—I'd been at Thornton long enough to have my soul crushed.

I delivered pancakes to the tables of other girls, and turned to face the seniors.

I know dropping off breakfast platters shouldn't be a big deal. But dozens of eyeballs stared at me like I was a lonely tree and they were lumberjacks, their faces dancing with visions of firewood and newspaper and Tinkertoys.

Kitchen duty wasn't so bad when my best friend, Dyna, did it with me—every student at Thornton had a job, and this was ours—but her father had pulled her out of school a month ago, after the Incident. Since she left, it felt like someone had opened my chest and scooped out my lungs and ribs. I pictured my insides like a hole dug in the ground, with feathery white roots hanging loose, with nothing to grip. I wasn't myself anymore—I wanted to get back to being myself, but who was that? I wanted to be a person without a hole inside her.

I glanced at the back of the cafeteria, at the longest and widest table, where Thing One and Thing Two sat with their fellow seniors. I dropped the pancakes off at their table without breathing, and moved away as fast as I could. I kept walking.

Something hit me in the back of my neck. Moist, slimy, and warm against my hair.

I peeled it off. Pancake bits and syrup stuck to my hand.

"Excited about tomorrow?" Thing One shouted across the room. "Your special day?"

5

Tomorrow was April thirteenth. A month ago, I'd received a letter:

THE WILLA THORNTON ACADEMY FOR THE YOUNG WOMEN OF TOMORROW

Educating and Improving Every Girl's Mind, Body, and Soul to Better the World

1400 Grackle Boulevard, Austin, TX

WARNING OF POSSIBLE SUSPENSION

This letter shall serve as official notice that Lucy Clark is under consideration for suspension from The Willa Thornton Academy for an extended period, due to the unfortunate incident on March 4 and her struggles to obey the school rules and meet the standards of this community. A final evaluation by the Headmistress will take place on April 13, and, if suspension is deemed appropriate, the terms will be given on that day.

Warmly,

Beverly Leery
Headmistress

Ms. Leery signed all her official letters "Warmly." Dyna usually scribbled next to Ms. Leery's "Warmly":

Warmly, with toads
Warmly, with pure hatred

Warmly, wishing you death by fire or another demise that is especially painful

I wanted to leave the school—somewhere, anywhere would be better than this place—but when I thought of how my parents would react if I got suspended, my blood thickened, clogging my body, and I could barely breathe.

After the Incident, on our video chat, my parents' shocked eyes had widened into full moons, as if they'd discovered that I was made of green putrefied alien flesh. "We didn't think you were the kind of person who'd do that," they'd said. "We're just so disappointed." The disappointment flowed out of their eyes as the love disappeared, and a distant sadness froze their features. A glacier of lost hope and faith in me, their eyes squinting as if they were trying to reconcile the daughter who screwed up with the daughter they hoped I would be.

I returned to the kitchen. Flo saw my face. "You don't look so good. Here. Eat this." She opened up the bin marked "Chia Seeds," which held her secret stash of emergency chocolate, and gave me a Kit Kat bar from Japan. She collected chocolate from all over the world.

Outside the kitchen, in the dining hall, everything had begun to deteriorate. The Ducklings had overstuffed themselves till their stomachs hurt and were being herded to the nurse; the Things and their henchwomen had squashed their pancakes into balls and thrown them at the ceiling, the lamps, and the "Choose Kindness" posters on the wall.

The bell rang for first period. Time for art.

"Take more chocolate," Flo said. She gave me an English Caramello and a Twirl. "Eat them today or keep them well hidden."

Thornton had a strict policy on candy: if you were caught eating it anywhere on the premises, your body would be sliced into pieces and fed to wild boars.

I stuck the bars in my pockets and walked to art, my favorite class, down the hall and past the Things, who smiled and whispered, "Tomorrow will be the day that you die."

The art room floated above the school on the top floor of the main building, with huge windows and treetops swaying outside. It was a sanctuary. It was also a total mess.

The room was filled with jars of paint and giant purple yoga balls to sit on, and a teacher, Mrs. Fell, who was legally blind and hard of hearing. Every day, she set out a bowl of wax fruit from approximately 1920 covered with dust as thick as squirrel fur, and then we ignored the fruit and drew whatever we liked— one girl drew her little brother with boogers coming out of his nose, and some people drew flying hippopotamuses, and one girl even drew a porno with naked bodies twisted like fusilli— and Mrs. Fell would nod at all of it and say, "Lovely, dears."

My drawings fell into the flying hippopotamus category. I'd been working on the same one every day for three weeks. Narwhal cats floating in the sky among thunderclouds, with Thing-like warthogs drowning in a lava sea. A blobfish, too, which resembled Ms. Leery. Today I added highlights to the blobfish's pus-oozing sores. I'd been learning cross-hatching from books that Uriah, our school librarian—he was Mrs. Fell's grandson—had gotten for me through interlibrary loan. It took hours to draw by making the tiny little lines in pencil, then black pen, but I loved it, while Mrs. Fell played oldies music and napped in her chair.

Ms. Leery never visited the art room—she viewed clutter and weirdness like a contagious disease. She thought mess was one of the worst things you could do, or make, or be. Mess was failure. *At Thornton we pride ourselves on teaching our girls the importance of tidiness and immaculate self-care.* The art room was the only cluttered place in our school.

As I drew tiny scabs on the blobfish's sores, I thought of how, soon after I'd arrived at Thornton as a first year, Ms. Leery had started commenting on my appearance. "Our presentation to the world matters, Miss Clark. Hygiene. Outside a mess, inside a mess. When your parents next see you, we want there to be less of you to see." She'd gazed at my stomach.

I finished drawing one scab and started another, and then a noise echoed down the hall. Everyone looked up from their work.

A heavy tap-clumping sound. Coming toward us.

Tap-clump. Tap-clump. It sounded like the clunk of Ms. Leery's thick heels.

Coming closer.

The porno artist girl peeked out the door window and said, "Shit!"

Everyone froze on their yoga balls and then tried to hide their artwork as fast as they could. We grabbed blank sheets of paper and began to draw fuzzy apples. The door squeaked open and slapped against the opposite wall.

Ms. Leery loomed before us. She was a tall, thin woman with wide shoulders and a pale face that had the texture of an omelet. A mole grew on her left cheek like a lonely olive. Her beige pantsuit was the color of a tea stain.

She tap-clumped around the circle of desks and stared at the students' art, working her way around the room. "What is this?" She reached under the paper on the booger artist's desk and pulled out the picture of her brother. "Repulsive. Zero marks," she said. She reached the girl who drew the naked fusilli. "Truly sick," she said. "I'm sending you to the guidance counselor for psychological evaluation."

"What a nice surprise to have you visit," Mrs. Fell said, suddenly fully awake. "I don't believe you've come to our room in years!"

"My flight to the conference was canceled," Ms. Leery said. "Thunderstorms in Oklahoma City. Three hours on the tarmac for nothing. How, I ask you all, will I be voted president of the Stars of Educational Leadership Society when my students produce this filth? How will our school maintain its status as having some of the highest test scores and one of the best college acceptance rates in Texas?"

She glared at me now. I kept drawing apples as quickly as I could, hoping she wouldn't see my narwhal cats, warthogs, and blobfish shoved beneath.

She approached my desk slowly.

A corner of a narwhal fin peeked out from under the apples. I tried to hide it, millimeter by millimeter, so she wouldn't see.

Ms. Leery had simmering moods and explosive ones; you never knew what might set her off. It was rarely big things that made her explode, but tiny things—if she saw you chewing gum or you accidentally dropped a wrapper on the floor, the volcano erupted and ash rained down for hours.

She drew in her breath. Her hand approached my drawing. She still wore her old wedding ring from long-departed Mr. Leery, with a pointed yellow stone that could cut glass, or flesh, people said, and her fingers were long and pale with brownish nails. Cadaver fingers, Dyna used to call them.

She whisked my drawing out from underneath the fuzzy apples. "What is this?"

"Nothing."

"If it's nothing, then it belongs in the waste bin."

I watched her hold it, the cross-hatching, hours and hours of it. She tore it in two and threw it in the garbage.

I flinched, and something broke inside me, but I tried not to show any reaction. I didn't want to give her the satisfaction.

She moved to the front of the room and stood behind the desk, surveying us.

I picked up a pencil. My hand shook. Her eyes fixated on my yoga ball while I tried to start drawing again.

"Stop that bouncing on your ball, Miss Clark. Reasonable bouncing only."

I kept drawing the apples, trying not to move. Being at Thornton froze you in time, sort of strangled you everywhere, this smashed feeling always, deep inside you. This fear. What were we so afraid of? Never measuring up to her standards. Those standards had been imprinted on us since we arrived and this slow and constant squashing began. I was sixteen now but short for my age, and I felt smaller at Thornton every day.

"The bouncing, Miss Clark. Enough. Come here. Bring me your ball."

I stood up and carried it to the front of the room.

"Hand it to me."

Twenty-five pairs of eyes watched me, sitting still.

It was only a ball. I didn't even care about it. It was the drawings I cared about—but I had plenty more of them, years' worth of artwork in my cubby. She couldn't touch those.

"You have no self-control," she said. "No restraint, no acknowledgment of how your bouncing affects others. Give it to me."

It felt like handing her a planet. She dug her fingernail into the valve and popped it open. It collapsed slowly, hissing for what felt like ten years, until finally it turned into a thick crumpled bag, a deflated animal. Nobody could look.

Only a few students dared watch as I returned to my desk. "Draw!" she yelled at them. "Work!"

She turned to me. "Clean out your cubby and collect all of your artwork—every single drawing, painting, every scrap of paper you've touched—and bring it to my office. Our meeting scheduled for tomorrow will be held today. Now."

three

'd come to Thornton over four years ago, fuzzy and duckling-ish myself, because my grandmother, Nana, died suddenly of a stroke.

She'd raised me. I hadn't lived with my parents since I was a baby—I knew the reason why, and it wasn't their fault, or anybody's fault. I developed serious asthma as an infant, and I had to be in an oxygen tent in the children's hospital in Austin. Nana, a retired nurse, helped take care of me. My parents struggled to pay my medical bills, and when they received a grant to teach abroad, they had to take it. Grants, teaching, and speaking gigs took them all over the world. They never stayed anywhere more than three months. Nana—she was my dad's mother—and my parents agreed I was safest staying with her, instead of being far from hospitals, with no stability or permanent place to live.

"We did what was best for you," my parents always said. "We had no choice."

Now they lived in Hawai'i on a fellowship with a wellness center, where my father gave workshops and worked on his latest self-help book. Twice a year, they'd swoop in for a few days in Austin, and then leave again. They'd been saying for weeks that they were looking to buy their own house in Hawai'i. They'd been there over seven months. Longer than they'd ever lived in one place.

A lot of kids at Thornton had parents who lived far away. One girl's mother was an actress filming a TV series in Iceland. Another had archaeologist parents researching in the Gobi Desert.

Dyna had arrived at Thornton a month after I did—she was sent there because her mother was undergoing treatment for cancer. Dyna had a Mallen streak in her black hair, a genetic stripe of gray that swiveled down from her temple like a silvery river; her mom called it her "unicorn streak." Her parents thought Dyna would be better off not witnessing her mother's treatments and suffering; they said Dyna would move back home after her mother improved. Our sophomore year, Dyna's mother felt an ache in her back—she thought she'd pulled a muscle—but it turned out the cancer, which had started in her ovaries, had spread to her bones. Dyna flew home. Her mom died eight days later.

The night Dyna returned to school, I woke up in the dark in our dorm room and she was crying. Her shadow shook above her narrow bed, across the room from mine. I sat beside her and held her. I didn't know what to say. I wanted to tell her, *Everything will be okay* and *It will get better*, but the moment Nana had died, I'd lost my whole life. I knew it sounded melodramatic. *Don't be a drama queen. No hysterics*, my dad would say. But after Nana died, the person I used to be disappeared. And when Dyna left Thornton, it had unearthed the old grief again.

I wanted to go back in time, to find some portal where I could be the girl again who'd sat on our back porch after school reading *Anne of Green Gables* while eating warm biscuits on a green polka-dot plate. Back then, in my old life, I stacked stones to make a hospital for ladybugs with injured wings. I took my stuffed hedgehogs for walks in the doll stroller, making sure each got a fair turn. I hid in our old redbud tree and observed the world. The girl who'd done those things was gone now, and I wasn't sure who'd taken her place.

Nobody had told me that it would feel so painful to think of Nana that I'd have to snap those feelings shut inside me like closing a book, or how my mind would focus instead on the things I'd lost that I hadn't even realized were mine—every corner of our little purple house, its windows with their white wood panes and windowsills deep enough to hold stuffed animals, old crumbling hardcovers, and my hedgehog drawings that Nana had framed. I missed every inch of our overgrown yard— Nana loved weeds and said they never got the appreciation they deserved. She didn't like to kill things, so she let everything grow. Our tiny backyard was a weed orphanage, a refuge for lost plant souls.

Why had I assumed, stupidly, that I'd always have that house and yard to go back to? I ached now for the purple cottage's ceilings with their patterns of chipped paint, for the wavy lines in the wood floorboards, for every bump in the limestone path to the street. At night sometimes I ached especially for the redbud tree with its strange doughnut-shaped knots that I worshipped, and the pink clouds blooming on its trunk every spring—*cauliflory*, my grandmother called it. I loved that word. That word was gone now, too, as if I could no longer speak an entire language.

The house had been sold to someone who, I saw on Google Street View, had painted it gray and torn out the redbud tree and the weeds. They'd paved the yard with concrete and gravel and built a driveway.

When we lived in the purple cottage, I felt like myself, I never doubted who I was. Maybe we're made up of the people and things we love—Nana, Dyna, the house, the redbud tree—and what's left of us when they're gone?

Most of all, her death felt like a landslide had come through and pulled my skin off. Except the skin grew back so I looked normal on the outside, completely untouched, but on the inside it had scrambled and roughed up all my organs, left rocks and sand and debris inside me. It hurt to move. It hurt to stay still. The weirdest thing was that after a while, I couldn't cry. It was like the tears had gotten trapped inside the mud and debris, stuck there, and that's what felt so heavy inside me all the time, the weight of all that water.

Then we found Gertrude, and for a while, everything began to change.

We'd been picking parsley in Flo's herb patch outside the kitchen when we found her. We heard a high squeak.

"What is that?" I'd asked Dyna. It was spring of our sophomore year, six months after her mom died. The squeak changed to a guttural yowl, like a singer who'd swallowed a toad. It came from under the lavender bush.

A gray fuzzy puddle lay under the spiky leaves. Gigantic green eyes gazed out. The kitten had a white spot on its back shaped like a three-quarter moon. Its tail had been injured, with a bloody wound in the middle and fur missing; its back paws were caked in dried blood, too. "We need to get him to a doctor," Dyna said, crouching beside me. "If Ms. Leery finds him, he's dead."

The kitten yowled again and started trembling. "Maybe Flo can help," I said. Pets weren't allowed at our school, of course. I picked him up and put him inside my jacket. He relaxed inside it; the trembling stopped. He felt lighter than a stuffed animal.

Dyna stared at my bulging jacket. "You look pregnant." She smiled a little, one of the few smiles I'd seen from her in ages. "And your coat is meowing."

In the kitchen, Flo said, "This isn't a he, it's a she. One

tough, battle-worn lady. Sweet girl, though, I'll tell you that. Knows good people when she meets them. Kittens like this, if you love them right up, they'll be healthy in no time. I can't take her myself, I got four cats already. Let's see what I can do." She called her brother-in-law, who was a veterinarian, and who met us in Flo's office next to the kitchen. He put a bandage on the cat's tail and gave her shots, and checked to see if she was microchipped—she wasn't. He said he could bring her to the shelter for us.

"Shelters are overcrowded," Flo said. "They'll destroy this one."

Destroy was worse than kill somehow.

"We're keeping her," I said.

"Can you keep a pet here?" Flo's brother-in-law asked, and then stopped himself. "What am I thinking? If I know Flo, she'll find a way. Good luck to you, ladies."

We snuck the cat into our room, and she took turns sleeping on each of our beds. Flo gave us cat litter and an old baking pan that we used as a litter box. "There's definitely no cat food in the bin marked 'Cornmeal' in the walk-in pantry," Flo told us.

That night, we slept better than we had in ages. The kitten changed our days. She loved to be cuddled and never had enough of it, meowing until I picked her up and held her to my chest and kissed her. Between classes, we rushed back to our dorm room to see her. We named her Gertrude Badass. Gertrude was Dyna's grandmother's name and Nana's middle name—one of the coincidences we shared, which we loved.

Maybe they'd sent this kitten to us.

Gertrude seemed happy in her new life. She liked to gnaw on socks. She chewed books, too, but only English novelists. She shredded *Pride and Prejudice* into confetti. Sometimes she lunged at the curtains and swung like a pendulum, staring out at the dark woods. Sometimes she slept with her paws on my shoulders like a cat necklace.

Flo snuck toy mice for Gertrude into the cornmeal bin, too, and even little tubs of catnip and extra large socks. "Be careful," she warned us. "Make sure nobody finds out."

"How would they find out? That will never happen," I said.

four
BOTTOMLESS DISAPPOINTMENT

I carried my portfolio from the art room, and I paused outside Ms. Leery's door. The thick gold plaque read "Headmistress." I knocked.

"Come in."

Gold brocade drapes hung from the windows; a hulking black lacquered desk stood in the center of the room, and on the wall behind it were various paintings of birds with dotted bellies, striped heads, and beady, accusing eyes. A fake tree leaned against the wall in a perpetual state of non-growth. My neck felt hot.

Ms. Leery hunched over the desk and looked me over, up and down, like a judge in a reality show. Her face was like a topographical map, with blue veins as the interstates and the mole as a capital city. I braced myself and stared at the side wall, which was covered with ornate frames filled with photos of Ms. Leery posing with semi-famous people, and dozens of black-and-white photos of Willa Thornton. She was Ms. Leery's mother, who'd died decades ago.

Ms. Leery saw me staring at the photos of her mother in various poses, like ancient selfies. Her mother in a 1950s dress with a cinched waist; wearing a cardigan with a tiger brooch; holding a pie. "Willa Thornton embodied perseverance, resilience, reinvention, and *grit*. Qualities that inspired me to start this school. Qualities that I've struggled to bestow on you." She loved the word *grit* so much that she had a whole assembly every year focused on it, which always made me think of grout, and every year I'd nod and clap along in the auditorium, thinking of bathroom tiles.

She rubbed a speck of dust off a picture of herself with the mayor of Austin. "Do you think I was able to meet these luminaries without learning grit and resilience?" She'd once served on the Texas Ethics Commission, a government job; she droned on about the photos of herself with the governor of Texas, local TV anchors, and Longhorn football players; of herself holding her little sister when she was a baby; with Willa and Barclay Thornton, Willa's well-to-do husband who she married late in life; and with Ms. Leery's students from her first job teaching at a military academy, decades ago, when she was unrecognizable, except for the mole. She pointed to a boy in that photo—it was my father.

That's how I came to Thornton after my grandmother died. Ms. Leery and my father had known each other since she was his teacher, before she started her own school. He always felt he owed her something because she was the first investor in his business when he was starting out.

She saw me glancing at the photo of my dad. "All your father and I want is to help you grow into a better person. To live up to the example your father and Willa Thornton and I have set."

Whenever I complained about her to my father, he'd say, "I just don't believe that Beverly would ever say that," or "That's not Beverly's version of the story. She can't show you a preference—wouldn't be fair to the other girls."

He hadn't spent much time with her in recent years, but when I pointed out that she'd gone bananas since he knew her, he wouldn't hear it. "That just doesn't sound true," he'd say. "We're paying Thornton money to see you become your best self, to achieve the levels of success they've had with thousands of girls."

During our biweekly video chats, my mother would nod beside him. "Listen to your father," she'd say. "Your father is right."

Now the blobfish's mole twitched. She tapped her fingers on a book called *Top of the Class*. It was an advance copy of her own book, which was going to be published in the fall. "If your low grades continue, how would that affect your test scores and Thornton's ranking? How would it affect everything my school has accomplished?"

She handed *Top of the Class* to me. It had an apple on the cover and a tagline: *Your Child's Success Guaranteed!* The back read: *Beverly Leery is a self-made business leader and award-winning educator who has held jobs ranging from teacher, member of the Texas Ethics Commission, field hockey coach, hospital administrator, coveted speaker, philanthropist, and writer.* And agent of emotional torture.

She picked up my portfolio. "Now let's review your work." She took out all my drawings and paintings from art class and surveyed them side by side. Flying narwhal cats and unicorn hedgehogs and dancing elephants. A cornucopia of weirdness.

"What is this? Can't you paint—normally?" She waved at the bird paintings behind her. "My sister, Bea, painted those when she was your age. You've taken art classes for years, and you've made *this*." She frowned at my work.

I knew my pictures weren't amazing or perfect and maybe not even art—who knew what they were—but I'd spent hours on them, letting the lines pour out of me while Mrs. Fell's old music played and the pencils and pens took over.

Her face twisted as she surveyed all of it. "What did you think you could do with this? Who would want to buy it? What use could this possibly have for your future? You've been ignoring everything Mrs. Fell has taught you, all the lessons, all the . . ."

She squinted at the drawings, side by side.

I hadn't realized until they were arranged together how the blobfish appeared in each drawing, and every one had a mole on the same spot on its face, exactly like her mole.

She pointed a long fingernail on each one. Her face turned red. She kept twisting her ring. I was afraid she was going to stab me with it. "This is inexcusable." She swept up all my artwork. "There will be a consequence for this behavior." She stood and disappeared through the door to the file room, in the far corner of her office.

My palms started to water—not sweat—this was a rogue wave of it, as if the tears that couldn't come out of my eyes had found another route.

No students were allowed in the file room. She stored everything in her meticulously kept secret files—all our handwritten exams, confiscated notes to friends, printed-out emails with curse words, and anything that might explain to parents why we had a lower grade or had received a punishment or "consequence." She saved all her Willa Thornton photos in there, and every month, she would pull out a new photo and tell us another boring anecdote about Willa's grit.

And now my artwork would live in the file room, too.

I held my breath until she returned a minute later clutching a brown package, a stack of papers, and two files—one was labeled "Lucy Clark" and one was "Willa Thornton History," as if her mother's grit and resilience could rub off on me through the file. My artwork was gone. "As you know, you've been on probation since March fourth. You're now receiving failing grades for art and citizenship, which brings your GPA down to a level that's below Thornton's minimum standard, and that requires long-term suspension, effective immediately."

She smiled and added, "Let's see what your parents have to say." She picked up the phone.

I gripped the arms of my chair, which felt slick against my hands. She dialed and pressed the button for the speakerphone.

My parents picked up. "Hello, Beverly! Cricket, are you there?" my father's voice boomed. He'd called me Cricket since I was a baby, when I made soft, chirpy sounds. "Your mother and I are both here."

I nodded, though he couldn't see me. Something pushed against my eyes, but I held it back.

Ms. Leery's voice was polite and calm, since she always put on a different persona around parents. "Unfortunately, Todd, I've calculated Lucy's grade point average, and under the circumstances of her probation, suspension is required. I know that you and I have previously discussed our options and our plan for what is best for Lucy now."

I blinked. I tried not to show anything, not to feel anything.

She glanced at my squinting eyes and seemed to enjoy watching me. "Ms. Clark is unfortunately quite upset," she told him.

"Let's slow down. Let's not get worked up," my father said. "Let's stay focused on the How here and the Future. How happiness and joy are right around the corner. We just have to walk through the Jagged Path to get there." In his writing, capitals popped up in his sentences like lost gophers. I could hear them through the phone. Recently, he'd sent me his latest book, *Your Authentic Path*, with a chapter on "Moving On" highlighted.

Focus on the Future, it said. *Chart your Path. Don't stop moving.*

I did move—during the three weeks since Dyna had left, I'd pace the room every night, from bed to dresser to desk to window. I'd walk this miniature Olympic track, thinking of how I'd gotten in this situation and how to get out.

"Cricket, are you listening?" he asked.

"Yes."

"Remember: Failure is essential on the path to Change. We expected this might happen since the Incident, so we've been talking to Beverly about next steps. We're going to take advantage of Thornton's renowned internship program—Beverly has generously allowed you to embark on an internship as a junior, instead of the typical senior-year adventure—and we have a life-changing Opportunity. We're going to send you to New York for the suspension period."

I clung to my chair. "What?"

"It's only for three months. You'll be living with your cousin Nanette," he said. "Nanette's secured a job for you taking care of an elderly woman who owns her building. I hear the elderly woman's quite ill—mentally impaired, unfortunately—but we believe it's a wonderful chance for Change, to show altruism and a selfless spirit."

I'd met Nanette once, when she came to Austin to speak at one of my father's workshops in January, as part of an Innovators Conference. She was a distant cousin on my mother's side, and was only twenty-four and already famous. She'd risen, in just a few years, to be the editor in chief of a women's magazine.

She was tall and glamorous and had been named to several *30 Most Powerful Women Under 30* kinds of lists. She scared the crap out of me.

"Sometimes we all need to press the Restart button on our lives. Reinvent ourselves. New York will be a Transformative experience," he said.

"Nanette lives in Greenwich Village, a beautiful neighborhood, in a gorgeous historic old building," my mother said. "I know you'll be happy there. I would've loved an opportunity like that at your age. Nanette is a role model for all of us. Remember to bring that book on manners that I sent you last year—that will come in handy, too."

My insides twisted. I hadn't even realized that before they said New York, I'd had a secret hope that they'd say I could live with them instead. My grandmother used to explain, when I pressed her, why they were always traveling, and she said their jobs—their calling—meant they could never settle down. "They wanted to," she said. "Someday they will—I know they will."

"I thought—what about—instead of New York, I could . . . Hawai'i?" I asked now.

"We'd love that, Cricket. I've been wanting to share our good news—we told you a while ago how *Your Authentic Path* had been optioned for a TV series," my father said. "Well, it's happening. Production has started!"

"This is a dream come true, Cricket," my mother said. "The work hours are shocking—sixteen hours a day. But production wraps in just six weeks. We're going to buy a house—we've been looking at beach houses—something big enough for the three of us. We're about to move into a rental that we might be able to purchase, too—you'd love it."

"Is it purple?"

My mother laughed. "Yellow. It's perfect."

"We're almost there. We've spent all our lives building this—we just need to be patient a little longer," my father said.

I tried to absorb it. I wanted to say the perfect thing—the words that would make them send me to Hawai'i instead—but they wouldn't form in my head. "Shit," I mouthed under my breath.

Ms. Leery's eyes narrowed. "Don't sass, Lucy Clark. Apologize to your parents immediately. Show them respect. You will do what is asked of you without whining and complaint. They're only trying to find an opportunity that's best for you."

I hesitated.

"Now," she said.

"I'm sorry."

"Like you mean it. You shouldn't feel resentment for people who are trying to help you." She waited. She loved watching my pain. I think it fed her, literally; her muscles seemed to grow and multiply, and she seemed taller and stronger as she sat there.

I stared at the phone, the landline, its clunky old shape. "I am very sorry." I felt so tired and empty. Exhausted. I didn't know what else to say. I knew I'd think of the right thing two days later.

"Apology accepted," Ms. Leery said.

"We just want you to try," my father said. "To help someone.

To help the poor woman you'll be working for."

"How do I help.her?" I asked.

"Stick by her side. Assist her caregivers. Even if the woman is losing her faculties, the companionship of a young person can give her a new life. Sometimes what we need is to be pushed out of our comfort zone. I know you can help her," he said. "This is your Path."

At his workshops and online classes, fans of *Your Authentic Path* shared their struggles and success stories. People loved his motivational videos—one even had two million views. My mother edited all my father's writing, and managed his schedule, website, and video channel.

"We know you can do it, Cricket." My mother's voice now. "And when your job helping this poor elderly woman is finished, then we'll be together." Her voice softened as she said it, and I felt something warm under my skin. She didn't say "I love you" as often as my dad did—she usually let my father do most of the talking—but her voice slowed when she spoke to me, and the spaces between words felt tender, filled with longing. "She has a quiet way," my dad often said. "Always know that she loves you very, very much."

She loves you very, very much. I carried that inside me, a tiny jewel buried in coal.

"I sent a package to Beverly to give to you, overnight mail. I think this will help turn things right around. Did you get it?" my father asked.

"I have it here," Ms. Leery said. She handed it to me—it was the package she'd brought from the file room. I ripped it open.

I took out a book—a blank book. A diary. It had a *Your Authentic Path* logo on the back, with a rising sun.

"If you look inside, there are prompts and exercises and at the top of each day, a space to write your daily goals and the food you've consumed—of course it's not only food, it's what keeps you nourished and energized to Change—and the habit of keeping it will help you stay on track. I think it will really turn things around. Maybe, down the road, you can share what you've written with us," my father said.

"Great." I'd never share it with him in a million years. He'd be too horrified to know what I really felt. My heart whirred every time I spoke to him—I wanted him to say I was actually not a bad daughter and everything was perfectly fine and it was wonderful that he'd been paying tuition to have pancakes thrown at my head.

"Your father needs to hear you agree to do your best on this internship," Ms. Leery said. "A commitment."

I felt a pressure in my forehead. "Yes. I will."

"Hang in there, Cricket sweetheart, chirp chirp! Chin up, eyes to the sky! We love you!" my father said.

Ms. Leery touched the file with my name on it. She thanked my parents and told them we needed to return to the school day. We said goodbye.

I stared at the now-quiet phone, as if it were a land mine or a meteorite that had blown up my life.

The phone stayed unnervingly quiet. "Now here is your independent study work during your suspension," Ms. Leery said, and handed me a gigantic stack of papers. "This will keep you busy and out of trouble in New York, on top of your work arrangements there." There were packets for every subject. "I've instructed Uriah to give you some texts from the library, a reading list. You can spend today picking up those books and packing your things. We're leaving for the airport first thing tomorrow."

I walked toward the library.

I weighed my options: Be a teen runaway? With no money, no phone—my parents had taken it away after the Incident, which felt like they'd amputated my leg—and nowhere to go? That wouldn't work.

On the way to the library, Thing One and Thing Two passed me in the hall, of course.

"We heard you're getting kicked out and sent to live with a lunatic in New York," Thing One said.

"I read about a girl from Dallas who went to New York and she was abducted by a taxi driver," Thing Two said. "She was found two weeks later chopped up inside a suitcase."

The night before, during the ten minutes I actually managed to sleep, I'd dreamed that Things One and Two ran an experiment in AP Biology and stripped my cell membranes away, and my cytoplasm and mitochondria and Golgi bodies spilled out all over the place while the teacher quizzed everyone on my cell parts. The Things were masters at sticking a knife in your soul (or your cell parts) while pretending it was a concerned pat on the shoulder. "You must . . . feel so terribly alone without your best friend?" they asked me after Dyna left, with a gleam in their eyes. Around teachers, they morphed into academic champions and field hockey stars, and a college sports recruiter even said once, "They're just so darn nice."

"People thought Mussolini was nice. Before he murdered them," Dyna said.

The Things coedited the yearbook; last year on the "Most" page they'd named Dyna and me "Most Likely to Shop at Forever 71" and "Most Likely to Live with 50 Cats." The Things labeled us the Two Spinsters and the Diversity Duo, because

I was Jewish and Dyna's mother was half-Jewish and half-Salvadoran, which meant the Things loved to ask her, "What *are* you?" And, "But where are you *from*?" They didn't believe her when she answered truthfully, "Florida." They loved calling us both "interesting looking."

"Their words have no power," Dyna would say, quoting her mom. Her mother used to tell her that the way to deal with them was to build a barrier with your mind. *An army of kittens,* her mother said. *Picture a wall of sparkly kittens protecting you from them.*

I tried to picture the kittens now. Orange, calico, gray tabby, and long-haired, extra furry. Sharp-clawed kittens.

"I read about that girl who was murdered also," Thing One said now. "Parts of her had been pureed in a blender. To make her fit."

My palms started to water again. "You're wrong." I stared at their shiny hair and plastic faces. How had they made it through seventeen years unscathed, with no big loss other than their favorite lipstick being discontinued?

"At least if she makes it out of the taxi, her job will be perfect. Taking care of a crazy old lady. Helping her go to the bathroom," Thing Two said.

"Emptying bedpans."

"Cleaning artificial teeth."

The air in my chest swirled, making it hard to breathe. "You're lying."

"The truth is so painful, you can't even see it," Thing One

said with a grin. They walked away.

I reached the library. Its paint was peeling, but seeing the books on the walls felt comforting. I was relieved to see Uriah. He was a quiet, gentle person Dyna and I called RBD (Raised By Deer).

When he saw me, his eyes brightened. He handed me a stack of the books on the list, and he gave me one other. Not a library book, but a paperback of his own. *Jane Eyre*.

He'd written a note on top of it.

You and Dyna are like Jane. You can survive anything. I hope you'll both come back. I promise I'll have lots of good things for you to read when you return.

"Thank you," I said. "I don't think I'll be back, though. I might run away to Antarctica and live on an ice floe or stow away on a ship or live in the woods or join a convent if they take Jews."

His eyes smiled. He gazed at the floor and tugged at the sleeve of his hoodie. He always wore hoodies, which he kept pulled over his head so just his brown eyes poked out. He almost never spoke a word. Rumors about why circulated all over school. Some people said he'd taken a vow of silence as a spiritual thing. Others said his vocal cords were damaged. Suddenly, it seemed like a good idea to not speak again, to not risk being shuttled around without a home, without anywhere you belonged.

Back in my dorm room, I started packing. I packed all my

stuffed hedgehogs and Nana's favorite nightgown—pale green flannel and velvet-soft. I'd saved it before they took all her things away. I kept it in my suitcase all the time because I was never sure where to put it. I just liked knowing that it was there.

I took out the diary from my father. The first few pages had rules and prompts for what to write.

1. Writing every day is essential to making lasting changes. Schedule the same time every day so your writing practice becomes a Habit.
2. Every morning, write down your Goals for the day.
3. Writing down your daily food intake is the first step on the road to Wellness.

The rules went on for three pages. They made my head hurt. I thought of how when I got a new sketchbook for art class, I loved its clean, stark, beautifully empty pages, with no instructions. All that space, open and ready, where anything could happen and no one was telling you what to do.

I started to write.

April 12
Goals:
1. Eat some chocolate
2. Do not get caught eating chocolate
3. Come up with better goals

I'd only been writing for a minute and I was already doing this diary-keeping thing wrong.

I ate the Kit Kat and the Caramello that Flo had given me, and then I pulled out a stuffed hedgehog that Dyna had sent to me after her father withdrew her from school. She had hollowed out the inside and hidden chocolate-covered caramels inside it, and sent it with a letter that had a secret code:

> *Look, I really miss you. Inside our house I keep practicing viola. This separation is the worst. Animals are making noises outside my door—I better say good night and send this letter!*

Look Inside This Animal. I stuck my fingers through the loose stitches and savored the last chocolate. Then I tore out the rules and prompts so the diary would be clear and blank and I could get that new-sketch-pad feeling back. I tried to sleep, but I couldn't. I stayed up all night, my palm rivers flowing, scared of starting my life over from scratch, among strangers, and of whatever awaited me in New York.

The next morning, during the ride to the airport, Ms. Leery kept glancing at me. Her eyes narrowed into brown slits. The windshield wipers swished and ticked like a metronome. I tried to tune her voice out as I always did, letting the sounds blend into the white noise of the highway, with only phrases coming through: *Some girls are beyond redemption but . . . your spectacular failures . . . I often say to my girls, "Who do you think you are?" because the entitlement of girls these days*— Swish. Clack. She's crazy. Swish.

We drove past tidy lawns. Thornton was in a suburban part of Austin with scrubby trees and flat beige houses, as if someone had sat on them. The city was growing so fast there were cranes and construction projects everywhere, like an erector set. Rosedale, the neighborhood where Nana and I'd lived, with its older houses with peaked roofs and candy colors, seemed a world away.

We reached the airport; she stopped at the curb. "You'll be an unaccompanied minor on this flight and I expect you'll be able to manage without any dramatics. Your father arranged for a car to meet you at arrivals. The car will take you directly to your cousin Nanette Sinclair's apartment, and she'll meet you there at four o'clock on the dot. The old woman will be paying you weekly, enough for incidentals. Follow all Nanette's directions and your father's directions at all times. You can manage it, can't you?"

"I can. I will."

The omelety blobfish was smiling. "I have tremendous hopes for you. Your parents do, too." She placed her long bony fingers on my shoulder. Her cadaver nails were pointed like talons.

I said goodbye. I waited on the check-in line. I turned around; she stood beside her car, studying me as I handed my passport to the airline employee—the first time I'd ever used it, so it didn't feel real, but like playing pretend—and she kept watching me until a security guard waved at her to move along. She drove off.

I walked toward security. I'd never been on a plane. My grandmother hated to travel—we rarely left Austin, except occasionally to go to Wimberley and Fredericksburg, and to Houston for fried chicken and waffles. "That is worth the drive," she'd say. She'd lived most of her life moving around, before she came to Austin for her nursing job. "Now I like to stay put," she said. "I grew roots here and I'm not chopping them off again."

I glanced out the airport window, as if I'd see rootless souls floating out there, untethered, between homes. I thought of how Dyna loved to play viola—she named her instrument Rosie—and if she were here, she'd play a calming song. A Concerto for Terrified Travelers.

My heart beat in wallops, like echoing howls. I wished I could see into the future. I felt strange inside, like all the molecules inside me were rearranging themselves and forming something new, as I boarded the plane to my new life.

part ii
WELCOME TO NEW YORK,
TRY NOT TO DIE

What delights us in visible beauty is the invisible.
—Marie von Ebner-Eschenbach

IF I CAN MAKE IT THERE

April 13
Goals:
1. Do not screw up
2. Stay away from men with blenders
3. Eat as much chocolate as is humanly possible
Breakfast: 12 airplane biscuits, 3 airplane hot chocolates, as much
ice cream as I could eat before flight boarded

I clutched the seat belt as my car sped through Manhattan to
Greenwich Village. My skin buzzed. So far, the driver didn't
show any signs of wanting to murder me.

We drove past brownstones the color of chocolate. Milk

chocolate and dark chocolate and red velvet cake. Cherry blossoms bloomed along narrow side streets, carpeting the sidewalks in pink. We passed storybook shops with striped awnings, and French bakeries displaying towers of macarons, like giant wizard hats made of dessert. Through the car window, I smelled magnolias one second and something ammonia—I think it was pee—the next. New York seemed nothing like the movies and exactly like the movies at once. We sped past a photo shoot of fashion models wearing white fluffy coats, two boys juggling on a corner, a woman in a ball gown, and a bearded man on a unicycle. It was like watching a circus for free.

The car screeched to a stop in front of 14 Summer Street, a large brick building with a red front door and ivy climbing up the walls.

I took a deep breath. *Do not mess up.*

This is your last chance. You can do this.

You cannot do this.

Open the car door. Do it.

I did it. I stepped outside into New York City, and the driver careened off. I was alive. So far, so good.

I'd been told to meet Nanette promptly at 4:00 p.m., but she didn't show up then. Or at 4:15. Or 4:30 or 4:45, either. There was no doorman. I kept sitting on the edge of a flowerpot outside the red front door. I wished I had my phone—after my father took it away permanently after the Incident, he gave me a fitness tracker watch instead. "Your phone is ruining your brain," he'd said, and quoted a phones-are-the-devil news article. "The internet has destroyed the way teenagers think."

I'd pointed out that he probably read that article *on his phone* and made his living off videos people watched *on their phones.* He changed the subject.

Thornton instructed all parents to "supervise" phone usage by adjusting phone settings so we had no privacy—my parents read my texts and my web history through the cloud, and even my fitness tracker history to make sure I was getting enough steps every day. Dyna was lucky that her father was technologically impaired and never put the right settings on her phone, but unfortunately, because of their business, my parents did it too well.

Now I was so hungry that my stomach groaned. I poked through my pockets looking for crumbs, but there was nothing.

My father's books also said, *Focus on what you want and you will bring it forth.* I focused on a giant chocolate cake. And candy.

The cake and candy didn't appear, but a hairy man in overalls and no shirt walked by twice. I took out *Jane Eyre* and read and tried to look like I belonged there. The man eyed me up and down, and his gaze settled on my behind. "Love me some big tushy!" he said.

Welcome to New York.

A moment later, I was saved from the hairy man. He scurried away when a tall woman hurried down the sidewalk and stopped in front of me.

I stared at her. She was unlike anyone I'd ever seen. She was beautiful—not magazine beautiful or movie-star beautiful, but like a painting in a museum that you can't stop looking at, and you're not sure why you love it, but you do. Her silvery, wavy hair sparkled in the sun and spilled across her shoulders like a waterfall. She was older but almost ageless at the same time: she wore cherry-red lipstick and was dressed simply but fashionably, in tailored navy pants, a crisp white shirt, red sneakers, and black-rimmed glasses. Stylish without trying. It was how most girls at Thornton wanted to look, but never did.

I glanced at my gray yoga pants and white T-shirt. My clothes looked like dish towels compared to hers.

The woman paused, took off her glasses and stared at me, and then her shoulders relaxed in relief. Her eyes were a color that looked almost violet. She said, "Are you Lucy Clark?"

I nodded.

"Your cousin Nanette told me you were arriving today, but she said it would be late tonight."

"I was told to meet her here at four o'clock."

"I'm sorry she kept you waiting. I'm Edith Fox."

This was the elderly woman I'd be taking care of? "Are you sure—you're Edith?"

She laughed. "Yes, I'm sure." She glanced down the street and winced. "Can you help me?" Her voice was urgent.

"Of course. How?"

"Can you drive?"

I nodded. "I took driver's ed at school—I have a learner's

permit, but I haven't taken the license test yet—"

She kept glancing down the street and around the corner. "Let's go." She walked ahead swiftly. I grabbed my suitcase and followed. We stopped beside a small red car. She unlocked it and handed me the keys. "Quick," she said.

"Where are we going?"

"No time for questions. Let's hurry."

She climbed into the passenger seat. A hundred things flew through my mind at once. What was I doing? What if Nanette showed up? They hadn't told me what to do if Nanette was late. Would my father want me to drive? *Help her*, he'd said. I put my suitcase in the trunk and slid in behind the steering wheel. I gripped it like a life preserver. "I don't want to get in trouble."

"Don't worry about that. I promise you Nanette won't mind."

"I've never driven in a big city. I mean, Austin is big, but I've never driven downtown, only in the suburbs around our school where the streets are much wider and—"

"You'll do fine." She patted my hand. She'd already buckled her seat belt. "*Go.*"

I pressed the gas and drove down winding streets, over potholes and cobblestones. Sweat began to pool down my back, but I kept going.

She glanced behind us. "Faster, please." Her voice was calm but with a creeping edge.

I turned on to Hudson Street and drove as fast as I could in the traffic. *Pretend this is a video game. You won't die.* A car honked at me and I screeched to a stop.

I'm in Manhattan and I'm going to die.

"What are we driving away from? Are you—in trouble?" My palms watered again, and I was glad I had my asthma inhaler in my bag, just in case. My chest hurt as I drove.

"Someone's following me" was all she said. "Turn here."

I turned into a street marked "PRIVATE: TRESPASSERS WILL BE PROSECUTED" and down a cobblestoned road. My heart tried to squeeze itself into my neck.

On Bleecker Street a dog crossed in front of us, its leash dragging behind him. I braked and came within two feet of hitting him. Its owner, a guy in a baseball cap, banged on our car hood. "*Slow down, assface!*" he yelled at me.

Edith lowered her window. "Where are your manners, young man?" she shouted. He crossed the street and ignored her.

Two blocks later, a guy who was staring at his phone and drinking coffee crossed in the middle. I stopped short again. He threw the empty coffee cup at our windshield. Edith clucked her tongue.

We made more turns and finally, on Perry Street, Edith began to look relieved. "I think we're safe now."

"Safe from what?"

"I'll explain when we stop. Please park up there—that's a spot. Oh good. I have a knack for this, you know, finding parking spots. My friend Mimsy calls it a gift from the gods."

I'd only parallel parked a few times before, but Edith talked me through it. I held my breath and a dozen tries later, I finally did it. We stepped onto the sidewalk. My legs shook.

"Are you okay?" she asked me.

I nodded. "What were we driving away from? Who were we driving away from?"

She glanced at the sky, then back at me. "The problem, you see," she said after a while, "is that someone is trying to murder me."

seven

A TRIAL BASIS

"Who's—trying to murder you?" I tried to say it calmly, to make it sound like a normal question.

"I'll explain in a minute. Let's sit down so we can talk."

We stepped into a tiny restaurant and a hostess led us to the back patio, which was filled with little marble tables. It was empty besides us. Baskets of ivy drizzled their leaves along the brick walls. A small potted tree leaned over our table, as if it were eavesdropping.

"Before I saw you, a tall man in a gray hooded coat and sunglasses kept walking behind me," Edith said after the hostess had left. "He turned when I turned. Every corner. For blocks. His body, his whole manner—I've seen him follow me before, one morning last week. I was scared he'd follow me into my building, or . . . do something." Her hand trembled slightly.

"Could you see his face, besides the sunglasses?"

"No. He was too far away. And I've been having trouble with my eyes. That's why I asked you to drive."

"Why was he following you?"

"I don't know." She touched the tree beside us and held on to it, as if steadying herself. "Three weeks ago, someone tried to poison me. I know it sounds crazy." She ran her fingers across the tree's bark gently, like she was soothing it to sleep. "This is a lot to spring on anyone. I'd planned for us to get to know each other a little before explaining the situation to you, but then I saw that man, and there you were. I apologize for the suddenness. It must feel overwhelming."

I thought of how my father had said she was mentally impaired. The thing was, when she spoke, she didn't sound crazy. She sounded sharp and together and genuinely scared.

"I'm happy to help. I want to help." The waiter placed a bread basket in front of us; the bread was pillowy and sweet and slightly sour at once, the opposite of the hardtack at Thornton. I gobbled three pieces. "Have you told the police about the—murderer?"

She nodded. "Of course. They said we didn't have enough proof. They can't do anything without concrete evidence. I took a picture of the man following me—" She took out her phone and showed me a photo of a sidewalk crowded with blurry figures. She sighed. "That won't do anything. This is exactly why my friend Mimsy suggested that I needed an assistant. A companion. Someone to be my eyes and ears. To help me collect proof. Evidence."

I ate another two pieces of bread.

"I'm sure this isn't what you expected. I know it sounds like madness. It's just that—when Nanette described you to me, you sounded perfect."

"I did? How did she describe me?"

"She said you were a unique person."

Good unique or sad-loser unique? I wanted to ask but didn't.

"She said you were resilient and gifted and you were having a hard time at boarding school, and that your father wasn't sure where you might go—he was looking for a good opportunity for you."

I wanted to actually enjoy the compliments from Nanette, but I didn't trust them. She barely knew me—we'd spoken for all of ten minutes when she'd visited Austin to speak at my father's workshop in January. She'd slithered around the convention center stage while she gave a speech called "Don't Be Afraid of Power," and when she spoke to me and the other workshop attendees, her eyes darted around, as if mentally computing our status and worth. Even Nanette's words seemed to slither. They snaked around, those compliments, wanting something in return. I wondered what.

"When she mentioned you, honestly, I thought of myself at sixteen," Edith said. "It seemed like a good match. Serendipity. You'll be safe, I'll make sure of that. When I spoke to your father, he said you had determination and perseverance and what a good opportunity it would be for you to come to New York."

At least he'd said that instead of, *She's a total failure and an embarrassment. Now I'm dumping her on you.*

Edith ordered iced tea for us. I added three packets of sugar to mine. I scanned the menu—it was in French, which I didn't speak—and she asked what I liked to eat and said it was her treat.

"That's not necessary—thank you." I didn't want her to pay for me.

When the waiter returned, she ordered six different things in French. "I insist. This is on me. I won't take no for an answer." She tapped the tree, as if waking it up. "I can't imagine how they described me to you. They probably made it sound as if you'd be assisting a decrepit geezer. A batty old lady." Her eyes sparkled. Her smile was like a light switching on in a dark room. "Things aren't always what they seem, are they? What's on the surface is never the whole story, is it?"

"No," I said, though I wasn't sure what she meant.

She picked her bag up from the chair. "Now, let's see. I received a document attached to an email from your father this morning. I printed it out to read more carefully later." She pulled out a piece of paper. She squinted at it.

I saw my father's business logo in the corner, with the name TODD CLARK and the small rising sun. My stomach clenched.

She read aloud:

Dear Ms. Fox,

Thank you again for hosting our Lucy and offering her this life-changing New York experience! Here are guidelines for her time under your supervision and employment (cc'd to Nanette Sinclair):

I braced myself.

1. Lucy must complete Schoolwork and Studying, two hours per day.

"They gave me a reading list," I said. "And assignments."

2. Lucy must follow a Wellness Program with Healthy nutritional choices. No sugar, no unhealthy fats, and all foods consumed must be from approved list (see back of this page) including TrueYou shakes.

I tried to discreetly sweep my used sugar packets under a napkin. She turned the page over and scanned the list, which was from his recent book. She seemed aghast, as if it were written in blood. "What's a TrueYou shake?"

"That's my father's new business. He's expanded into canned smoothies. In his books, he says it's not just about weight loss or nutrition, but that eating and drinking these things can change your telomeres. Your genetic material." I was glad she didn't seem to know anything about him and his social media fame.

She took her glasses off and gazed at me, as if I'd just told her I was from Pluto. "Why would you need to change your genetic material?"

"I guess, well, my father says—it's so we can improve ourselves. Change for the better."

"You look perfectly lovely to me." She frowned at the paper. "Telomeres," she repeated.

3. Lucy's internet usage shall be restricted to study time and conversations with Mr. and Mrs. Clark during prescheduled video chats on Nanette's phone and/or computer. No exceptions.

4. Lucy must behave with politeness, kindness, helpfulness, and respect for her elders at all times.

5. Lucy must be chaperoned in the city and not wander alone. She must follow all rules and directions from Mr. and Mrs. Clark and Nanette Sinclair. No exceptions.

She crumpled it up and handed it to the busboy as he walked by. "Well. That's that," she said. "Let's have a fresh start, shall we?"

I gazed at her. I hoped she actually meant this.

"Now, a little bit more about my expectations. What I'm looking for in an assistant. I'll explain more in the coming days, but what's most important is to notice things. To see. To observe and let me know what you think. And of course, to help in daily tasks—they told you about the garden, didn't they?"

I shook my head.

She sighed. "Of course not. For over thirty years I've designed and cared for one of the largest private gardens in Manhattan. My most recent partner is no longer working for me. Your father said you had gardening experience?"

"We had an herb garden at school," I said. "Flo, the school chef, planted it, and my best friend, Dyna, and I took care of it. Except it gets really hot in Austin, so it's hard to keep things alive sometimes."

She looked a little sad at the words "herb garden," as if I'd just boasted to Picasso that I could finger paint.

"I'm sorry I don't really know how to garden. But I can learn. I want to learn," I said.

"I'm happy to teach you. We can start our arrangement on a trial basis. It's important that you feel comfortable in this job, too, that you feel good about it, and it feels right for you."

Comfortable? Good and right? No one at Thornton had ever asked if I was comfortable.

"My ideal assistant would take notes and help me make sense of what's happening. Stay by my side. Help me remember things, and handle complications, and . . . oh no." She squinted at the door. "Speaking of which. *Peter.* I should've known we might run into him here."

An older man in a sweater vest and button-down shirt talked to the waiter, who pointed at us. The man carried a bouquet of daffodils, and as he approached us he bumped his way around the other tables, which had started to fill up with other diners. He held the flowers in the air, saying "*Sorry, sorry, so terribly sorry*" in an English accent.

Edith looked at me and whispered, "Help."

"Is that who we were running from?" He looked more like a kind woodchuck in a children's fable than a murderer.

"Oh no. Not him. He's harmless," she whispered. "It's just— he wants—I'm not sure."

Before I could ask what she wasn't sure about, the man pulled up a chair beside us.

"Peter," she said to him in a strange tone, "how wonderful."

He glanced at me. "Excuse us," he said, and took out a blue handkerchief to wipe beads of sweat off his forehead. "May Edith and I have a moment alone?"

Edith shook her head. "Lucy can stay. She's my—new assistant. On a trial basis. Lucy Clark, this is Peter Lloyd. I'm so glad you two are getting to meet."

He nodded, and then took a long time to speak, as if carefully considering every word. "I hoped I would find you here. It's Wednesday, and I know you love the mushroom tartine special here on Wednesdays."

"I do," she said. "It's extra mushroomy and not too salty."

"You haven't been returning my calls. Not since the party," he said.

"I'm sorry," she said. "I've been so busy."

He gave the flowers to her. "I'm asking you if you might please—take *the trip* with me in mid-May. As we planned."

A strange expression crossed her face. He said "the trip" in an odd way. His whole face softened when he looked at her, with what seemed to be a deep and genuine kind of love—I'd almost never seen anything remotely romantic outside of movies and TV series, and I felt sort of shocked to watch it. Thornton occasionally held dances with the Chester Wallfinger boys' school, where their idea of tender affection was to launch a spitball at you. This was like being transported to the 1800s.

Edith was silent. The waiter brought our food—Edith had ordered plenty for all three of us, and the waiter set an extra place for Peter. I ate the tartines—fancy toasts drenched in so much butter Ms. Leery would faint—while I watched them.

"I'm just not sure that I'm ready for the trip," she said finally, and smelled the daffodils he'd given her. "Are these a new hybrid?"

"I bred them in the field. Narcissus 'Eveline' crossed with jonquilla."

"They're beautiful," she said, and they pattered in some kind of secret plant language, with Latin names flying and words I'd never heard before, like *bulbocodium* and *biochar* and *fimbriated*.

Then he said, "I understand if you've changed your mind about the trip," but he looked crestfallen. "Are you certain?"

She shook her head. "I'm not sure. We've been friends for forty years. I don't want to be unfair to you. I think the deadline for a refund for the hotel was May tenth?"

"Yes."

Edith seemed lost at what to decide or to say. She turned to me.

I wanted to ask her, what was the trip? What were they talking about? Whatever it was, her eyes seemed to plead with me to give her more time to answer him.

I cleared my throat and tried to summon my most polite, ancient, Jane Eyre-ish voice. "Mr. Lloyd, I'm sure you can understand that a person needs time to make a decision about . . . travel. I'd be happy to schedule a time for Edith to meet with you to follow up, before May tenth?"

He brightened. "You'll definitely have an answer by then?"

I turned to Edith and tried to read her expression. She seemed to be waiting for whatever I said.

"We'll work as hard on it as we can," I told him, and Edith nodded happily.

Peter sat up. "Good! That's a plan. Thank you both. Edith, wonderful to see you as always. Miss Clark, lovely to meet you."

He patted his vest, said goodbye, and walked out of the restaurant.

Edith watched him go. "Thank you. I think this might work out brilliantly, with you and me." She paused. "In early February, he and I made plans to have a romantic getaway in May, to a garden in Maine. But that was before all these strange things started happening in my life. I'm not sure if I should take the trip anymore, with everything that's been going on lately." She touched the chair where he'd sat. "I'm afraid I've been unkind to him—I haven't been returning his calls or texts or voicemails."

She looked embarrassed.

"That's totally normal. We call that ghosting now. You don't like him?"

"I do like him. It's just—so much has been happening lately, it's almost like I feel muffled. Like I feel so overwhelmed that I can't hear what I think or want."

I nodded. "I know how that feels."

She looked me in the eyes. "Honestly, the main thing I'm looking for in an assistant, above all else, is this: I'm looking for someone who can help me see the truth."

"I can see the truth," I said.

"Can you?"

"I think so." I hesitated. I wanted to say the right thing. To not screw up. I liked her. I liked her open-mindedness, how she'd crumpled the rules, and that she already seemed to trust me.

I also felt terrified. What was I getting into?

She continued to study me. Her eyes were so intense and piercing, I looked away. I was almost afraid to look up at her again. Afraid that she could see through me, could see all the broken things inside me, my flaws and failures.

She extended her hand toward me. "Our trial basis officially begins. A week or two and then we'll reevaluate. Of course, you can tell me anytime if you're unhappy and want to go back to Texas, or to your parents."

"I don't want to go back to Texas." I didn't know how to say that I couldn't go to my parents.

I shook her hand, and when she let go, I had a good look at

her hands for the first time—the grooves and cuts and scars, the roughness.

"Gardener's hands," she said, inspecting them. "That's what you get for working with plants for decades." She seemed proud of them. "Do we have a deal?"

"Deal," I said, with a whirling feeling that I had no idea what I was agreeing to.

eight
DYNA'S DILEMMA

Nanette wasn't home yet when Edith and I returned from the restaurant. She'd texted Edith:

Can u let Lucy in pls? Her room is maid's room in the back. Sry I'm late! Still at work—thx!!

Edith had the keys, since she owned the building. She'd unlocked the door for me.

Nanette's apartment was white and shiny and clutter-free. Except my room, which was filled with giant stacks of my father's canned shakes. It looked like a grocery store. Edith invited me to stay in her apartment if I didn't want to be alone, but I said I'd be fine. We agreed to meet at nine a.m. the next day.

Under a stack of cans, an old clunky laptop sat on a white desk in my room.

I moved fast. I pressed the power button and created a new account on Upchat with the username GertrudeCatTx, so Dyna would know it was me.

Her face popped onto the screen. "*Lucy!*" She leaned in and whispered, "Hold on." She shut the door to her room. "Is this account trackable? I don't want you to get in trouble. Are you okay? Where are you?"

"In New York." I explained everything that had happened since I arrived. I thanked her for the stuffed hedgehog she'd sent me with the chocolates hidden inside it.

"I wish I could've sent a real hedgehog. An emotional support hedgehog," she said.

"I could use an emotional support hedgehog." Something squeezed my throat. I studied her face, the gray unicorn streak in her hair. I told her about driving Edith around and there being a possible murderer.

"No. Is there really? Or is she 'mentally impaired' like your dad said?"

"I don't know. I wish you were here to help me figure this all out."

There was a knock on her door and the murmur of words. She turned and shouted, "I'm just practicing! I need privacy!" She picked up Rosie, her viola, and played a loud measure by the doorknob, then came back to the computer.

"Hairy Tomato," she explained. Hairy Tomato was her

father. He worked for Fantasy Cruise Lines in the marketing department, which meant that he traveled all the time and sent her postcards from the Cayman Islands and Alaska and Southampton, England, where he shot promotional videos of himself opening giant bottles of champagne. He was like an overgrown frat brother with no fraternity, posting selfies on ships in his fashionable glasses and pastel shirts tucked into his pressed pants, wineglass in hand, always.

Two days after Dyna's mom died, he'd returned to work and sent her back to Thornton. "Right now my dad is in the Virgin Islands drinking cocktails out of a coconut," she said that night. "When we said goodbye at the airport, he actually said, 'It's a relief now in many ways. Her suffering is over. We can finally move on from this chapter of our lives.' I wish I'd said, 'I am moving on, because I truly understand now that you're a dick.' But I can't say that, because if I did he'd cancel my phone service. Also he started dyeing his gray hair brown, and with his perpetual sunburn he looks like a tomato in a wig." That's when we started calling him Hairy Tomato, which worked well since his real name was Harold Thomas, and he signed all his cards to her with his initials, like a business memo: *Happy Valentine's Day, Beloved Daughter—H.T.*

Now she put her viola down. "Guess what? Hairy Tomato is sending me and Lois, my homeschool tutor, on a cruise. He thinks I'm too provincial and I need 'to see the world.' Really he just wants me out of here so he can be alone with his new twenty-three-year-old girlfriend."

"Oh no."

"The girlfriend has a giant head. She looks like a balloon with a tiny string body."

"Hairy Tomato and Helium Balloon."

"What a couple."

"So off I go on a freaking cruise." Dyna hated cruises and got seasick within twenty minutes of stepping on a ship. Her father used to send us cruise brochures with their company tagline in swirly letters: *Let us take you to the place where all your dreams come true.*

Let us take you to the place where all your dreams are crushed, Dyna would say.

"It's the 'Grand Baltic and Northern Isles' one for *four weeks*. To freaking Norway, Iceland, Finland, and the Faroe Islands. I'd love to go if it was with you and not 2,400 people, Lois, and Herb, her boyfriend—Lois convinced my dad to let her bring him. I asked if I could bring you, and my dad laughed. He still says I can't be in touch with you, the jerk. So it's a month on the high seas with Lois and Herb. Herb is a ferret breeder. I kid you not. They make a photo calendar of their ferrets every year, dressed in little outfits that Lois sews. Ferrets in Santa hats in December. Ferrets in yellow skirts in June. The ferrets fight all the time, snapping, biting, and hissing. When she holds lessons at her house I'm surrounded by mad weasels."

I laughed.

"She's one mad weasel away from animal hoarding," she said. She picked up a giant book, her mother's copy of the *Diagnostic and Statistical Manual of Mental Disorders: DSM-V.* Her mother had been a psychologist. "I wish there was some way you could come with me on the cruise. The ship leaves from New York next Saturday—I was thinking at least you could come meet me before it sails, but Hairy Tomato is going to be there to see me off. Whenever the subject of you comes up, he acts crazy."

"I wish you could escape the cruise and come here. It could be your first step toward your career on Broadway," I said. Dyna's dream was to play in the orchestra for Broadway shows. She'd never been to New York before. We didn't even have a theater group at Thornton; Ms. Leery didn't believe it was "a good use of funds."

"I'd do anything for that," Dyna said quietly.

She heard a noise and glanced at the door; her father called her name in the distance. His voice grew louder. "I have to go," she said. She put three fingers on her lips. It was a gesture she and her mom shared during her mom's treatments, when her mom's throat hurt too much to talk. It meant *I love you.*

I put three fingers on my lips also.

"More soon," I said.

"More soon."

The chat window disappeared.

My chest felt hollow again. When Edith and I had left the restaurant, I'd glanced into the window of a shoe shop and saw a girl who looked like Dyna. My heart thumped—it wasn't her, of course. A Dyna mirage. All hope and longing.

I opened my diary. I wrote about missing her, and about

everything that had happened, and it felt like a tsunami pouring out of me. On the opposite page, I drew a picture of Dyna and me together, with thick weeds winding down the page and all around us.

nine

I MEET MY FIRST MURDERER

April 14, Nanette's apartment.
Goals:
1. Do not get ~~murdered~~ by lunatic
2. Do not let Edith get murdered by lunatic
3. Find some chocolate
Breakfast: 1 sip of ~~tastes-like-mucus~~ TrueYou lemon and kale
smoothie

I fell asleep on top of my diary and *Jane Eyre*, and woke up as the sunlight streamed in the window, and the fire escape outside sliced up the sky. I wrote again for a half hour, and then fell back asleep.

Soon after, a sound woke me—my door creaking open.

A half-naked man stood in the doorway, wearing only a towel. He gripped a hammer.

I screamed. I picked up a vase and threw it at him. I hid behind the bed.

He laughed.

This is it. I'm going to die. The murderer is going to kill me.

I searched for something else to throw or to use as a weapon. A sharp pen. A book.

"I'm not going to hurt you," he said, and stepped around the shards of the vase. "Put that book down." He placed his hammer on the dresser and folded his arms. "I'm sorry I scared you. I didn't mean to."

He smiled. He seemed to be enjoying watching me cowering. "I just wanted to welcome you. Nanette's still in the shower—we got in late last night. Had a work party. I'm Cyrus, Nanette's . . . partner. Sorry I look like this—did I leave my shirt in here? And my jacket? I can't find them anywhere."

He seemed Nanette's age or even younger—maybe twenty-two. A cloud of cologne surrounded him; it smelled like vanilla and burnt wood.

I dusted off my legs. My throat felt tight. I wasn't sure what to say in this situation. This was not in the etiquette book my mother had given me. *When a hammer-wielding-nutbar-possible-murderer appears, this is what you should say.*

I decided to observe every detail, as Edith had asked me to. *Uncreased hands, not those of a laborer. Snake-like expression. Disgustingly hairy chest. Lies about "losing shirt." Distinctive hideous cologne.* "Um, what's the hammer for?"

"Home improvements. Your window sticks—it needs a new locking mechanism so you can access the fire escape. Safety hazard, apparently. I told Edith I'd fix it, save her the hassle, since she's giving Nanette a break on rent. Shame about the vase. I think Nanette got it from Edith. It was probably worth a million dollars."

I froze.

"Don't worry, she won't mind, she's got plenty more. You're a fan of Fox's Fruit Syrups?"

Strawberry, raspberry, blueberry—I'd eaten them on pancakes and sundaes with my grandmother. "Edith Fox owns Fox's Fruit Syrups?"

"Her family did. She's a multimillionaire. And the best landlady ever. Kind to her tenants, practically a benefactor. Batty as hell but very, very rich." He looked me up and down, his eyebrows raised, like I was an injured exotic animal they were harboring, a reject from the zoo. "How exactly are you related to Nanette? You look nothing alike."

"She's my mother's cousin's daughter. Second cousin, I guess."

"Hmmm."

"I'll clean this up. Is there a broom?" I touched the shards. There were dozens of them. I tried to ignore the weight in my stomach, thinking of how mad Edith might be. I'd once broken a drinking glass at Thornton, and they'd taken the cost out of my weekly allowance. I might be paying this vase off for the rest of my life.

"Check the supply closet down the hall, one door down on your right."

I swept up the shards from the floor. Cyrus took the laptop out of the room—I was glad I'd deleted my search history—and he left. I jumped in the shower and put on my softest hoodie, which had once belonged to Uriah. I went to the kitchen and braced myself to say hello to Nanette.

She was almost six feet tall and even more glamorous than I'd remembered. She shared some of my mother's genetics, which somehow had completely skipped me: the honey-colored hair, the willowy body with pointed hip bones, and the arched, perfect feet. Even my toes went in every direction, like they didn't know where they wanted to go or what foot they belonged to.

She waved at me while talking on the phone. "Here's my cousin—distant, distant cousin—how lovely to see you, Lucy, how wonderful that you're staying with me! What a gift!" She spoke with a strange affect, like she was trying to be European. She twirled the belt of her silky black dress, and went to the refrigerator to remove one of my father's shakes.

"You wouldn't believe what I'm holding now—yes, they bought major advertising in *Clique*. Just have to babysit her for a few months," she said into her phone, and handed the can to me. "Drink more. Your father sent a million of them."

So she had meant sad-loser unique. I was only here because my father bought advertising in her magazine. I knew it had to be transactional, that she wouldn't have told Edith I was resilient and gifted unless she was getting something in return.

I took a sip of my dad's shake and tried not to spit it out. If they had a flavor called flu, this would be it.

She pinched my sleeve. "We're writing about hoodies in our next issue for a 'Relaxation Days' piece. What label is this?"

"Uriah," I said. He'd given it to me because it had shrunk in the wash and no longer fit him. It was extra soft from lots of washings and had a faded strawberry color. Uriah wore hoodies like they were armor. He often gave little gifts to Dyna and to me, left in our mailboxes—viola music for Dyna, a hedgehog bookmark for me, and little toy mice for Gertrude, wrapped in brown paper. "How did you know about Gertrude?" I'd whispered to him in the library one afternoon. He pointed to a lone cat hair on my sweater. He said little but seemed to see everything.

"Have you heard of the fashion label 'Uriah'? Me neither. Must be an Austin thing," Nanette told her friend on the phone, and shrugged.

She ended her call. "Lucy! *Lucy.* What a treasure to have you here. Edith told me she let you in yesterday, had I really said four p.m.? I didn't write it down. Your father sent strict instructions for your stay here and all your food." She opened a closet, where she'd stacked four more boxes of TrueYou shakes. "These were delivered yesterday along with the ones in your room. So glad I have all these since I have so much closet space. This is exactly what I wanted to do with my life. Harbor a teenager and store cans."

She looked me up and down again, the way she had when I'd

met her at the workshop in Austin, computing my status. Dyna once said that certain people seized on the sadness in you—the Things, Ms. Leery, Nanette now, too—as if they could sense the pain, the weak spot in you.

"When I spoke to your headmistress—she was so kind, she said I was a perfect role model for you, that I came to mind immediately when she sent you here, to change your life—but she hinted that something bad happened at that school of yours. Something you did. That's why you had to leave. She wouldn't tell me what, exactly. Your father didn't tell me, either. Can you tell me?" She blinked her giant, possibly-surgically-enhanced doll's eyes, their lashes like a Venus flytrap.

My insides crumbled. I couldn't tell her. They'd promised me that no one would ever know.

ten

NOT MOVING ON

At Thornton, one afternoon in early March, a package had arrived from Dyna's father. Inside was a jumbo bottle of black hair dye—*Jolie Femme Professional Premixed One-Step Color. Say Goodbye to Your Gray Fast*—and a note:

> *I know you said you didn't want to do this, but you don't understand the power of fitting in. —H.T.*

"My mom kissed the streak in my hair every night," Dyna said. "She never thought I should dye it. Never."

The next morning, while Dyna and I worked in the kitchen, we heard the screeches and whoops of other girls outside. The

Things had organized a scavenger hunt for their friends, for fun.

We later saw the hunt list:

2 grackle feathers
10 erasers from teachers' supply closet
1 cardigan from lesbian spinster couple

They'd taken a key to our room from the front office to steal a cardigan. That's when they found Gertrude. "We hit the jackpot," I heard them say later to their friends.

They called animal control. From the kitchen window, Dyna and I saw the van park outside our dorm. We sprinted to our room. A man in a uniform held Gertrude in a cage.

"Look what we found," Thing One said, standing beside him. "The crazy cat ladies have a cat."

"*Stop,*" I said. Dyna began to cry.

"You are in so much trouble," Thing One said with glee. I thought of how she'd taunted us for years, the constant looks of contempt and disgust; the comments, the "What's wrong with you?" and "That outfit is disgusting" and "It's heartbreaking that your parents barely come to visit. They must've forgotten you exist." *Build a barrier with your mind*, Dyna's mom would say. *Walk away.* But I couldn't.

My eyes settled on the bottle of hair dye on Dyna's dresser. I picked it up.

It happened so fast, the bottle in my hands, squirting it at Thing One from behind. The liquid spread over her blond hair and down her back, a big darkening reddish-black blotch on her white shirt and white jeans.

"You fat, ugly bitch," she said.

She backed out of our dorm room, into the hallway. I followed.

"Everyone hates you," she said to me. "Even your own parents."

She stood at the top of the landing. "The whole school knows they never wanted you. They never loved you. You never even lived with your own parents. What a joke."

The next seconds happened almost in slow motion: another force took over me, and I shoved her. She stumbled at the top step, lost her footing, fell backward and down the stairs.

She lay there on the landing below, not moving.

I froze. Someone screamed. I ran down the stairs. She was breathing. "She's breathing," I said. Her nose bled. A teacher came and pushed me out of the way. Time sped up, and Dyna's arms were around me, the police and an ambulance arrived, the animal control man took Gertrude, and paramedics came with a gurney and carried Thing One, whose real name was Victoria Jones, to the hospital. I couldn't stop shaking.

The police officer had an expression on his face, looking at me: *Who are you? What kind of person would do that?*

Victoria spent time in the emergency room with a concussion and bruises on her face, arms, and leg. Her parents threatened a lawsuit against the school and me, and my father negotiated with them to drop it. Ms. Leery said he paid them an enormous amount of cash.

I felt sick every time I thought of it. An accident. Was it?

I'd had secret fantasies, for years, of bad things happening to Thing One and Thing Two: they'd catch leprosy; they'd be whisked away by a tornado; they'd disappear into the forest to be eaten by a witch in a gingerbread cottage.

"It was an accident. You didn't mean to do it. She's a horrible human being," Dyna said. "Anyone would've fought back."

Who are you? What kind of person would do that? A bad person, the policeman's eyes had said.

Thing One shared photos of her bruises with everyone, and on campus girls looked away when I walked by. They hurried down the path.

My father called me yelling a number of times—"press the mute button," Dyna kept saying, and eventually he calmed down.

He finally sent an email.

Hello, Cricket, I've reviewed everything with my lawyer and you are a minor, so no matter what happens this will not be reflected on your Permanent Record. That is a relief, I know. Being young comes in handy sometimes. Gets you off scot-free, really, after time passes, with the documents sealed. Remember, though, you are a Representative of our family and you must never stop thinking of your Reputation. There will be Consequences for this.

Love, Dad

Three days later, Dyna's father withdrew her from school because he'd decided he wasn't comfortable exposing his daughter "to a roommate with severe issues."

Flo let me use her phone to call every animal shelter in town, and Flo searched them in person, but we couldn't track Gertrude down. We never saw her again.

My parents and their lawyer wrote a formal apology letter to Victoria that was officially from me, which I signed.

After Dyna left, I replayed what happened every night, with twists and turns and changes—what if we'd thrown the hair dye out when it arrived? What if Victoria had turned toward the hall instead of the stairs? What if I'd walked away? *Don't follow her, don't listen to her, walk away walk away walk away.*

And then, around midnight, when the halls were quiet and nobody else was awake, I began to relax a little. The dark covered the world like a blanket. I liked the idea of everyone else being asleep. There was no one judging me. No one disapproving. No one to taunt me or be cruel, or to demand anything, to take something away. No one to disappoint.

And then, just as suddenly, sometimes the nighttime turned on me. My thoughts took over—thoughts about how I had no one anymore. No family. My parents didn't love me. Victoria was right. My parents never wanted me. Did they know that something was wrong with me, deep inside?

One Monday morning, I slept through my classes, and I was sent to Mr. Fell, the school nurse, to check on my "mental health and well-being." He was Uriah's grandfather, and the only other male staff member. He drove a giant black hearse-like sedan, and was the opposite sort of nurse from my grandmother—he was gaunt, with a thick beard flecked with dandruff like frost crystals, as if he'd spent time in a freezer. Maybe Mrs. Fell made him sleep in the walk-in. "Good night, Frosty," Dyna used to imitate Mrs. Fell saying. "Sleep tight and don't bump into that frozen ham."

His office smelled like chemicals, like fungicide and preservatives. He handed me an herbal sleep supplement, a square packet of tiny green pills.

I was grateful for those pills. The insomnia felt unbearable sometimes. I missed Dyna and Nana and Gertrude most at night—I missed how when Dyna and I both couldn't sleep, when it felt like our beds were life rafts unmoored and adrift, Gertrude would hop from one bed to another, calming us like a sea captain, as if she could tell we needed extra help. After she was gone, I tried to pretend her soft paws were hugging my shoulders. A phantom cat.

Often, during the few hours I slept, I dreamed of Hawai'i. The air seemed golden and green, and I lived in a tree house with Dyna, Gertrude, Flo, my parents, and Nana, too, who said, *I'm still alive, I was just lost. It was all a mistake.* The tree house had endless rooms, one after another, filled with leafy branches. I woke up drenched in sweat.

Until they took Gertrude and Dyna away, I hadn't realized our life in 302 Thornton East was fragile; it seemed like the play forts I used to build when I was little, flimsy houses made of blankets and chairs and string.

eleven

JACK AND WIGGY

"Fine," Nanette said. "Don't explain. Though Cyrus can tell you, no one keeps secrets from me. I have ways of finding things out."

Cyrus nodded half-heartedly, scrolling through his phone and looking bored.

"How did you two meet?" I asked. On a dating site for shallow people?

"Cyrus works for Fairchild's auction house—they supplied antiquarian books for a cover shoot we did for our December issue—you must've seen it? It went viral? Of a model setting a pile of books on fire," Nanette said.

I had seen it. Everyone had. That issue of *Clique* was all

about new technology, and the cover had blared the words "No Longer Necessary!" The model had a deadened expression as she aimed a blowtorch at *Great Expectations, Pride and Prejudice,* and even *Jane Eyre.*

Cyrus saw my face. "We didn't really burn classic literature—we used worthless books and photoshopped the titles in. They were going to be pulped anyway. Nanette's genius is that she can take an image and twist it to find new meanings."

Nanette smiled at him. She caught sight of the clock. "Time to go. You can wait for Edith downstairs, outside," she said to me.

"I'm not meeting her till nine," I said. "It's only seven fifteen."

"Fresh air is good for you. Just don't wake her up at this hour. She controls our rent, so I don't want you to piss her off." She picked up her bag. I grabbed my backpack with my diary and asthma inhaler inside it, and followed them out the door and into the elevator. Hopefully the day would get better as soon as I was away from them.

On the street, as they started to walk away, Nanette's phone rang. She answered it. "Todd! How lovely." My father. Her voice turned sugary. "Yes, I'm so grateful to have her here. Indeed. I'll put her on. So grateful. So happy." She handed the phone to me.

My father's voice boomed, loud and cheerful. "Just wanted to check in! Isn't your cousin the most wonderful person? A perfect role model?"

Nanette leaned toward me, eavesdropping.

"Wonderful," I said.

"I'm so glad you're getting to know her. Did you meet the elderly woman? I'm so proud of you for helping her."

"Yes. She's actually really nice. She—" I paused.

"What?"

"Everything's fine." *I've been on a wild drive escaping a murderer and fended off a half-naked man with a hammer and my cousin is a sociopath.* "I'm moving forward. Onward."

"That's good to hear! I really think you've been listening. I think this opportunity will turn things around for you. I'm proud that you're embracing Change."

"Thanks. I really am."

Nanette pointed at her phone. I said goodbye to my parents and handed it to her. She rolled her eyes as my father kept talking. "Yes, of course," she said sweetly, "she won't be unchaperoned in this city. Not for a moment. Goodbye." She hung up and glared at me. "Shit," she told Cyrus. "I might be screwed if I leave her alone."

The front door opened and out came a young, lanky guy with floppy black hair, walking a cat on a leash.

Something warmed in me at seeing a cat, though I felt a pang for Gertrude. I remembered how, when I was eleven, my father told me I should clip photos from magazines to help me figure out who I wanted to be. He sent me a giant corkboard. I pinned pictures of fluffy orange cats to it, cats playing piano, cats in flowerpots, a cat riding on a vacuum cleaner, and a woman with three kittens sleeping on her forehead. (The Things' yearbook prediction wasn't exactly untrue.) When he came to visit, he saw the board and a look of horror crossed his face.

"Jack!" Nanette said to the young guy. "This is my cousin Lucy. Can you babysit her? Till she meets Edith? They're meeting at nine. I have to get to work."

Babysit? My face caught on fire.

"Sorry?" he asked. He looked barely older than me.

"Look, just make sure she doesn't get into trouble, okay? Or whatever. Lucy, this is Jack, er—"

"Jack Zuo," he said.

"That's right. This is Lucy. Fantastic kid. Real gem. We're in a rush. Have fun. Bye!" She and Cyrus hurried off, her heels clicking down the sidewalk.

I watched them turn the corner. "Nanette is my cousin from the space alien side of the family," I told Jack.

He smiled. "They only moved into the building a few weeks ago—up until last week, she kept thinking I was the janitor and handed me her trash bags."

His cat lay down on the sidewalk and swatted at the leash. He was brown with long-haired fur, like a fluffy hedgehog. Jack took a step, trying to get his cat to follow, but it refused to budge. Jack dragged him a few inches, sweeping the pavement. I tried not to laugh.

"As the janitor, it's my job to clean the sidewalk in front of the building," he said.

"Efficient method," I said.

"I made a promise to my mom that I'd walk him. He used to—well. He used to like it. You're Edith's new helper?"

I nodded. The sunlight turned the brick buildings across the street to gold. I breathed on my hands to defrost them in the cold morning air. Spring in New York felt like winter in Austin.

"People have been talking about you coming—this is a small building. You look like you're freezing. I'll buzz Edith? She wouldn't mind."

I shook my head. "I don't want to bother her this early."

"Do you want to wait inside? You could wait in the entryway." He had a kind, gentle face and a steady voice.

"I'm fine. I'm good," I said.

"Your lips are turning blue."

"That's their natural color. I'm part Smurf."

He gazed at me with a searching look, as if he could see my hollow insides and could tell I wasn't good. He watched my hands shiver a little. I stuck them in my pockets.

He tugged the leash again. His cat yowled and refused to move.

"What's his name?" I asked.

"Wiggy. He's named after Vincent Wigglesworth, a famous entomologist—one of my mom's heroes. She was a scientist."

Was.

I didn't know what to say. He looked at Wiggy and there was something heavy and lost behind his eyes. His shoulders slumped. So he was a member of the same club as Dyna and me—those of us who'd lost someone. You could tell when people carried that around. Other people seemed to stand up straighter, certain they were invincible to the world. They didn't realize.

"Wiggy, come on. Please. We need to get coffee." He tugged the leash. Wiggy glared at him, and then lunged at his leg and nipped him. Jack winced. "This is going well."

"Do you want me to hold his leash here while you get your coffee? I don't mind. I used to have a cat."

"Are you sure you don't mind? He won't bite if you don't force him to move. The coffee shop's right over there, so if he tries anything I can run back in a second. Usually I end up carrying him there with me. Not embarrassing at all to bring your cat to a coffee shop. Yesterday the owner made a 'No Felines' sign for the front door."

"Ridiculous policy."

"I know. Next thing they won't let Wiggy eat at the counter, either."

I took the leash, and he gave me a pouch of cat treats. He walked quickly to the coffee shop and waved, then disappeared inside.

I leaned down and petted Wiggy. It felt good to touch an animal, its fur and softness. I fed him a treat, and then he sniffed my hand and let me scratch his face. I found the spot by his whiskers where Gertrude loved being scratched, and after a while and many treats, he let me really pet him, and he went melty into the sidewalk. Then he rubbed against my leg. He sat still at first, and then I miraculously got him to walk a little. I coaxed him over to a square in the sidewalk in front of the building where lots of plants grew, by the street.

Wiggy lay down beside a fern and pawed at the dirt.

I thought of Nana's yard, weedy, messy, and enchanted, with dandelions galore. My father hated it. He begged to mow it every time he visited, and she refused. And I thought of the herb garden at Thornton, how lonely the plants looked in the dried-out soil, like they longed for company. Here the plants seemed like a festival, gathering to celebrate the world.

Jack came back holding a coffee cup and a hot chocolate piled high with whipped cream; it had sprinkles shaped like tiny gold stars. He handed it to me. "Thanks for watching him. This will warm you up."

I thanked him. It looked like a hot chocolate constellation. I took a sip. I loved New York.

"How did you get him to come over here?" he asked.

"I don't know—I think he likes this spot." We crouched down beside Wiggy. The tiny plot was filled with lots of ferns and strange plants I'd never seen before, a miniature forest sprouting from a cement sea. The ferns were still growing, their tops unfurling, their ends like curlicue snail shells, like green lollipops.

Wiggy let out a funny cat sigh. Cat happiness. He sniffed the dirt and turned over, his belly in the air.

One flower in front of me seemed from a fairy tale—white bells with tiny green dots like hand-painted china, hanging from a tall stalk. I touched it. "What is it?"

Jack said a Latin name but the name wasn't what I was asking for—I meant, how can this be? How can this grow from the sidewalk? I touched its pointed petals. "It looks like a lantern for a fairy ball."

He smiled. "I like that one, too. It's a perennial, so it will die back in a week or so and then bloom again next year."

"A whole year till I see it again?"

He nodded and touched the flower. "I keep asking it to stick around longer, but it hasn't listened." He paused. "My mother planted this little space—she put the perennials in years ago. I've been maintaining it. Or trying to." Sun shone through the leaves, lighting up their different shades of green. A rainbow of green. "She used to live—we shared the apartment in Edith's building. Until she died. Now I live there myself. With Wiggy." He sipped his coffee. "Though I think he'd be happier living right here, napping under the ostrich fern."

"Who wouldn't," I said.

His black hair fell in front of his face and he pushed it back, and then it dropped over his eyes again. He was good-looking but didn't seem aware of it. He stroked Wiggy's back. Then all of a sudden Wiggy turned, and he lunged at Jack's wrist like a flying Muppet. He bit him and swiped at him with his paw.

Jack hollered. Tiny teeth marks and four streaks of blood appeared, like red railroad tracks.

"Are you okay?" I asked.

Edith poked her head out a second-floor window—she'd heard him scream, too. "Is everything all right?"

"Sorry! It's fine. Just a scratch." Jack held up his wrist.

"I'm coming down," Edith said. Ten minutes later, the front door opened. She gave Jack a large Band-Aid, and Jack thanked her and put it on his wrist. Edith wore a long gray silk skirt today with a white blouse tucked in.

She patted the cat's head. "Wiggy's had a hard time lately. I think he misses Wenli. We all do." She turned to me. "I'm glad you two have met. Jack has lived on the fifth floor since he was two. He used to rip his diaper off and run down Summer Street waving it like a flag and singing 'This Land Is Your Land.'"

Jack gazed at his feet.

"Wenli, Jack's mother, was one of my closest friends—she conducted pioneering research on bumblebees, and she loved to garden, too. Lucy was such a help yesterday—she drove for me," she told Jack. She glanced both ways down the street, and relaxed. She handed me her keys again. "Are you ready? Everything seems safe today. We can get an early start."

"You have your license already?" Jack asked me with a look of surprise. "You look young."

Edith peered at him over her glasses. "You're only nineteen yourself. She's an excellent driver." I was glad she didn't mention almost hitting the dog yesterday, being honked at, the hood-banging and thrown coffee cup, et cetera.

"Can I see your license?" he asked.

"What? Why?" I asked.

"Jack." Edith had the tone of a mother gently reprimanding her son. She turned to me. "Jack is interning with his father, Scott, in the police department."

"I'm sorry—I'm trying to help," he said. "My dad said they're cracking down lately—I don't want either of you to get in trouble."

I opened my wallet. "It's a learner's permit." I handed it to him.

He looked it over. "It's actually illegal for you to drive here."

I'd broken the law. I knew I was capable, as Ms. Leery said, of spectacular failures, but this quickly was a new record for me.

Then, because the universe must have known I needed a character witness or a ringing endorsement, the hairy man from yesterday walked by. "Hey, my girlfriend! Love that tushy!" he said. I wanted to disappear into the manhole in the street. Thankfully Edith and Jack pretended not to hear him.

"I didn't think it through when I asked you to drive—I'm sorry," Edith said to me. She turned to Jack. "The man was following me again yesterday. I'm hoping I can drive myself soon, once my eyes are healed."

"Is it cataracts?" I asked Edith. I'd assumed she couldn't drive because of that, or simply old age. "My grandmother had those—she had to have surgery. After her eyes healed, she felt great."

"My eyes were damaged by the murderer," Edith said. "Poison in my eye drops."

Jack studied his shoes once more.

"Jack doesn't believe me," Edith said. "Because his father has decided I've made it all up."

"I think—I'm—" Jack said, and then seemed at a loss for words.

"Jack's father had the lab test my eye drops, and the toxicology report came back negative. But the bottles could have been switched." Edith paused. "We can be honest here. I know your father thinks I'm crazy."

Jack fidgeted with the bandage on his wrist. I glanced at Jack's hedgehog-on-a-leash, and back at Jack—who was the crazy one here? I wanted to point out.

Edith seemed to be thinking the same thing. "Aren't we all a bit crazy, though?" she asked him. "Aren't we all odd and strange." She said the last part as a statement, not a question, and her voice was so accepting and honest, it shook my world a little. We all were a bit odd and crazy—or a lot. My insomnia. My parents, Thornton, Dyna's father. The whole universe was sort of bananas. Clearly.

I wanted to tell Jack and his hedgehog that I believed Edith. That I wanted to help her. Not because my father told me to—but because I wanted to.

"I'm going to help Edith find the truth," I said. "About what's really happening. I'm going to help her solve this." My heart began its howling beats again, but I meant it.

"I hope you will." Jack said it in a trusting way. His eyes were kind.

Edith smiled at me and touched my shoulder. She took a cloth out from her bag and cleaned her glasses, and said we'd take the bus. "It's safer, anyway. No one would try anything in front of all those witnesses. I don't trust taxis or car service drivers—did you see that *Sherlock* episode where the taxi driver was the murderer?"

"I did. It was terrifying," I said.

Wiggy yowled again. "It was nice to meet you, Lucy," Jack said. "I should get to work. Welcome to New York—don't hesitate to ask if you need anything."

He shook my hand; his felt rough and weathered, like Edith's hands.

He took a step, but Wiggy wouldn't budge again. He picked him up, and Wiggy extended his raptor-like claws and swatted at him. Jack carried him as if holding a cactus.

The door behind them closed, and Edith sighed. "He was a really sweet boy once, before the world began to stomp on his soul." She looked down the street. "Now let's catch the bus to the garden."

"Let's do it," I said, my stomach churning at whatever lay ahead.

part iii

WONDERLAND

Watch with glittering eyes the whole world around you
because the greatest secrets
are always hidden in the most unlikely of places.
Those who don't believe
in magic will never find it.
—Roald Dahl

twelve

A FOX'S RULES FOR LIVING

The bus let us off on a cobblestoned street in the Far West Village, not far from the Hudson River, a mile and a half from Edith's place. We walked toward a giant stone town house standing alone, unattached to other houses like the rest of the block. Its window boxes overflowed with pink and yellow flowers, which cascaded down the building like a rainfall of petals.

We climbed the marble steps and Edith gripped the brass door knocker. She knocked twice.

After a moment, the door opened a crack. "Is it safe?" a voice whispered from the darkness.

Edith glanced down the block. "Yes. No one's following me."

"Well, come in quickly, then." A six-foot-tall woman emerged from the darkness. She waved us inside. She wore a gray braid wrapped around her head like a crown, and earrings shaped like sunflowers.

She shut the door behind us and locked it. "These are times that try the soul."

Edith introduced us; she was named Alice, though her friends called her Mimsy.

"How do you get 'Mimsy' from 'Alice'?" I asked.

"*All mimsy were the borogroves.* From the 'Jabberwocky' poem. My father was a Lewis Carroll fan. He called me that since the day I was born." She shrugged. "Lucky he didn't call me mome wrath, though that does have a certain ring to it. Gladys made tea for us—I hope you're hungry."

"Starving," I said.

"As am I, in so many ways." Mimsy led us down the hallway. Framed black-and-white photos from stage plays lined the walls. *All's Well That Ends Well, The Delacorte, 1978*, one engraved gold label said. *A Midsummer Night's Dream, The Mount, 1984*, said another. I stared at a picture of a woman in fairy wings gazing at an elf-like man up in a tree.

Mimsy leaned in beside me. "'Love looks not with the eyes, but with the mind.' That's a Helena line, though you know Titania was always my favorite role. Loved enough asses in my time, is why I was so good at it. Came naturally."

The hallway opened up into a giant living room and a wall of windows, the sun in the distance, a glittering pom-pom.

They led me out a glass door and into the back garden, to

a sea of daffodils and cherry trees. White daffodils with pink cups, and ruffly yellow ones, and some like orange meteors. There were hundreds of flowers, kinds I'd never seen before and didn't know the names of, which resembled starfish and moons and tiny pink spaceships. The flowers swayed—they seemed to be almost laughing—and the cherry blossoms floated down like pink snow. The air smelled of sugar and honey.

"This isn't real," I said.

Mimsy laughed. "It is real. It's Edith's work. Edith's magic." She spoke of magic matter-of-factly, as if it were an accepted thing.

We followed a narrow stone path through the walled garden, past hand-carved chairs hidden behind hedges, a miniature fairy village, a tiny reflecting pool in the shape of a question mark, and a gravestone that read "SMUSHY, YOU WILL ALWAYS BE LOVED," for Mimsy's old bulldog, she said. At the end of the path was an outdoor library filled with stone books with titles like "HOLY SCHIST" and "IT'S NEVER TOO SLATE." A magnolia stood against the library wall, its buds like pink baby owls.

It was different from any place I'd ever been—it felt like being inside a strange work of art that was alive.

"You do know that Edith is one of the most famous horti-culturists in the world?" Mimsy asked me. "That she's authored three bestselling classic gardening books?"

I shook my head. "Nobody told me."

Edith waved the compliment away and pinched off flower

heads that were turning slightly brown.

"Always editing," Mimsy said. "That's what she calls it when she clips and trims. 'Editing.'" She waved her hand around the garden. "What do you think?"

"I've never seen anything like this." Something fell away from me, being there. It was as if the beauty scrubbed your shallow surface off.

Mimsy explained that the property was less than an acre, but it seemed larger because it was next to a church garden, which made it feel as if the grounds stretched on and on. A lot of thought had gone into engineering this magic, she said.

We walked over to a cherry tree, and hidden behind it was a white metal table set for tea, and a tiered tray filled with scones and tiny muffins. Yellow birds and red hearts decorated the teacups; everything at Mimsy's was brightly colored.

"I feel like a white rabbit with a pocket watch might say hello any second," I said.

"Which would be lovely," Mimsy said. She poured tea into our cups. Her long orange nails scooped up a muffin.

I gobbled a tiny scone with clotted cream and lemon curd. It tasted like lavender and sugar and everything good in the world.

I had an odd feeling, being there—Nana used to say that homes had souls, like people do, and we loved them like people. Maybe gardens had souls also.

Mimsy cleared her throat. "Did you tell her?" she asked Edith in a stage whisper.

"Yes. She knows. Not the specifics."

"The specifics?" I asked.

"Of what's been happening. Of who might be trying to kill Edith," Mimsy said. She sounded more theatrical than alarmed.

Edith leaned back in her chair. "Mimsy enjoys playing detective." She had a half-amused, half-stern look. "This is serious, though."

"I'm very serious. I'm just confident that we can stop him. Don't forget, I played Miss Marple in *What Mrs. McGillicuddy Saw* on the radio. I picked up a lot of skills."

"You were wonderful in that performance," Edith said. "Your acting days are not over, I promise you."

Mimsy devoured another muffin. She turned to me. "I'm surprised it's not me they're after. There have been lots of people who've wanted to do away with me over the years. Or simply drive me crazy. Wanting things." She paused and lowered her voice. "Money and love. Reveals who's truly evil and who's not."

"Is that why you think Edith's in danger? Because of money? Or love?" I asked.

Mimsy nodded. "Absolutely. We'll tell you all the suspects. Maybe you should write this down. When Edith told me about you, I thought, that's exactly what we need. The perspective of someone who isn't old and jaded like us."

I was glad they didn't know about the jaded—or worse than jaded—parts of me, and the real reason I was on an "internship" from Thornton.

I took my diary out of my bag and wrote down what Mimsy said.

LIST OF PEOPLE WHO MIGHT WANT TO MURDER EDITH FOX

"Write down 'Peter,'" Mimsy said, and described him.

Peter Lloyd, Edith's longtime friend and professor of botany and ecology

"Please. I'm a hundred percent certain Peter doesn't want to do away with me," Edith said.

"Do you ever really know a person? I think it's smart to remain suspicious." Mimsy added an extra sugar cube to her tea.

"I met Peter at the restaurant yesterday. He asked Edith to go on a trip with him," I said.

"Again? Let's hope he doesn't go postal if you say no. Peter's been in love with Edith for forty years—he wants to marry her. Love makes people stark raving mad, you know. Put that down as 'Possible Motive.'" Mimsy picked up a butter knife and pretended to run it across her neck.

I wrote:

Love é stark raving mad

Edith sighed. "Peter is not going to attack me with a butter knife. Or poison me."

"I didn't want to tell you this, but yesterday I asked the tarot cards, 'Do we trust Peter?' and the Moon card came up reversed. It means there are secrets and skeletons deep in his closet."

"Everyone has skeletons and secrets," Edith said.

"And maybe commitment issues," Mimsy whispered to me.

"I can hear you," Edith said. "I might be half blind, but I'm not deaf."

"And, Lucy, write down Cyrus Shaw, please," Mimsy said.

"Nanette's boyfriend?" I told them what had happened that morning.

"Be extra careful around him," Mimsy said. "Are you sure it's safe to stay there? You're always welcome to stay here." Edith said the same thing.

"Thank you—but it's part of my arrangement to stay with her because she's my cousin," I said, though it felt good that they'd offered. "I think it'll be fine." I shrugged.

"If he makes you feel uncomfortable, come here anytime." Mimsy paused and tapped her finger on the list I was writing. "Please put down 'A Stranger' in case it's some mad stalker or something," she said. "And Clifford."

"No. Not Clifford," Edith said. "*No.*"

"And Liliana," Mimsy added. "Though I know . . ." She fiddled with a muffin wrapper.

"No, absolutely not." Edith glared at Mimsy. "Enough."

I gripped my pen. "Who are Clifford and Liliana?"

They didn't answer. Edith shook her head. "This isn't getting us anywhere. I think we have to accept that we don't have a clue who it is yet, or why. Let's show Lucy the evidence of the first murder attempt."

"There's evidence here?" I asked. "In the garden?"

"This way," Edith said.

They led me to a small greenhouse along the side wall, which was filled with rows of seedlings sprouting everywhere. Mimsy pointed at the plants. "See?"

I eyed the plants. What was I looking for? A bloody knife nestled among the pots? A torn piece of clothing? A note from the murderer saying *I'm after you*? "What—am I looking at?"

"The missing seedlings," Mimsy said.

I realized that she was pointing at empty spots among the rows, behind labels that read *Aconite, Digitalis, Sanguinaria, and Brugmansia.*

"Four seedlings—all highly poisonous and deadly—were stolen the night of March twenty-first, during my annual spring equinox party," Mimsy said.

"Why are you growing poisonous plants?" I asked.

"Many plants are toxic. Nobody plans on eating them. We never thought anyone would steal them," Mimsy said. "We've never had anything like this happen before, and I've been hosting this equinox party for a decade. It's an annual benefit for UNICEF." She picked chocolate chips out of the scone she'd brought with her and ate them one by one. "That night, men and women swirled about in their fancy dresses; we had music and dancing, and a firepit for roasting marshmallows. Edith's eyes bothered her from the smoke, so she went into the potting shed to put in her eye drops. She uses them several times a day for her dry eyes."

"Later that night, my vision changed—it became cloudy. I could barely see," Edith said.

"The tiniest drop of sap from any of those plants would be all it took," Mimsy said.

"Jack said the eye drops were tested?" I asked.

"The killer could've easily switched the bottle. It's a generic. Put the poison in, wait till she uses it, then switch it so it tests clear. That night, they also tampered with Edith's drink. She came down with a violent illness. Nausea and vomiting. Three days later, Edith noticed the seedlings. Gone."

"I ordered a blood test and we finally received the results two days ago—they found traces of *Brugmansia* in my system. Scott, Jack's father—he's a homicide detective—he said it's not evidence enough for a murder attempt—he said it was 'likely accidental' since we had a bartender that night mixing drinks with fresh herbs right from the garden, and they could've been 'easily harvested by mistake,' he said." Edith shook her head. "We don't 'mistakenly' harvest." She looked as if he'd accused her of the worst sin imaginable.

I thought of Jack's reaction earlier, how he seemed to agree with his father.

"I'm sure the police would have a hard time getting a search warrant for missing seedlings," I said.

"Yes. They didn't believe us in the slightest. Just two demented old ladies, they thought. Imagining things," Edith said. "I know it sounds far-fetched. Believe me. The police said I need concrete proof."

"I believe you. I'll help you find proof," I said. I liked how they were taking action and trying to solve it, and how they looked at this—at life—as a challenge and almost a game. Not something that squashed you until you couldn't recover.

"So we know the murderer was at the party," I said. "Were the people you mentioned—Peter, Cyrus, Clifford, and Liliana— all there? Do you have a copy of the guest list?"

They nodded.

I thought of every mystery novel I'd read and detective show I'd seen. "We should probably start with the major suspects," I said. "Gathering more information about them, their motives, and whereabouts yesterday to see if they could've been the person following you. And what their behavior was like at the party that night—if anyone saw them sneak into the potting shed and greenhouse alone."

"Yes," Mimsy said. "Perfect."

"This all sounds good," Edith said, though she looked uncertain. She glanced around the garden and checked her watch. "I need to change into gardening clothes and get to work now— we have a lot of planting to do today."

"I'm ready to help," I said. I remembered something. "This morning in Nanette's apartment—I broke one of your vases. I'm so sorry. It was an accident. You can take the cost out of my pay." I braced myself for her response. At Thornton I'd be scrubbing toilets and washing dishes for weeks to make up for it.

"Don't worry—it wasn't worth anything," she said kindly, and I relaxed with relief.

Mimsy stood up. "Let me show Lucy the folly first, and then I'll bring her right back?"

"All right. Be quick," Edith said.

Mimsy led me down the path to the back corner of the garden. "It wasn't only that I wanted to show you the folly," she said when we were out of earshot. She lowered her voice. "I wanted to tell you I think Clifford is the murderer. He's Edith's son— she gave birth to him when she was only sixteen and gave him up for adoption. They only reconnected three months ago. He was at the equinox party that night."

I tried to imagine what it must have been like for Edith to have a baby at my age. My chest hurt, thinking of it. "Do you really think he's guilty?"

"I'm not sure, but all these strange things started happening after he arrived—the poisoning at the equinox party, the man following her, and the problem with her eye drops. Edith won't believe it's Clifford—she's convinced it has to be someone else. The night of the equinox party, before the poisoning, she introduced Clifford, and told everyone how she'd found her son. She also recently added him to her will. Clifford and Liliana— Edith's stepdaughter—they'd both inherit millions if anything happened to Edith."

"Edith's married?" I asked.

"Divorced. Her ex-husband died a decade ago."

"Could Clifford have been the man following her yesterday?"

"It's possible. I think that's why he poisoned her eyes. So he could follow her and make another attempt on her life, and she wouldn't be able to identify him."

We reached the folly, a small stone cottage near the back wall of the garden, under a crabapple tree. It looked like it had been built by gnomes, with a moss-covered roof and a chimney.

"Why is it called a 'folly'?" I asked.

"It's from the French word *folie*—it means both madness and delight." She paused, not seeming too delighted. "Next Saturday night, Edith is hosting her annual Passover seder. Clifford will be there. It will be the perfect time to get evidence. Maybe he'll even try something. We'll catch him in the act."

"On Passover?" Something lifted in me at the thought of going to a seder, since I hadn't been to one since my grandmother died. I hadn't known Edith was Jewish, too. I felt glad she was—it was like finding a fellow member of a secret society.

"Do you think I should try to get to know Clifford at the seder, then? Ask him questions?" I asked.

"Exactly," Mimsy said. "I asked him a few questions two days ago, when Edith's blood test confirmed there was *Brugmansia*—angel's trumpet—in her system. He was so upset that I suspected him—it didn't go well. Hopefully you'll have better luck."

We went inside the cottage and sat in two rocking chairs. My eyes settled on a picture frame on the stone wall above the fireplace. Inside it was a yellowing page from a vintage black-and-white magazine, *American Housekeeping*. Flowers curled around the edges of the page, with a tiny fox leaping out. The first letter of each rule was in a fancy font, with leaves and flowers winding around them.

"Edith wrote that when she was around your age. One of her gardening columns. She took over the column after her mother died—she used to help her mother write them, and they were so popular that the editor asked her to keep writing it. She wrote this one a year before Clifford was born, before her life changed."

A Fox's Rules for Living
April 1956

Spring has sprung! New beginnings, fresh starts, and freedom. The whole world is awakening and making itself new. City dwellers, if you stay in your apartments this month, you'll miss it. Some blooms will be gone in a flash. Get to a garden, a real garden. It will change you.

This month's rules:

1. TRUST. Plants want to live. I can't tell you how many letters readers send me every day that say, "I have a brown thumb and can't grow anything." Most plants will do anything to survive. They'll tolerate unhappy conditions and questionable soils and pests. Trust that they want to live and you won't kill them. (Or at least you won't kill all of them.)

2. DORMANCY IS NOT DEATH. At this time of year everything looks dead, gone, kaput, like the depths of despair. Be patient: give everything a chance. Don't overwork the soil and pull up roots in a rush. Wait for the plants to rise from their dormancy.

3. RECORD EVERYTHING. The best way to learn is to write down everything: what is planted where and when and what grew, and also why. Why do you love what you love? Why do you think it's beautiful?

4. WE ALL STAND ON A PRECIPICE. On one side of the cliff is despair and gloom, a wasteland. On the other is a garden in full bloom. Which side will you choose?

This month, design a bed of annuals in a perfect rainbow to shock the neighbors: red petunias, orange poppies, yellow pansies, blue ageratum, and violet snapdragons. Recommended reading this month: The American Gardener *by William Cobbett,* Down the Garden Path *by Beverley Nichols, and* The Gardener's Year *by Karel Čapek.*

We all stand on a precipice. It made me think of my mother, and how, during one of my parents' visits to Austin, on my thirteenth birthday, after I'd started boarding school, my mom took me to the Barton Creek mall to celebrate, just the two of us. I was so excited to be alone with her that I couldn't even eat breakfast that morning; my stomach wouldn't stop twisting.

My mother had glossy shampoo-ad hair, fawn-like eyes, and expertly applied makeup. Somehow, I'd gotten my father's dark circles under his eyes, not my mother's and Nanette's perfect, smooth, moon-like faces.

I loved being alone with her. My heart whirred as if I were onstage, and I never wanted the day to end. Every minute with her felt alive, electric.

We walked by Picture Paradise, a place that took professional photos. "I know what we're going to do," my mom said. "Get pictures taken. We'll surprise your father."

We went to Sephora first and she did my makeup, and then she bought me a blue silky dress that made me think of a waterfall, and then we went to Picture Paradise.

I'd never had professional photos taken before. We gathered props and chose different backdrops and spent a half hour in different poses. In one photo she held a sign that read "Best Friends," and in another I wore a tinsel tiara that read "Birthday Girl" and we held a plastic cake.

She bought the most expensive package, $200 for the digital images and prints of all sizes. "Your dad will love these."

Later, he put them on his website with a line that said, "The ladies in my life." The photos had so many different backgrounds that you'd almost think they were taken at different times, in different places, not all in one afternoon.

We ate lunch at California Pizza Kitchen. She ordered a salad, and I ordered the same thing. I wanted to be like her. "I'm so sorry that I don't see you more. But you know that I'm always thinking of you. You can't ever leave your family. Family is here forever. I'm always with you," she said, and squeezed my hand. "Sometimes life isn't fair. It isn't what you planned. But that doesn't mean it's a bad thing." Her eyes were steely. I wished I could feel strong like her, and not like I would collapse as soon as she left.

After lunch, we stopped by the mall bookshop to see my dad's books. "There they are!" my mom said. "I always feel so proud of them when I see them. If people knew who we were, that we were related to him—well. Imagine. We're so lucky to be who we are, you know?"

"I know," I said. I wanted to freeze that day with her, to keep it forever, to always be included in that *we*.

"Why are you crying, sweetie?" she asked me.

"I don't know. I'm happy," I said, but that wasn't the truth exactly. "I feel happy and sad," I tried to explain. I couldn't put it into words.

"Me too. I love getting to see you. It makes me feel so good. You know how much I love you. You know I have no control over any of this. Sometimes life deals you a rough hand. Sometimes it's a struggle. I've done my best."

"I know."

"I know our situation hasn't been perfect, but I love that you accept it," my mom said.

The power of acceptance was from my dad's books, too. I wanted to do that.

"Do you love me?" I squeaked out.

"Of course, Cricket. Never doubt that. I'm sorry I don't say it more. You know, my own parents never said it to me once, not in their lives, not one single time. It's not that they didn't feel it, they just didn't know to say it. I'm trying to not be like them. It's hard for me. They used to say children should be seen and not heard as a joke, but they actually meant it. The only thing they cared about was that I married well." She shrugged. "At least I did that."

Before she said goodbye, at the end of the day, she said, "Let's do this every year." She'd bought the Picture Paradise frequent customer card. "Every time I visit." Then came more travel for them, and stress over my father's income and book sales, the TV show, and the Incident. And now here I was.

"Are you okay?" Mimsy asked me, bringing me back to the present.

I nodded. I looked at Edith's column again. "I love her rules," I said. "I bet nobody believed this was written by a teenager." I touched the frame, my finger hovering over the black-and-white engraved illustrations of flowers.

"Of course not." She hugged her elbows. "People look down on teens as much as—or worse than—they look down on old ladies. Like we're all idiots."

I laughed a little. It was true. I liked that Mimsy and Edith were old, and not only because of my grandmother—it was that thinking about being their age was like peeking into another realm where the shallow things didn't matter.

A precipice. On one side I had Thornton and misery, and on the other side this strange blooming world. I wanted to find a way to stay in this one.

thirteen

SUGAR FIXES EVERYTHING

April 23
Goals:
1. Do not screw up
2. Observe suspects and look for clues
3. Meal plan: chocolate, chocolate, matzo ball soup, chocolate

Every morning in Mimsy's garden felt like unwrapping a present—seeing what had bloomed, which buds had formed, and which corners of the garden had turned into new tiny worlds.

The week had been a crash course in plant education. "A flower you've grown yourself is different from one bought in a store," Edith told me. "You've tended it, nurtured it—you'll see." Mimsy loaned a stack of gardening books to me, including the three that Edith had written, and I studied them every night. Edith gave me potted plants for my room and fire escape to practice tending to, and I learned all about amending soil and fertilizing, deadheading and pinching off. One of Edith's books, *Strange Botanicals*, included a whole section on poisonous plants, and I studied the plants that had been stolen. And I learned more about Edith and Mimsy—how Mimsy had an agent who she kept calling to get her auditions, but the agent never returned her calls, and how Edith had a heart condition called atrial fibrillation and took a medicine for it, digoxin, once a day. I barely saw Nanette and Cyrus; I only heard the locks on the front door click and unclick. I suggested to Mimsy that we invite them to the seder, to observe Cyrus more closely, too. "Excellent idea!" she said.

At night sometimes when I couldn't sleep, I'd sit on the fire escape outside my bedroom window, to look at something besides the cans in my room. I'd stare up at the windows of the apartments around me and at the tiny courtyard below, where the cherry tree bloomed. I'd touch my fire escape plants—pansies and violas, baby fuchsias, chocolate mint.

One afternoon, when I came home from Mimsy's garden, an ostrich fern was outside Nanette's front door with a tag on it.

For Lucy—
I heard you were growing a garden on your fire escape—here's an addition for the shady side.
—Jack

It smelled fresh and strange and new, and its leaves felt feathery and soft. Its fronds stood tall like an all-green peacock.

On Saturday it was Edith's Passover seder. After breakfast, Edith, Mimsy and I sat at Edith's dining room table, counting the Haggadahs, the texts for the seder, and arranging the place settings and the ceremonial foods for the meal.

Nothing in my life had prepared me for Edith's apartment. We'd been spending all our time at Mimsy's—this was the first time I'd seen beyond the entryway of Edith's home.

It was an 1800s mansion plopped inside the six-story building: an open living room with a spiral wood staircase to the second floor, elaborate moldings and ceiling plaques, chandeliers and marble fireplaces, wood shutters, and honey-colored plank floors that creaked with every step.

I couldn't believe this gigantic home could exist inside an apartment building—it was like wandering into another world. And Edith owned it.

"This whole building used to be one house," Mimsy explained. "A thirty-room mansion. Edith's father, Robert Fox, bought it from Henry Alton, an old New York shipping magnate. Later on, her father broke it up into one- and two-bedroom apartments—this is the only original part of the building that remains." She waved her arms around. "It's amazing, isn't it?"

"I've never been anyplace like this," I said.

"It's the only home I've had in my life," Edith said.

"You're lucky to choose who to rent to." Mimsy turned to me.

"That's why, when Clifford and Edith reconnected, he was able to have his choice of two different vacant apartments, and he chose the one on the third floor. Nanette rented the other one."

Edith noticed our expressions. "I didn't realize what Nanette was like. Or that she'd bring Cyrus along. She had such stellar recommendations."

Of course she did. A perfect role model, my parents and Ms. Leery had said.

The formal dining table held dozens of flowers in antique vases. A pot of matzo ball soup simmered on the stove, making the entire apartment smell good. I peeked in the oven, where Edith's cook and housekeeper, Cora, roasted a turkey.

Edith set the place cards out in front of her on the dining room table. "Where should we seat everybody?"

"I think Clifford would be happy sitting over here by this lovely painting," Mimsy said, moving his seating card far from Edith. "And since Lucy is new here, let's seat her across from Jack's father, Scott. Can't hurt. Police protection."

Edith rolled her eyes. "There are only eight people coming besides us. There were a hundred at the equinox party. I'm certain it's not one of these eight friends, neighbors, and family."

Mimsy examined a place setting and picked up a knife. "Maybe we shouldn't use the ones that are quite so sharp."

"Here we go." Edith rolled her eyes again.

Mimsy felt the knife's edge. "Probably couldn't do too much damage. Maybe take off a pinkie finger if you really sawed away at it."

"Ewww," I said.

Edith ignored Mimsy and finished writing out the shopping list for the last things we needed. I offered to get everything on the list: a flourless cake, macaroons, and meringues from three different bakeries—her favorites—in the neighborhood, as well as some appetizers and items for the seder plate.

As I walked down the street, I thought of how, my first Passover at Thornton, I asked Mrs. Hipp, the school secretary, if there would be a seder. "A what?" she'd asked, her face blank. I'd explained the eight-day holiday to her, and she kept squinting at me as if I was describing some imaginary thirty-day holiday celebrating broccoli.

Both my parents were Jewish, but neither had any interest in Judaism and worshipped what they called the "Life Force" of the world instead. Dyna's grandfather was similar—he pretended he wasn't Jewish at all and raised Dyna's mom completely secular. Nana had been a tiny bit religious, celebrating the Jewish holidays. My parents insisted we celebrate Christmas so we wouldn't feel "left out of the fun"—we stayed in Austin's Dellamark Hotel for three days at Christmastime every year.

The Dellamark had cowhides on almost every surface. I called it the Cow Murder Hotel. I refused to eat the steak my parents ordered in front of the hides. "It's mean," I said. "Like eating their babies while they're watching."

My parents loved Christmas at the Dellamark; they liked to dress up and order cocktails in the grand lobby, and to sit near the tall tree covered in gilt ribbons with fake presents at its base.

I tried to like it, too, but this pit would grow inside me there. It felt like we were performing in a video called "Christmas Cheer." I found myself complaining that the hotel was always freezing, and the free cookies in the lobby were burnt on the bottom, the Santa too obviously fake. The complaints felt like I had these bad things inside me and I had to fling them out, though I knew I sounded ungrateful. I missed Nana's house, its soft overstuffed couches and its reading nooks, fluffy rugs, and deep dishes of mac and cheese. I missed Nana's squeezing hugs. My parents hugged politely, as if they didn't want to wrinkle your clothes.

Dyna and I used to talk about having this heritage that felt chopped off from you—when Nana died, that's how being Jewish felt to me. Nana was born in Germany in 1938, and escaped with her mother on one of the last boats this country allowed in. She showed me her birth certificate with a swastika in a circle beneath a bird. All her aunts and uncles had been killed. She grew up speaking German and Yiddish, and regretted never teaching either language to me.

"When my mom died I didn't only lose my mom but my whole identity, my entire world," Dyna said once. "I can't believe I think this, and I hate thinking this, but I wish my dad was the one who died." Her mom was an only child and had lost her own parents when she was young; she only spoke English to Dyna. "When I study Spanish now it makes me feel like this whole part of me was cut off." We both felt like our family trees had been chopped down.

On Thanksgiving, Dyna and I both stayed on campus, and Flo cooked a feast for us, making all the foods we longed for: Nana's brisket recipe and Dyna's mom's pan con chumpe and leche poleada, and plain chicken for Gertrude.

Now, in New York City, Passover was everywhere: shops hung glittery blue Stars of David in their windows, bakeries displayed "Kosher for Pesach" signs over their flourless cakes, and towering stacks of matzo filled the windows of the West Village Market. I loved it.

I stopped outside the last bakery on the list, on Perry Street. It was called Sugar Fixes Everything, and when I peeked inside I saw a girl browsing at the counter, her back to the window—she was my age, in sunglasses, with black hair flowing out from under a blue hat. Another Dyna mirage.

I walked inside. It was crowded. I almost wanted to talk to the girl, but what could I say? *Hi, you look like my best friend. Wanna hang?* That would be humiliating.

The girl stood at the front of the line and put her hand on the glass case, staring at the croissants and buns and tarts. She asked the man behind the counter, "How do I get to Summer Street?"

"*Dyna?*"

A million feelings flooded me at once. She hugged me and we laughed and squealed, holding each other in a crazy sort of dance, and because this was New York City, no one even noticed.

She held up a crumpled piece of paper in her hand—a rough

sketch of a map. "I've been walking around looking for a way to find you! I Google-stalked Edith Fox and found an article about her, but no exact address. I've been wandering for an hour."

"How did you escape the ship?"

"Long story. Who designed this freaking city? Why does West Fourth Street cross West Tenth Street? How can anyone find their way around? I can't use my phone's GPS—I turned it off—I'm afraid if they notice I'm missing, they'll try to track me with it."

"I can't believe you're here. I thought I was imagining you. How did you get here?"

"I escaped. I jumped ship. Literally. I was on the ship and then I left." She pointed to the viola case at her feet. "We boarded early—my dad was antsy to get rid of me—and we had extra time and I saw the musicians and I talked to the viola player, performers on the cruise. They were meeting musician friends in New York until the passengers finished boarding. I snuck out with them. Then I walked here all the way from the pier on Fifty-Fifth Street." She glanced at the clock on the wall. "The cruise ship left the harbor twenty minutes ago." She shook her head. "I have so much to tell you."

We sat down on two white stools by the window. "How did you get Lois to agree to it?" I asked.

"I had to give her a thousand dollars."

"Whoa."

"Yep. It's crazy. I lost my mind. I had to give her all the cash

119

my dad gave me for port days in order to keep quiet, and some of the money my mom left for me before she died. I just couldn't stay on that ship. It was like my body wouldn't let me. Like my mom was telling me, 'Get off this hulking boat. Get away from these mad weasel people. Go find Lucy.' Lois promised that she'll tell my dad I'm fine. I even wrote postcards for her to send to him from all the ports. She and Herb are probably going to start an online ferret clothes shop with my money, but who cares."

"You're sure Hairy Tomato won't find out you're missing and freak out?"

"The whole reason he shipped me off is because he and his girlfriend are planning to elope. I'm not supposed to know—I peeked at his texts. They leave tomorrow for a cruise themselves to Bora Bora. Believe me, he won't be checking up on me. He's happy to get rid of me."

"I can't believe you're here." I hugged her again. I felt everything inside me melt a little. Dyna had this inborn poise, this sense of herself—she always carried herself with confidence, and when she played her viola, it seemed like it was an extension of her body. "Does this mean you can stay for the whole four weeks of the cruise?"

"Well . . . I didn't exactly figure out that part of the plan yet." She smiled sheepishly and touched the strap on her black duffel, next to her viola case. "I haven't figured out any part of the plan, actually. This is all I brought—I didn't want to look suspicious getting off the boat with a big suitcase."

"Don't worry. I know who can help us."

. . .

"I live in a huge house. If I can't share it, then what's the point of anything? Why live?" Mimsy told us. She insisted that Dyna stay with her in her house and showed her the guest room on the top floor, which was Mimsy's daughter's room when she came home to visit. Mimsy told us that her daughter was an actress who lived in Australia now. "It's my favorite time of the year when she comes home. I love hearing the pitter-patter of little feet up here."

"How old is your daughter?" Dyna asked.

"Forty." Mimsy sighed. "I know. But she's still my baby."

Mimsy brought us glasses of sparkling juice and a tray of snacks. Dyna took out her viola, Rosie, to make sure she'd survived the journey. She cradled her.

"That's her soul mate," I said.

"I'll have to introduce you to the group of musicians—Juilliard students—who play around the neighborhood. They perform at cafés and sometimes play in the Christopher Street station."

Dyna's face lit up. "I'd love to meet them."

I told Dyna about the seder that night, and Mimsy insisted that Dyna join us. "We'll need to invent a story to explain why you're with us to the other guests," she said. "So nobody knows you're a cruise runaway."

"We could say you're my old friend and former classmate from Thornton—all true—who's now studying viola at Juilliard," I said.

"That's my dream," Dyna said.

Mimsy fluffed the pillows on the bed. "Perfect."

Dyna put Rosie back in her velvet case. "What if they ask me about Juilliard and I don't know what I'm talking about?" She snapped the case shut. "Maybe I won't say much tonight. I'll be shy. Like Uriah."

"Who's Uriah?" Mimsy asked.

We told her all about him, how he wore hoodies every day so you could barely see anything but his eyes and nose poking out, and how he barely ever said a word. We told her how he was the epitome of gentleness.

"It's an art, too, expressing things only with your eyes," Mimsy said, wiggling her eyebrows at us until we laughed.

Dyna and I told Mimsy about Flo and Ms. Leery, too. "I texted Flo before I left for the cruise and she said Leery's worried about her book promotion," Dyna said. "Flo said Leery even sold off some old artwork she owned, her old wedding ring, and some real estate to invest more money in advertising for her book. Then Leery called my dad to ask him to enroll me in the fall again, and to consider donating money to the school and 'her mission' and to give away free copies of her book on his cruises. He told her to bug off."

"I bet she loved that," I said.

Mimsy glanced at the clock. "We better get ready for the seder tonight."

I took out my shopping list. "Edith asked me to get a few things for the seder plate."

"I'll come with you," Dyna said, and I showed her the list.

"What's a quail egg?" she asked.

Mimsy smiled. "Edith always has quite the seder plate—every year she has unique-looking eggs and an array of salts for the salt water—Hawai'ian red salt, Himalayan black salt, and *fleur de sel*, and the maror, the horseradish, is imported from France, and for the karpas last year it was anise hyssop and lemon verbena, and this year it's a lovely purple sage variety. The matzo is handmade by a young man in Brooklyn. It will be amazing. I promise."

Mimsy gave us all of her exotic salts from around the world, and she showed us where the purple sage was to pick, and she wrote down directions for the gourmet shop to buy the quail eggs. "I'll see you both at the seder," Mimsy said. She raised her juice glass. "L'chaim! To life!"

fourteen
ON ALL OTHER NIGHTS WE DO NOT WORRY ABOUT MURDERERS

The apartment was ready, the seder table set with an extra place for Dyna, and the food simmered on the stove and in the oven. Cora carved the turkey and made stuffing with the sage Dyna and I had brought, and we helped arrange the seder plate. As we shopped, I filled Dyna in about everything that had happened to Edith, all the suspects, and how we hoped to observe everyone tonight.

At four o'clock, Edith's doorbell rang—the first guests arrived. Mimsy opened the door to greet them. It was Jack and his father.

Jack carried a giant floral arrangement, a flowering cherry

branch and lilacs. You could barely see him behind it.

"He brought a bush," Dyna whispered to me.

"Thank you for inviting us," Jack said politely as he peered out from behind the blossoms. He introduced us to his dad, Scott, also known as Detective McShea, who had a giraffe-ish neck. His dad seemed embarrassed by the flowers. A branch poked him, and he gave it a look like he wanted to arrest it.

"Thank you—this is beautiful," Mimsy said, taking the arrangement from Jack and giving Scott a hard look. She introduced Dyna and calmly explained that she was an old friend of mine and a student at Juilliard. Mimsy used her best acting skills—even I believed her. She set Jack's flowers by a window in the living room, and then she excused herself to help Edith in the kitchen. Dyna smiled at everyone and barely said a word, Uriah-like. She excused herself to help Mimsy and Edith, too.

Jack's giraffe father frowned; he didn't seem to want to be here. He pursed his lips and kept glancing around the room, as if trying to find an escape route. He settled on the sofa, plopping himself down near the appetizer tray. He took out his phone.

Jack and I stood by the window where Mimsy had placed Jack's flowers. The cherry branch arched above us, the flowers like cheerleaders' pink pom-poms with tiny yellow-and-green tendrils in their centers.

"Thank you for the ostrich fern—it's growing really well," I said.

"You're welcome. We grow them in the greenhouse at school. I'm glad it found a good home." He touched a cherry branch and a few petals floated down. "'Pink rain,' my mom used to call it when the flowers fell. This is from the tree she planted in the courtyard." He pointed out the window, down to where it bloomed.

"I like that tree. My fire escape looks out on it, too," I said.

"So does mine."

Jack stood with his head to the side, as if trying to listen to the faint hum of the world. He had a gentleness to his face when he touched the cherry branch, an openness. It seemed to be the opposite of the hardness in his father's face.

"How did she die?" I asked. "I'm sorry—I don't know why I'm asking. When I tell people my grandmother died—she raised me—people always ask me, 'How?' I guess when they know how it makes it real, or they think they can avoid it. She died from a stroke, but sometimes I want to say that she was eaten by bears, or something shocking. People have a traffic-accident look when you say someone you loved died, so it feels sort of good to shock them."

He smiled. "I know what you mean—I don't mind you asking. She had leukemia. She'd had it for a long time."

"I'm sorry."

"Next time I'm going to say she was eaten by bears. I'm sorry about your grandmother, too."

I stared down at the cherry tree below. I paused. "Have you been to a Passover seder before?"

He nodded. "Here at Edith's every year. 'Next year on Summer Street,' we say at the end. It was always just my mother and me—my parents have been divorced since I was three. This is my dad's first time here. I told him it was important that he come."

Jack's father was hunched over his phone. He must have sensed us staring at him; he looked up. "Hey, how long did you say the meal's gonna take?"

"A while." Jack gave him a look.

I touched the lilacs next to the cherry branch. The lilac petals almost seemed fake because they looked so perfect, but they were soft and real, and smelled like candy.

"The cherries will bloom for a little while but the cut lilacs might only last a day," he said. "Still."

"Still. What a day," I said.

"What a day."

He cleared his throat. "How's it going for Edith?"

"I like it. How's Wiggy?"

"Wonderful. He was just sleeping on my lap purring and letting me rub his belly."

"Really?"

"No." He held up his arms: fresh red scratches.

"Ouch. Sorry."

He stuck his hands in his pockets. I glanced around the room, taking in the ornate ceiling plaques and marble.

"It's beautiful, isn't it? Has Edith given you the full tour? It's twelve rooms," he said. "There aren't a lot of apartments like this left in Manhattan. I've never been to one like it."

"She hasn't yet—she told me I was free to explore, but I

haven't had a chance. It's been busy working for her—I'm learning a lot. Her eyes are healing, so that's good." I remembered the skepticism he had about her eye drops. "I know that you said you had doubts—or your father did—but I really believe her that someone is after her."

Something came over Jack's face; his features rearranged themselves in a strange way. "I should show you something." He glanced at his father. "I'll be right back," he told him, but his dad was too busy scrolling on his phone to even hear him.

Jack led me down a long hallway. "Where are we going?" I asked.

He didn't say. He seemed tense and a little nervous. We turned a corner. "Here we are," he said outside a closed door. He opened it.

It was a room filled with stuff. Piles of books towered from floor to ceiling, hundreds of books everywhere, and cardboard boxes precariously stacked; there were shelves of old yellowing copies of the *New York Times*, bronze menorahs and silver kiddush cups, canvas paintings stacked against each other, dozens of copies of *American Housekeeping*, Royal Horticultural Society gardening encyclopedias, art supplies, wooden boxes imprinted with "THE SEED EXCHANGE," cigar cases and broken lamps and wool scarves. A moth fluttered out. I spotted the top of a grandfather clock, its hands frozen at six thirty.

I picked up a magazine from a stack near me. On the back cover of an *American Housekeeping* from 1930 was a jolly Santa Claus illustration, his red mitten holding an open pack of

Camel cigarettes. *Season's Greetings from R. J. Reynolds Tobacco Company*, the ad read.

"Whoa. Santa's smoking," I said.

Jack frowned.

Despite his reaction, something thrilled in me, seeing this mess—discovering this treasure trove of the past. I loved the smell of antique paper, of things that had a long life, that were held on to and loved. These magazines seemed like peeking into another world. Time traveling. I loved that Edith lived in this crazy mansion and had this secret mess tucked away, this holding tank of her past. I longed to read these old magazines and to look through the books and learn all their secrets.

He touched a kiddush cup. "My dad saw this room when Edith first told him someone was after her—he searched her apartment to make sure nothing seemed out of order, no signs of break-ins or anything. He told me this room made him think of the Collyer brothers."

"Who?"

"Hoarders. Two men who died from their own stuff. Famous case in New York. They lived in a brownstone on Fifth Avenue where they obsessively collected things and set up traps everywhere because they were paranoid that someone was after them. In the late 1940s they died in their home. From starvation and getting trapped by their possessions. The body of one of the brothers had been eaten by rats."

"But what's that have to do with this? With Edith? It's not the same." I looked around at the mess. "The rest of the apartment—I mean, I've only seen the living room and dining room and kitchen, but—those rooms are perfect, and this isn't that bad. It's just some mess. Nobody's dead in here." I smiled, but he didn't smile back. "She's human. Not flawless."

And I thought, but didn't say, that as gruesome as his story about the Collyers was, it was also sort of appealing in some weird way. Not the part where they starved to death from obsessive hoarding, of course—but something about those brothers breaking society's rules, living in a mansion with all their beloved things that they couldn't part with. *At Thornton we pride ourselves on teaching our girls the importance of tidiness and immaculate self-care.* Dyna and I often let our dorm room turn into a slob's den—the only reason we didn't get in trouble for it was that Flo was in charge of room inspections.

The Collyer brothers—and Edith—would tell Ms. Leery to go screw herself.

Jack seemed to sense what I was thinking. "I know that tons of people keep stuff in garages and attics. But this is Manhattan—this room, which was once a bedroom or parlor or a sitting room—this room itself is at least three hundred thousand dollars' worth of real estate right here. People in Manhattan don't have unused rooms."

"Well, it's not unused exactly, and it obviously could use some organizing and sorting and cleaning, but—it's storage," I said, deciding that was the right word. "Here. Look at this." I pointed to the Santa cigarette ad. "This is amazing." I read it to him:

There's no more acceptable gift in Santa's whole bag than a carton of Camel Cigarettes. Here's the happy solution to your gift problems . . . Enjoy Camels at mealtime—between courses and after eating—for their aid to digestion. Get an invigorating "lift" with a Camel. Camels set you right!

"My grandmother used to say that people thought cigarettes were healthy way back when—but I've never seen it. It sort of makes you think about the stuff we're being told now. Whether it's true." Lemon and kale shakes. "At boarding school, you could get so caught up in the school's rules and its tiny universe, it was as if nothing else existed." I paged through the magazine. "This is like jumping into history."

I wanted Jack to see what I was seeing—that all this stuff was a window into a whole other world. A treasure chest. Something amazing. Like Edith herself.

He looked away, then back at me. "I don't think you understand."

"What don't I understand?"

He paused and lowered his voice. "Edith has dementia."

I put down the magazine. "That's not true."

His voice was quiet. "My father's sure—he's seen this before with his own mother. And at work. Edith has memory loss. Confusion and disorientation. Paranoia. Agitation. Delusions." He took a deep breath. "My father and I were just talking about it before we arrived. He's absolutely sure no one is trying to kill her."

"She seems sharp and smart and together." I looked around at the mess. I couldn't put into words what I felt about Edith. Her warmth. Her sense of wonder. Her comfort with herself. "I believe her."

"I know it's hard to hear," he said. "It was hard for me to believe at first, too. My father explained all this to me. She goes in and out of clarity. I love Edith—I've known her since I was born—but no one is trying to murder her."

All of a sudden, I thought of Edith's column: *We all stand on a precipice.* Even here, in this room. I saw it as a treasure trove, and he saw it as a sign that her mind was falling apart.

"How do you know what her diagnosis is for certain? Has she been tested by a doctor?"

He shook his head. "She refuses to have a brain scan. But my father spoke with a medical professional who evaluated Edith and is certain."

Jack seemed to have two personalities—the gentler, cat-walking, cherry branch one, and this harder side, imitating his father. He touched a stack of magazines and neatened them, putting their corners in alignment, as if that might actually make a difference in this cluttered room.

I tried to choose my words carefully. "What if—I mean, even if her mental state could be—an issue, as you say—but what if these things are still actually happening, that there's a chance she's not imagining them? Mimsy witnessed that the seedlings went missing. They said the seedling theft was never properly investigated. She said the police didn't take them seriously."

"I've been trying as hard as I can to have my father take it seriously. He's been to this apartment twice to help Edith, and he inspected Mimsy's greenhouse. He thinks the seedlings were stolen as a prank by drunken people at that party." He straightened a stack of cigar boxes, turning them into a neat, small tower. "You wouldn't believe what I've seen since I started interning with his department. Do you know what people steal? Posters from bathrooms. Cash registers. Bibles. People steal garbage. They'll take anything."

"They took *Brugmansia* and foxglove—highly poisonous," I said.

"The plants she said were stolen are ones she highlights in one of her books. My dad thinks that's a sign of paranoia and delusion."

"I'm reading that book now—*Strange Botanicals*. It doesn't seem like a delusion to me. It seems possible."

"We all want Edith to be okay," he said. "To protect her. To keep her safe. To get her the help she needs."

A voice came from the hall. "Lucy? Hello?" Mimsy's voice.

"In here." I opened the door.

"There you are! I've been looking for you. Oh, hello, Jack." She saw our expressions. "Ooh. Did I interrupt at a bad time?" She saw the magazine I'd put down, with the jolly Santa holding the pack of cigarettes. "Oh, he's handsome! I've always had a thing for Santas. Men in costume. With nice tummies." She smiled at the picture.

I gazed at Jack warily, afraid he was going to accuse her of having dementia, too.

"I'm here to help. All of you. And Edith," Jack said.

"Thanks," I said.

We opened the door, and Jack walked down the hallway in front of us. Mimsy and I lingered till he was out of sight and we could no longer hear his footsteps. I told Mimsy what he had said.

"Don't listen to him. I've known Edith all my life, and she's sharp as can be. Trust me. I would know. I'd like to go peek in his closets and see what I find. And you know what? If we were men, they'd believe every word we said. No doubts. No belittling us."

I nodded—that seemed true.

Mimsy squeezed my arm. "Dyna is waiting for us, keeping an eye on everything in the living room while I looked for you. Are you ready? Because Clifford and Liliana just arrived."

fifteen
MAD WEASELS GALORE

We reached the living room. Dyna came over to us, nibbling a piece of matzo, and I filled her in on what Jack had said.

"He arrives carrying a forest, and you said he walks his cat on a leash, and he's the one assessing other people's mental health?" she asked.

"He's listening to his father," I said. We looked at his dad, who'd fallen asleep on the couch and was lightly snoring.

Mimsy glanced toward a woman who was walking toward Edith now, taking a dancer's tiptoe-like steps. "That's Liliana," she whispered. "Edith's stepdaughter."

Liliana kissed Edith on both cheeks and said, "You look

radiant, Mother. How are your eyes?"

"Much better, thank you," Edith said.

Liliana's blond hair waved down one side of her body, nearly to her waist; her skin was so pale and papery that you could see her veins beneath. Her mouth twitched. Edith introduced her to Dyna and me. She grasped our hands and said, "Mother has told me so much about you, Lucy. And look at your beautiful friend. What strong, gorgeous young women you two are. You must've heard of my company on social media? Trillium? Tons of our followers are girls your age. We're a dance company but I've also launched a line of botanical skin care products under the Trillium Wellness brand."

"Um—sounds familiar," I lied.

"I'm not online much," Dyna lied, too. "I'm a student at Juilliard? All I do is practice, practice, practice."

Liliana squeezed Dyna's hand. "We're always hiring young musicians for our rehearsals and performances—I'll give you my card."

She opened an expensive-looking white leather wallet and gave Dyna a business card. "Don't you love being with Mother?" she asked us. "I'm her only daughter. Stepdaughter." She had an awkward laugh. "I hate the word 'stepdaughter.' There aren't good words for complicated families, are there?" She smoothed her hair as if it was a pet.

She turned to face the door, where a nurse was helping Clifford take off his coat; another nurse was leaving—they were changing shifts. Clifford was tall, with thick eyebrows, pale skin, and black hair, and he walked slowly, with a cane; small movements seemed to pain him.

"Clifford, I was just saying how there aren't good words for family, for step-half-siblings? How complex family is," Liliana said in her fragile voice.

"That's true," Clifford said. "Complicated. Messy. Endless fun." He smiled slightly and looked around the room with an expression I liked—as if the world was enormously absurd, and he sort of enjoyed it and hated it at the same time. His nurse helped him into his chair.

Edith went to him and hugged him. "You look well. The Levion is working?"

"Today it is," he said. He touched Edith's hand lightly. "We've been gradually increasing the dose to make sure I tolerate it. So far, so good."

Edith introduced all of us. The current nurse, Trish, wore a navy uniform and had a kind face. Edith brought Clifford a drink, gingerly placing it on the table beside him.

Clifford shifted in his seat. "Polio, in case you'd like to know. People usually do. They're too polite to ask, so they stare and wonder. I was one of the unlucky ones who caught it as an infant before the vaccine eradicated it. Getting worse now. Post-polio syndrome. Muscle weakness, pain, fatigue. Fun."

"I'm sorry," I said.

"It's not your fault. You weren't staring. But people usually do, eventually. I like to get my cards on the table when I meet strangers." He picked up the drink beside him and held it carefully.

"Clifford is doing better than ever with the top-notch medical care in New York," Liliana said to Dyna and me. "And I gave him samples of my new Trillium Wellness creams."

I tried to observe every detail about Liliana and Clifford—Mimsy hadn't mentioned that Clifford had a disability. How could he have been the person following Edith? I noticed he had dirt under his fingernails. It looked like potting soil, which lately had taken me forever to scrub out of my own nails.

"Have you tried the comfrey and coltsfoot?" Liliana asked him. "And the arnica? I know they'll help the Levion work its magic even more."

"It's not magic. It's an experimental drug. We still don't know yet how effective it is, or how long its effects will even last. I'm a guinea pig," Clifford said. "And I don't think it's wise to mix herbs and serious medicine."

Liliana looked away and rearranged her hair.

Edith kept staring at Clifford with a concerned expression, surveying his movements. "Have you noticed that the Levion's taking effect, too?" Edith asked his nurse, Trish.

"Absolutely." Trish smiled. "I've been testing his movements each day and overall muscle strength has improved, and there's been a substantial decrease in pain." She was around Edith and Mimsy's age, or even older; she had short, sparse white hair held back by a navy headband that matched her uniform.

"Its effectiveness comes and goes, though," Clifford said. "But I'm hopeful." He said *hopeful* with a resigned tone.

Of course there was no polite and subtle way to ask, *Are you resentful of Edith, as Mimsy said? Do you want to harm her and get her money?* So I tried: "What do you think of New York?"

"I'm not sure. It's not—home," he said.

"Home is but a state of mind," Liliana said in a saccharine tone. "It's a feeling we conjure in our souls."

"No. I don't think we do," Clifford said.

Liliana's face crumpled.

The doorbell rang; Nanette and Cyrus arrived. Nanette wore a low-cut, skintight black dress made of a scaly material, like serpent skin. Cyrus wore a silver suit with black trim.

"He looks like a hubcap," Dyna whispered to me.

Nanette carried a huge stack of *Clique* magazines. "Thought everyone might love a sneak preview before this hits the newsstands next week." She held up the cover, which featured a naked woman in high heels pushing a lawn mower below the words "SUMMER FASHION SPECTACULAR." She placed the stack on the coffee table.

Jack picked one up. "Is that what's in fashion this summer—being naked? Though I guess at least there's no burning books."

Nanette scowled at him. Mimsy handed her a glass of wine; Nanette held the glass's stem like it was a kitten she was about to strangle.

"I think it's a wonderful cover," Liliana said, and beamed. "Cyrus, did you help?"

"Yes. I picked out the model's clothes," he said.

Everyone laughed.

"You were all at Mimsy's equinox party," I said, looking

around the room. "Quite an event, I hear."

"I try to go to all the best society parties," Nanette said. "We run pictures in the magazine after."

"Nanette's at one party or another every night," Cyrus said.

So that's where they were in the evenings—at least it made living in their apartment bearable, since I never saw them.

Nanette's eyes settled on me, and the piece of matzo with whitefish salad in my hand. "Oops, that's not approved, is it? Let's put that right here." She picked up a plate and held it out.

Mimsy intervened. "Really? Don't be ridiculous."

"She's under strict rules," Nanette said. "That is not on the list." She put the plate down, then reached into her black bag and pulled out two shakes. "These are for you tonight."

I froze. This was the first meal, since I'd arrived, that Nanette and I'd be eating together. I tried to think of what to say. Mimsy took the shakes and plopped them back into Nanette's bag. "These are not dinner. Under this roof, everyone will eat what they like," Mimsy said.

Nanette narrowed her eyes. "Didn't I see a rerun with you on TV recently—a small role in *Evil Twins' Revenge*? I'm sure that was quite the Oscar winner. It's been a while since you've acted, hasn't it?"

Mimsy's face fell. Dyna glared at Nanette and Jack gave her a hard stare also. Nanette's phone rang; she stepped into the hallway toward the kitchen to take the call, still carrying her large handbag.

Liliana watched Nanette disappear, then smoothed her

yellow hair and approached Cyrus. She flushed when she spoke to him; she seemed to have a crush on him, even though she was about twenty years older than he was. "Cyrus, I have a beautiful antiquarian book I'd like to show you in the library. I'm sure you've never seen one like it, not even at the auction house."

I whispered to Mimsy, "How does she know him so well?"

"She's invited him here for drinks when Nanette works late, she told me. Liliana always asks Edith if she can entertain friends here, since she lives in a small apartment in Bay Ridge."

"I'd like to see the library, too," I said. I didn't want them to go out of sight—I didn't trust either of them.

Peter arrived just as we were leaving the living room—he was the last guest—and he held up a bag containing a bottle of wine, and herbs and flowers.

When Peter saw Edith, he said, "It's been over a week—any chance you're closer to a decision about our trip?"

"I think—well—I'm still not ready to decide, I don't think. I'm sorry," Edith told him.

He looked crestfallen. "I'll just bring this to the kitchen."

Everyone relocated to the library, except Jack's father, who was still snoring on the couch. Clifford made his way slowly, with his nurse's help, and Nanette came in after her phone call was finished.

The library was two stories high, with built-in wooden shelves covering every wall from floor to ceiling, a deep window seat, and a ladder and walkway along the second story.

It was a more organized, less cluttered version of the unused room—it held tons of stuff, but in an acceptable, presentable way. Books were stacked everywhere, and old magazines with crumbling edges teetered on the shelves and side tables. It was like an old bookstore or the best ephemera shop. I saw a *Woman's Day* from 1945 with a price of two cents, and magazines called *Home Life* and *Lady's Almanac*. Antique typewriters balanced on the stacks, and tchotchkes and old handwritten letters; all these antique books and papers calmed and thrilled me at the same time, all these old, beloved things.

The vintage book that Liliana showed Cyrus was called *A Gentleman's Style*. Cyrus snaked around, reading the spines on the shelves. He seemed like a snail who'd leave a trail of slime behind. He ogled everything Edith owned—vases, books, framed paintings, and potted plants. Nanette nodded approvingly, drinking in Edith's wealth, as if money were contagious.

Dyna moved to a quiet corner of the library where an antique wooden stand held a gigantic ancient dictionary.

"Look at this," she said.

It was open to the word *love*. There were pages of definitions and related words—*love-apple, love-bird, love-child, love-hate, love-in-a-mist, love-lies-bleeding, love-potion*—it seemed almost endless.

I read the verb definitions. *Be unwilling to part with or allow to perish.* I liked that one. I ran my finger down the page, past *lovesick, loveworthy,* and more *love* words. "I never thought there could be so many," I said.

Next to the dictionary stand was a desk with a thick book on it. Edith picked it up. *An Encyclopedia of Engineering.* "Ah! This I have to show you," Edith said.

"That's not worth anything," Cyrus said derisively.

Edith laughed. "It's one of my most valuable possessions of all." She opened the encyclopedia's cover. The pages had been hollowed out and it held a secret compartment. Inside the compartment was a small brown leather book with gold edges.

"A diary," I said.

"I love seeing you write in yours," Edith said to me. "I used to write in one all the time when I was your age, filling up a new one every three months. My diaries had little pockets in the back where I could stash photos and things. My father tried to read them sometimes, so I had to keep them hidden from him or I'd never feel like I could write the truth. This is a really old one from when I was thirteen."

Peter entered the library and came over to us. "Did you find the one you were looking for?"

Edith shook her head. "No. Not yet." She explained, "I've been looking for the diary that I kept when I was pregnant with Clifford." He sat in the corner, absorbed in a book. "I've told Clifford already how I want to show it to him. It has all my memories of that time. Everything. But I haven't been able to find it. I stopped writing in it after he was born, and my father tried to read it, so I hid it. It was such a—difficult time for me then, I wasn't sleeping,

I was—so unhappy." She gazed at Clifford.

"I'm not sure which book I hid that diary in," Edith continued. "It's not exactly organized in here, as you can see. I was always moving the hidden books around so my father couldn't find them—and then I couldn't find them, either." We looked up at the rows and rows of books. There were hundreds of them—maybe even a thousand or more.

"I've been suggesting to Edith that she find her old teenage diaries for her memoir," Peter said. "And to have closure from that time in her life."

"You're writing a memoir?" Dyna asked.

Edith smiled and shrugged. "I've been trying."

"Edith's gardening books are classics, but I think she could tell her own story, too. It would mean a lot to others to read it," Peter said.

Liliana cleared her throat. "While everyone is here, before we start the seder, I have an announcement to make." She reached into her purse and pulled out a stack of what looked like theater tickets. "I'd like to take this opportunity to invite you to the spring benefit for Trillium Dance Company. I'm the founder and artistic director. The performance this year is a new piece titled *Natural Freedom*. It's a fundraiser for 'The Bumblebee Initiative,' the fund that my mother and Peter and Wenli—Jack's dear mother—all conducted research for at Mandragora. Please bring friends!" She peeled tickets from her stack and gave them to everyone. "Here are order forms as well, to fill your tables, and the link for donations. The benefit is going to be held at Mandragora."

Mandragora. I liked the word. "What's Mandragora?" I asked.

A hush came over almost everyone. Clifford closed his book and looked up.

"It's the most beautiful garden in the world," Jack said.

"It is. The loveliest. Makes my own garden look like a postage stamp," Mimsy said.

"Mimsy's garden is a miniature, urban version, but Mandragora is like entering another universe," Jack said.

"It's where I was born," Clifford said, taking a sip of his drink.

"You were born in a garden?" I asked.

Edith smiled. "It wasn't a garden then. In the 1950s, it was a maternity home. That's where I had Clifford."

"Edith bought it and turned it into a public garden thirty years ago. It had been overgrown and neglected for decades," Mimsy explained.

"I named it Mandragora because the garden felt like it had magical powers," Edith said.

"I visited it three weeks ago," Clifford said. He stared at his lap. "I wanted to see it. It started to rain so we didn't get to see much of it—I didn't realize it would be so big."

"It will be a different experience in May," Peter said, and smiled. "So much more will be in bloom. Edith designed the plantings, and a small staff of horticulturists maintains it. It's not open to the public every day—only once a month, and for fundraising events and scientific research."

"It's paradise," Liliana said. "I hired an artisanal gardening company to plant an herb garden on my roof, because I don't have the gardener's gene the way Mother does. Flowers die if I look at them. Yet I find that absorbing the botanical arts feeds the souls of performance artists—our endless, insatiable hunger for natural beauty. Wouldn't you agree, Mimsy, as an actress?"

"You could put it that way," Mimsy said.

"Of course, Clifford, this must all be very new to you, since you've only just gotten to know Mother recently," Liliana said with a slightly jealous tone. "I know you must appreciate living in this beautiful building. I used to live in one of Mother's apartments before my dance company became successful, before I was able to make it on my own in New York. I've always been careful to never take advantage of Mother's generosity." She gazed at Clifford.

His face turned slightly red. "I believe *Mother* is the benefactor of your dance company," Clifford said. "And I believe it's likely her fortune pays part of your rent, still."

"Even if that were slightly true, I built my dance company from nothing. It's saving the bees. Our Trillium Wellness brand is helping scores of people—our creams—our—"

"Saving the bees—and the world—with creams," Clifford said. He held up his ticket. "Who does this 'benefit' really benefit? How many millions has Mother put into financing your hobby?"

Liliana's serpentine hair suddenly seemed like it might uncoil and bite him.

"They both say 'mother' as if it's a curse word," Dyna whispered to me. "They're like Lois's ferrets—mad weasels."

Everyone gazed at them awkwardly. Edith's face was pale. Jack caught my eye and gave me a look that seemed to say, *Welcome to the crazy family.* Trish quietly stepped aside, politely pretending not to hear. I thought of how my grandmother told me it was an art form to not get involved in patients' family dramas.

Nanette and Cyrus loved it; all they needed was popcorn to keep them entertained.

Edith said, "I think it's time to start the seder."

"I'm sorry," Clifford said. "I didn't mean to upset everyone or cause a scene."

"I'm sorry also," Liliana said. "Our first squabble. I guess we really are siblings."

"So we are." He stared down at the floor, lowering his thick eyebrows.

"All right, everyone—please join us in the dining room," Edith said, changing the subject. Out the windows, the sun began to set.

Nanette slithered over to the table, and Cyrus inspected the silverware, probably judging its worth. Jack woke up his father and told him the seder was starting. At the end of the table, there were yarmulkes for the men, and Jack's father looked reluctant to put his on. Jack wore it easily. Cyrus didn't put one on at all. He probably couldn't bear the thought of messing up his hair.

Everyone scurried to their seats—Edith at the head of the table, with Jack's father on the side near her for protection; Dyna and I sat on the other side of her, across from Jack. Nanette and Cyrus were at the far end of the table, thankfully.

Peter said to Jack's father, "Your son has been a big help to me at the lab. Keep hoping we'll see him there even more."

"Peter's my favorite professor," Jack said.

"Jack's been busy with his internship. No time for flora and fauna," his father said.

Jack winced. *I know how you feel,* I wanted to tell him. *Bottomless disappointment.* It was a common disease afflicting parents everywhere.

Edith and Mimsy passed out the Haggadahs.

"Clifford, you've been gardening," I said, eyeing his fingernails. I tried to bring it up in a casual way.

"Seems to afflict most of us here," Peter said. "Plantsmen and plantswomen. It's the best of passions."

"I haven't," Clifford said. Why did he have so much dirt under his nails, then? Was he lying?

"I haven't, either," Nanette said, taking a piece of matzo even though we hadn't blessed it yet, which was part of the meal. Her manicured, polished nails were painted gold. "I've never really understood the houseplant thing. I moved to New York to get away from nature. Lucy has those plants on her fire escape—it's like some kind of jungle there."

How often was she looking in my room at my fire escape?

Edith started the prayer. *Baruch atah adonai, elohenu melech ha-olam*, we sang.

"As we light the candles and welcome Passover into our homes, we hope that everyone who is suffering will find light in the dark," Edith said.

Jack's father's phone rang and he answered it at the table. "Yeah. Got it. Sure. Look, I'm at a Jewish, uh, dinner, call you in ten," he told the person on the other line, in a loud voice. Jack looked like he might take the bread knife and stab him.

Edith cleared her throat. "Now it's time for the first cup of wine."

"Even though Nanette has already had four," Dyna whispered to me.

Edith sang the prayer, and we took turns reading the Haggadah, and Dyna and I filled our glasses with grape juice. We passed around a ceremonial pitcher and cloths for the ritual washing of hands, and it was time for the ceremonial foods.

It was Peter's turn to read from the Haggadah. "The karpas, the vegetable, represents struggle and aspiration. When we dip the karpas into salt water, we see the tears of all who suffer injustice mixing with our hope for life, rebirth, and new possibilities."

Jack's dad yawned.

The bowl of herbs sat by Edith's plate. Peter gazed at her as she dipped the leaves in the salt water and opened her mouth to take a bite.

Peter stood up. "STOP! DON'T!" he screamed. He reached across the table for the bowl and threw it to the floor. It clanged and shattered.

"Oh my god, he's truly lost it," Nanette said.

"That's not sage." Peter examined a leaf. "This is digitalis. This is poison."

sixteen

FOXGLOVE

Mimsy gasped. Edith held a leaf up to the light, close to her face. "You're right. My eyesight isn't perfect. But it's foxglove."

"Digitalis—foxglove—was one of the seedlings that was stolen at the equinox party. This is evidence," Mimsy said, turning to Jack's father. "Here's the proof you've been needing."

Jack's father had an expression on his face that seemed to say, *This is too much cuckoo.* He looked at all of us as if we were actors in a deranged performance. "Let's keep calm, everyone. It was probably a simple mistake. Harvested by accident," he said in a measured voice. "Who brought the greens?"

"I did," I said. "But—"

"When foxglove are young plants, their leaves look similar to sage," Edith said.

"I know I picked the sage," I said. "It was a purple sage plant, and I remember picking the most purplish leaves that I could find." My chest hurt.

"I was there—I remember, they were purple," Dyna said.

"I brought some greens also, for the salad," Peter said. "Not foxglove, certainly. I brought lettuce from the greenmarket."

"Anyone could've switched the herbs in the bowl. People have been moving from the dining room to the kitchen to the living room and library all night," Mimsy said, looking around at everyone in the room.

Jack took charge. "We'll take it right away and have it analyzed." He went to the kitchen to save all the greens and have them tested.

"Let's not get carried away and jump to conclusions," Jack's father said. His voice was calm. "We saw a case like this just last week with wild mushrooms. A forager picked the wrong ones for a farm-to-table restaurant in Brooklyn. Six people ate them and nearly died. Let's stick to the facts. Why would someone poison every single person at the table? That makes no sense."

"The bowl was by Edith, and everyone knew she'd be leading the seder and would eat it first," Mimsy told him. "Or this is all part of someone's plan to gaslight her and make people like you believe she's going insane. It seems to be working. You had the same theory of it being an accident, of 'mistakenly harvesting' after they found traces of *Brugmansia* in Edith's blood test after the equinox party."

Jack's father looked unconvinced.

Jack finished collecting all the herbs and greens from the kitchen, and Mimsy announced that unfortunately we couldn't continue the seder under these circumstances. Jack's father looked relieved that he could go. He had an all-in-a-day's-work expression. He took the bag of greens Jack had collected. "We'll get these to the lab right away. Thank you so much for having us. It's been—different. Thank you."

Jack nodded. "I'm sorry this happened," he said to me. He turned to Dyna. "It was nice to meet you." He thanked Edith. He and his father were about to leave when Nanette whispered something to them. They all left together and fifteen minutes later, they returned.

Nanette had a zealous look on her face. She was carrying a plant. "I just showed this kind police detective how I saw this earlier on Lucy's fire escape. I had a feeling there was something off about all those plants she keeps out there."

It was a small, young foxglove plant.

"Where did you find that? That isn't mine," I said.

"Outside on your fire escape, as I just said, in that tropical forest out there," Nanette said.

Jack's father folded his arms. "Any plants on a fire escape are illegal, for fire safety reasons, according to RCNY Section 15-10," he said. "Now you're saying this one isn't yours?"

"Absolutely not." I tried to sound strong and believable and not how I actually felt, which was a terrified mess.

"You're saying someone else put this plant there? Potted plant reverse stealing. Big crime spree in New York, people giving away plants. First seedlings stolen, and now they're giving you unwanted plants," Jack's father said dryly.

"I didn't give her that plant," Edith said.

Jack's father's voice was resigned. "We'll take this to the lab, too. In the meantime, get the other plants off your fire escape," he said to me.

They left. The rest of the guests followed, murmuring among themselves as they made their way out the door.

My stomach kept whirring. I hugged my elbows.

After everyone had left, Edith, Mimsy, and Dyna and I were alone in Edith's living room. Edith sat still, paralyzed. "It could've been anyone here tonight. They all had access to the kitchen and dining room. They could've arrived with it in their coat pocket or handbag, snuck into the dining room, switched the herbs, and been done with it in thirty seconds."

"And anyone could've put that plant on Lucy's fire escape beforehand," Mimsy said. "All the fire escapes are connected and accessible from the courtyard."

"It wasn't a stranger, then. We know that. It was someone at the table tonight," I said.

Edith looked exhausted. "I need to get some sleep."

"Do you want company? We can stay with you here tonight, or you can stay at my place," Mimsy said, putting a hand on her shoulder.

"Thank you—I'll stay here, though. I need to sleep in my

own bed. To get some rest," Edith said.

We said good night to Edith and gathered our things. "You can't stay at Nanette's tonight," Dyna said to me. "Not if she's snooping on your fire escape, trying to implicate you. You need to stay with us at Mimsy's house."

"I wish I could. My dad would freak out, though, if I didn't stay with her—living with Nanette is a condition of me being in New York. Also I want to keep an eye on them. At least they're almost never home—maybe I can look through their stuff and find some evidence of how Nanette knew the plant was there. Maybe she and Cyrus put it there themselves." I thought of something. "When I got to New York, Cyrus fixed the lock on my window to make sure I could open it. He said it was for fire safety, but—maybe they planned something then. If they did, I want to catch them. Also it's good to be on site near Edith, too—to have one of us close to her."

Mimsy thought for a moment. "I have an extra phone to give you. So you can call us anytime. And you can call Jack, too, if there's an emergency—he's only one floor up from you. Call us if you feel scared or anything—even in the middle of the night—and we'll come get you." She fiddled with her bracelet. "What would Nanette and Cyrus's motive be to harm Edith?"

"To steal her things—I thought Cyrus was going to pocket something in the library," Dyna said.

"He works at an auction house, so it would be easy for him to resell them," I said.

155

"That would be an extreme motive for murdering her, though," Mimsy said.

"Liliana seems extra crazy," Dyna said. "With all that 'Mother' stuff—and that fight with Clifford. She has serious issues."

"She has a strong motive, not wanting to split her inheritance with Clifford," Mimsy said.

"Did you see the dirt under Clifford's fingernails?" I asked. "It looks like he's been gardening."

"I did—why would he lie about that?" Mimsy asked. "Maybe he was hiding that he stole the seedlings. Maybe he's growing them in his apartment." She raised her eyebrows. "Here—come this way." She led us through the kitchen and pushed through a door to a back stairwell.

I didn't even know there were stairs back there. "Where are we going?" I asked.

"To find out some more information," Mimsy said excitedly. "Follow me."

seventeen

BREAKING AND ENTERING

Mimsy led us up the back stairs. We reached a door one flight up.

"Now, let's see—I have a key from when Edith asked me to help decorate before Clifford moved in—I picked out the yellow curtains." She burrowed into her purse and pulled out a key ring that held a dozen keys. She found a blue one. "Ah. This is it."

"Where are we?" Dyna asked.

"The back door to Clifford's apartment. Maybe he's raising foxglove plants in here, or the other missing seedlings. Or maybe he has a gray coat, like the man who followed Edith. Now's our chance, while he's out to dinner—he and Liliana went out to eat, 'to make up,' so they said, so they'll be gone at least an hour," Mimsy said.

My heart banged away in my chest, and my throat felt tight.

Mimsy opened the door, which led into the kitchen. We checked the fire escape outside the kitchen window first. We found potted plants—daffodils, pansies, and violas—but nothing poisonous.

Next to the kitchen was a coat closet—we searched it, and there was a plain, short black coat, but there was no gray hooded coat like Edith had described.

"How could he have been the person following Edith, though, with his disability?" Dyna asked. "He's not physically capable of it."

"Isn't he?" Mimsy asked.

"What do you mean?" I asked.

"As an actress, I often think other people are acting."

"Isn't that ableist?" Dyna asked. "To think he's faking it? To not take it seriously?"

"I don't think we can take anything at face value. It's Edith's life at stake. She's my best friend. I can't lose her." Mimsy stood at the doorway to his room. "As his nurse said, he's regaining a lot of muscle strength. Of everyone, he's got the strongest motive—Edith wrote him into her will just as all these strange things started happening."

It was a two-bedroom apartment—Clifford had the larger room, and the second bedroom was the overnight nurse's room; it was tiny, down the hall from his, the size of a large closet. The entire apartment was perfectly tidy. Ms. Leery would give it the highest marks.

I felt a strange mixture of dread and thrill—I felt guilty at trespassing, but at the same time, Mimsy had a point. If it saved Edith's life, then it was worth it. I hoped.

We entered Clifford's room, and Mimsy opened the door to his closet. There were neatly pressed men's shirts, but no sign of a gray coat. His nightstand held a stack of the three gardening books Edith had written.

"Who was Clifford's father?" I asked.

"He was Edith's boyfriend whom she loved and hoped to marry," Mimsy said. "He was two years older than her and he went into the army before Edith knew she was pregnant. He died in an accident—his army jeep rolled over. Edith was devastated—it happened right after the death of her mother. She barely survived that time."

"That's so awful," I said.

"It was—it is," Mimsy said.

Dyna stuck her hands in her pockets. "I can't imagine losing two people you loved only weeks apart."

We checked the nurse's room. Mimsy said that Trish did all the overnight shifts, and some daytime shifts, so she was the one who lived with him. The closet held her navy uniforms and plain dresses, and her nightstand held stacks of medical books and printouts from medical journals about post-polio syndrome. On her desk there was a notebook with a chart featuring the Levion dosage and Clifford's improvements and side effects: *200 mg, range of motion and muscle strength, 10%*

improvement. 210mg, muscle strength, 15% improvement. Hand grip test, 30% improvement. In the corner, she had a small craft table covered with jars of scissors, markers, a stack of paint palettes, and containers of Mod Podge decoupage glue. Her current project was decorating a pencil cup with tiny pictures of baby penguins.

"As his caregiver, would Clifford's nurse gain anything if he inherited millions—would she get some of it?" Dyna asked.

Mimsy shook her head. "Nothing at all. All his nurses are paid through Clifford's insurance company. Edith offered Trish extra pay since she puts in the longest hours, but she refused to accept it."

We searched the tiny kitchen and living room, too, but we didn't find any evidence.

"Let's check Clifford's room once more," Mimsy said. We returned to his room, and she picked up a stack of papers on his dresser. There were restaurant receipts, a laminated map of the Village, a subway and bus map—and underneath, a stack of letters. From Edith.

"Ah," Mimsy said. "These are the letters Edith sent to him when they reconnected. Before he moved in here."

Next to the letters was a silver necklace in the shape of a fox. The silver chain had been polished to a bright sheen, and the fox looked well-worn and well-loved, its orange enamel rubbed off at the edges to show the silver beneath. I picked it up and felt its cool weight in my hands. GRAYSON JEWELRY COMPANY was printed in tiny block letters on the back.

"Edith left the fox necklace with him when he was born, with instructions that it be given to his adoptive parents to keep for him. He also volunteered to have a DNA test done to prove she was his mother. One of those mail-in things—I googled if it could be faked."

"Could it?"

"No." She sounded disappointed. "They're accurate, unfortunately. He's her son. But I get a feeling—I don't trust him."

Mimsy picked up the letters from Edith.

"Would she mind us reading these?" I asked.

"She wouldn't mind. She showed them to me as she was writing them," Mimsy said.

Dear Clifford,

I am so happy to be in touch with you. I've been hoping for this all of my life.

Mimsy touched the fox necklace, its orange enamel and worn edges. "I can't believe it survived all these years. Edith wore two pieces of jewelry to the maternity home—this necklace, which was a gift from her mother, and a watch from her father."

"Is this valuable?" I asked, running my finger across the enamel.

She shook her head. "It's not worth money. But it meant everything to her. She doesn't have many of her mother's things, since her father threw most of them out after she died. The watch her father gave her is gone now, too. That was priceless. Worth a million dollars or more, probably, by today's standards. Edith's father was very wealthy—Fox's Fruit Syrups was one of the most popular brands back then—he built a fortune. The watch was beautiful—the band was made of sapphires, rubies, emeralds, and rare diamonds in flower shapes. She told everyone it was costume jewelry."

"What happened to the watch?" Dyna asked.

"When Edith went into labor with Clifford, they put her under anesthesia. That's when the watch was stolen. It was never found again." She paused. "At the maternity home, babies were taken away seconds after the birth, and their mothers never saw them again. It was brutal," Mimsy said.

Mimsy touched the stack of handwritten letters. Beneath the letters was a legal pad, where Clifford had started a letter to Edith on his own.

Dear Edith,

I have been wanting to tell you how it feels

I have been feeling

The mother-son love is messy, as you said, but what I feel

Your generosity has meant the world to me

I am not good at expressing myself

I do feel I love you and I am sorry that I can't say it

I want to write this because it is hard for me to say in person that

I do love you

He never finished the letter, never sent it.

"This is really sad," I said.

"Oh," Mimsy said. "That is quite sad." She paused.

"Maybe he's not out to get her after all?" Dyna asked.

"Unless he doesn't actually mean it, and he's sending her a letter to throw off suspicion," Mimsy said.

There was a noise in the hall outside the apartment door. Footsteps. We froze.

The rattle of keys.

"Hide!" Mimsy said. "Quick!"

We ducked behind Clifford's bed as the apartment's front door creaked open slowly. Someone approached down the hallway, heading toward Clifford's room.

eighteen

POPSICLE TOES, BUMBLE RUMBLE, GINGEROO,
AND OTHER CURES FOR WORRY

Liliana stood over Clifford's bed, staring at us. "What on earth are you doing here? Why are the three of you crouched on the floor?"

Mimsy stood up. "What are *you* doing here?"

"I came back to fetch a sweater for Clifford. We're at Metamorphic Café around the corner. He was cold," her wavering, fragile voice said.

"We were searching for my lost bracelet," Mimsy said. "Months ago, before Clifford moved in, as Edith and I were discussing some fixes for this apartment, I lost a bracelet here." She held up a gold bracelet—she must've taken it off while we were hiding behind the bed. "Found it!"

Liliana gazed at her. She wasn't buying it.

Mimsy smoothed her pants. "Well. I'm so excited for your show at Mandragora. I'm inviting all my friends."

Liliana brightened at this. "Your society friends?"

"Maybe I can purchase some extra tickets? The whole lot!" Mimsy lowered her voice. "If you wouldn't mind not mentioning to Clifford that we were . . . bracelet-hunting."

"I won't." Her eyes shifted as she said it. She opened her purse and handed Mimsy a stack of tickets. She sat down on the corner of the bed. "I don't think you should be suspicious of Clifford. Even though we're having our—adjustments in our relationship—he wouldn't hurt Mother. We had an open-hearted discussion about our quarrel and he doesn't want Mother's money. He told me he's even found a job here in the Village."

"What sort of job?" I asked.

"In a florist shop. Apparently he's been inspired by Mother to learn flower arranging. It's at Enchantments on Bleecker Street. They do fantastic living arrangements—potted succulents and moss and lovely things."

"Why didn't he tell the truth when I asked if he was gardening?" I asked.

"He wants to surprise Mother. He's planning to give her a giant living arrangement he's working hard on—a rectangle of succulents, like a painting, that she can hang in her living room." She moved her hair to the other side of her neck. "It's funny that Clifford and I squabble like siblings already." She touched a corner of the quilt. "I don't mind it, you know. His honesty. It's refreshing. He has no filter. He says exactly what he means."

"Quite refreshing," Mimsy said.

"I think Clifford's feelings about Mother are just so complicated. This is all so difficult for him. I feel terribly for him." She shrugged. "I think he can't accept why Mother gave him up."

"That's why Edith wants to find the diary. So he might understand it," Mimsy said.

"Maybe it would help," Liliana said to her hair.

"What do you know about his life before he came here?" I asked her.

"I know his adoptive parents both passed away, just before he got in touch with Edith. They always told him how lucky he was to be alive, and how his birth parents didn't want him because of his illness—even though Edith told him that wasn't true. She never knew about his illness. She didn't even know she'd had a boy. But I think deep down, Clifford believes she gave him up because he wasn't a 'perfect' baby."

I thought of my own parents and my asthma. His situation was so much more severe, so much worse.

She stared off into the distance. "His adoptive parents weren't kind to him. I think they thought they were saving his soul by adopting him, that he was a charity case that would make them feel good about themselves. But they treated him like a burden. I don't think he ever got over it," Liliana said.

"His adoptive parents let nurses do all his caregiving. He's had quite a number of nurses, apparently—he hasn't gotten along with most of them. His adoptive parents brought Trish back when his post-polio syndrome worsened years ago, since she's trained in physical therapy, and she's always patient with him and kind. He's lucky she's covered by his insurance, since he said his adoptive parents never would've paid for it. They left him with very little when they died." She paused. "Mother is paying for the Levion—Clifford's insurance wouldn't cover that. And I do think he could benefit from my Trillium creams, if he'd open his mind to it."

Liliana turned to me. "You're lucky, you know, to spend so much time with Mother at your age. I was ten when my father married her, and I chose to live with her after their divorce. My father worked all the time. I spent more time with Edith than I ever did with Father." She glanced at the clock and stood up. "I better get back—my food's probably gone cold and Clifford is waiting."

"Thank you for—not telling him about my bracelet," Mimsy said.

"Thank you for buying the tickets. For the bees," Liliana said, and she left.

After she was gone, we closed the door to Clifford's apartment, and we walked back toward Edith's.

"Ick," Dyna said. "All that 'Mother' stuff again. No offense, Mimsy, but these rich people are kind of nuts."

"Don't I know it," Mimsy said.

"Did you really bribe her silence by buying tickets?" Dyna asked.

"Yes. I did." Mimsy shrugged. "Well—maybe Nancy Drew didn't bribe anyone, but I have much lower standards."

"I'm not sure it will work," Dyna said. "I think she's going to tell him."

"It's fine if she does. Maybe that would even be a good thing—he should know that we're on to him. If he's the one behind this, he needs to know we're going to catch him. Same for Liliana."

"Should we tell Edith about Clifford's letter to her?" I asked. "And that we searched his apartment?"

"Yes," Mimsy said. "We have to. I don't want to keep secrets from her. I think she'll forgive us. I hope."

We stopped back at Edith's apartment. She was ready to go to sleep. We told her everything we'd found, and she seemed moved to hear about his attempted letter to her. "I told you he's not a suspect," she said. "I think what we all need is some rest and to think this through tomorrow morning. And maybe it's not such a good idea to break into my tenants' apartments." She gave Mimsy a hard look.

"We want to keep you safe," Mimsy said.

"Let's try to do that legally," Edith said.

We said good night to Edith again. Mimsy, Dyna, and I weren't sleepy at all, and we spent the rest of the evening eating pizza at a place a few blocks away—not a Passover food—but that was okay. "I always think that knowing it's *trayf*—not kosher—makes it taste even better," Mimsy said.

While we ate, we made a plan. "First on our to-do list is paying a visit to Enchantments. A florist shop indeed—that would give him a perfect place to stash hidden foxglove plants," Mimsy said.

"I'll see what I can find in Nanette's apartment, too," I said.

Dyna squeezed my hand. "Are you sure you can't stay with us at Mimsy's tonight?"

"I'll be fine," I said.

"Please be careful. We'll come over in a second if you feel unsafe at all," she told me.

The tests from the Passover seder food came back—they confirmed that the herb was foxglove—and foxglove was also found in the herb stuffing Cora had made, "but that was to be expected," Jack's father said, "if someone had switched it with a bunch of sage in the kitchen."

"Maybe Cora is a suspect," Dyna said as we talked it over the next day in Mimsy's garden. "If she's the one who was cooking that day."

"She's worked for Edith for three decades. Why would she be after her now?" Mimsy asked. "She doesn't have a motive. Also Jack's father said that the herbs being switched was clearly an honest mistake, too, because there wasn't enough to kill anybody—only to make them sick."

"Maybe they just wanted to scare everybody," Dyna said.

"Wait a second." I picked up my bag and took out a thick

book I'd borrowed from Edith's library on medicinal herbs. "I think there's a mention of foxglove in here." I opened the cover and turned the pages, then read them a passage that said that for those taking certain heart medications, an overdose of foxglove could cause a heart attack. "It makes perfect sense. Foxglove would make everyone sick, but it would only kill Edith, because of her heart medication. She'd be the only one to overdose."

Mimsy thought it over. "I think you're right. I still don't think it's enough to convince the police, though," she said.

I told Mimsy and Dyna how I'd searched Nanette's apartment, but there were no plants at all, and no evidence that she or Cyrus had put the foxglove plant on my fire escape. The only things I found were three bottles of Cyrus's Pure Man cologne, with 75 percent off discount stickers on them, and a lot of beauty products for men and women.

Dyna and I stopped by the florist shop on Bleecker, and they said Clifford was doing an excellent job, and they'd never had a foxglove plant in their shop, or any of the seedlings that had been stolen. They showed us Clifford's work table in the back, where he was making a giant living arrangement of succulents.

The next morning, and throughout the week, Edith self-medicated by planting dahlias, her favorite flower.

"This helps me think," she said. "To get clarity."

She was right—it felt good to take a break from thinking and do physical work.

"Dahlias cure everything," Edith said.

She showed me how to make a spiderweb out of twine for the dahlia plants to grow through. Boxes kept arriving that contained more and more dahlia tubers—they resembled dried-out deformed giant's toes.

"In three months, they'll be the most beautiful flowers you've ever seen," she said.

I loved seeing the bags labeled with their names: Bumble Rumble, Fuzzy Wuzzy, Gingeroo, Otto's Thrill, Mandragora Moon, and even one called Pooh.

As I planted them, it did feel like a cure to stick my fingers in the dirt. I was in the midst of planting one called Popsicle Toes when Mimsy came outside holding her phone. She mouthed the words "Your father."

"Nanette gave me this number—we've been trying to get ahold of you, Cricket. We spoke to Nanette this morning and we've been a bit confused by something she told us? Something about a poisonous plant on your fire escape? I know it could have been an honest mistake, but it did worry your mother and me. We have half a mind to send you back to Thornton, if this internship isn't working out. Beverly said she can arrange a work program for you on campus as an alternative."

Visions of chain gangs flashed through my head. "Please—I want to stay here. I know I can do a good job. I'm trying to. If you could only see—"

"I want to believe you. Your mother and I do. I know it was only a plant. We're just very confused about what is going on there."

Mimsy motioned to hand the phone to her, and she

talked to my father. "Hello! I'm sorry I didn't have a chance to properly introduce myself when you called—this is Alice Luddington-Stein. I'm so glad Lucy is here—she's doing a wonderful job. We can't praise her enough. She's been a huge help to us, to me and to Edith Fox," she said. "Of Fox's Fruit Syrups," she added.

Edith spoke to him also. "We had a trial basis, but the trial's approved now. Her help has been beyond our expectations." They talked to him for a long time—I didn't think he'd ever heard so much praise about me in my whole life.

They handed the phone back to me. My father seemed almost speechless, drunk on hearing good things about me for the first time. "Those ladies you're working for sound rather nice. Edith doesn't seem as crazy as Nanette said." He paused. "Do they have my books?"

"Um—no. I don't think so."

"I'll send them a set. If you think they'd like them."

"Sure. Yes. Definitely." Ugh.

"I think we're going to be able to purchase this yellow house we told you about," he said. "And just wait till you see the TV show. The producers say it's going to be a giant hit. It's going to cause lives to Change."

"Wonderful."

"Are you writing in the diary? Sticking to the food plan and the Goals?"

"Completely," I lied. I said goodbye to him and hung up the phone.

Edith said, "As I told your father, our trial basis is over, but I'm not sure if you *want* to stay here. I understand if you want to go to your parents' where it's safer. I'm afraid it's more dangerous here for you than I realized."

"I'm staying," I said.

Dyna walked into the garden right then, carrying her viola. "Me too—I'm staying—I'm never leaving New York." She told us how she'd spent the morning playing with the musicians Mimsy had introduced her to, especially two named Julius and Ramona. "We made a hundred dollars playing in the Christopher Street station! And Mimsy, I went to that old shop you told me about in the basement on St. Mark's Place, and I got all this." She showed us the sheet music for viola solos she'd bought, for songs ranging from Billie Holiday to the new band True Revolution. "My dad always said, 'Music is a hobby, not a profession. I'm not donating to Princeton every year for them to reject my kid because her dream is to play in a subway station.' Well, guess what? I love playing in the subway station." She hugged her sheet music. "I love New York. Here, almost everyone's parents or grandparents were born in a different country. *Everybody* is everything."

I nodded. "I love it, too." Dyna set up her music stand and practiced while Edith and I planted more dahlia tubers. I loved hearing her play.

"It will help the plants grow, too," Mimsy said. "Listen up, tubers!"

On break time, I took out my diary and wrote and drew

cross-hatched pictures of the plants in the garden. I copied the black-and-white tulip illustration from the bottom of one of Edith's framed columns, which was hanging in the potting shed. Dyna looked over my shoulder, and I told her about how Edith used to write them when she was our age. Together, we read the posted column.

A Fox's Rules for Living
APRIL 1957

1. KEEP GROWING. These are trying times for all of us. Everything in the world may be getting you down, but this isn't the time to be afraid.

2. LOOK FORWARD. These dark and endless rainy days are the time to prepare for what's to come: order seeds and design your cutting beds.

3. HAVE FAITH IN THE NATURAL WORLD. Behold the dahlia tuber. How could anything so ugly turn into something beautiful? The world isn't what men tell us, all wars and strife. What looks like despair now will change with water and feeding and sun.

4. EMBRACE THE MUD. Life is like planting things, isn't it? Everything grows beautifully and then it gets knocked down and there's mud everywhere and it's all a mess. You have to start over.

5. NEVER GIVE UP. That's the hardest thing in the world to do. For all of us.

By the end of this month, if this spring stays warm, you can

plant your dahlia tubers in the ground. Try the dinner plate
variety to break rules and have fun. Recommended reading this
month: We Made a Garden *by Margery Fish,* In Your Garden *by Vita Sackville-West, and* Children and Gardens *by*
Gertrude Jekyll.

"I love it," Dyna said.

Over lunch, while Edith went to a doctor's appointment, Mimsy and Dyna and I discussed the investigation.

"Next Saturday is Liliana's party at Mandragora. Everyone who was at the seder will be there," Mimsy said.

We decided we'd go to the party and observe all the suspects. Mimsy said she'd hire bodyguards to come also, to mingle and keep Edith—and all of us—safe.

At five o'clock, after Edith returned, Edith and I said goodbye to Mimsy and Dyna and waited for our usual bus home.

The streets filled with businessmen going home from work, women walking their dogs, wearing heels and sunglasses like a street fashion parade, and I took mental notes of what was beautiful: velvety black suede boots, red sneakers, a striped scarf. A well-groomed sheepdog with hair falling over its eyes stared at me and seemed to say, *Everybody looks good in New York.*

Edith peered down the street, looking for the bus, and glanced at her watch. "Might be a while," she said. We were the only ones at the stop. I looked around at the window boxes and the architecture. I never looked up like this, living in Austin. Almost all the buildings in the neighborhood I grew up in were only one or two stories high. Here the buildings had little surprises on top: gargoyles of tiny dragons and scrolls and black sculpted dots under the rooftops. Air conditioners jutted out of them like gray Lego pieces, or tabs in a pop-up book. There were so many things to see and drink in. I probably looked like a gawking tourist, but I couldn't help it.

It happened in a millisecond above us: someone adjusting an air conditioner at a sixth-floor window, a flick. Two black-gloved hands, their fingers at the window's edge, pushing the air conditioner out.

A sudden forward movement, a flash, dropping toward us, Edith a yard from me, it came so fast—I pushed her back toward the stoop, I tried to hold her, to cushion her fall—

It crashed. A giant boom and bang and Edith screamed.

nineteen

DO NOT DIE. REALLY.

April 29
Goals:
1. DO NOT DIE
2. DO NOT LET ANYONE ELSE DIE
3. Oh, screw the goals. Just don't die.

𝔚est 𝔙illage 𝔊azette

ACCIDENT ON W. 10TH STREET

An elderly woman and a teenager were injured yesterday when an air conditioner dropped from the window of a building undergoing renovations on W. 10th Street.

The women were identified as Edith Fox of Summer Street in Manhattan, and Lucy Clark of Austin, Texas. They were taken to Village Hospital and released that evening.

No one was present in the building at the time of the accident, and West Side Builders, the company managing the renovation, said, "It was a freak accident. The air conditioner had been properly secured and we're not aware of what might have caused its sudden release. Our workers had left for the day and the building was locked and empty."

Ms. Fox, when reached by telephone, told a reporter, "I believe this was intentional. I was a target." The other injured party could not be reached for comment.

I wasn't sure what they gave me at the hospital, but after they sent me home I slept for twelve hours. When I woke up in Nanette's apartment, it felt like a hippopotamus was sitting on my head.

Two fuzzy figures appeared over my bed, hovering.

"Dad? Mom?"

Nanette flinched. "You look terrible. You scared everyone. I don't know what I'd tell your father if you *died*."

Cyrus elbowed her. "The questions." He wore the heavy cologne again. He seemed to have taken a bath in it. Its smell made my head hurt more. I pulled the sheet up over my face, but Nanette pulled it back off.

She took out a piece of paper. "The doctor said it was a minor bump on the head, but we had to ask you this when you woke up. Name? City? Country? Are your pupils of equal size? Look up at the light, please."

"Lucy Clark. New York. United States. Is Edith okay?" I started to panic, thinking of her.

"She's fine," Nanette said. I relaxed a little. Cyrus took out his phone and showed me the article in the *West Village Gazette*.

I didn't tell them that I'd seen gloved hands at the window, that someone pushed the air conditioner toward us.

Cyrus handed me one of my father's kale shakes. "You're supposed to have this." I took a sip and could barely make myself swallow. It tasted like rotten lawn clippings.

"Time for you to get up. Police want to speak with you. Investigating the accident," Nanette said.

"Police?" My knees ached. My whole body ached.

"Don't worry, they won't arrest *you*," Cyrus said. "I don't think."

"Where were you both last night when it happened?" I asked them.

Nanette rolled her eyes. "At a party, of course."

They left the room. I looked down at my knees: red and bruised, with giant bandages on them.

My chest hurt and I kept coughing, so I used my inhaler, and then I took a shower and tore the soggy bandages off my knees and tried not to grimace at the sting. I kept replaying what had happened: the air conditioner falling toward us, the flick of the black gloved hands. Why did the builders tell the newspaper that no one was inside the building then?

I got dressed quickly and was about to leave the apartment to go to Edith's when I heard a knock on the apartment door. I unlocked it.

It was Mimsy and Dyna. They hugged me. "I'm so glad you're okay," Dyna said. "I wanted to stay the night with you here, but Nanette wouldn't let me. Mimsy wanted to take you back to our place, but Nanette said your father wouldn't allow that, either."

"How's Edith?"

"She's fine, but scared. That was way too close a call." Mimsy shook her head.

"It wasn't an accident." I told them about the black-gloved hands.

Mimsy jabbed the elevator button. "When you tell the police, you have to sound confident. They're going to question what you saw and decide whether you're a reliable witness."

The elevator pinged at Edith's floor, and we walked to her front door. A deliveryman waited there with a cart overflowing with flowers, like an entire florist shop on wheels.

Another man waited beside the deliveryman—it was Jack. "Are you okay? I stopped by this morning, but Nanette wouldn't wake you—"

"I'm all right," I said.

Mimsy leaned over and talked to the flowers. "Oh, you peonies, we need you now more than ever. Who sent you?" She peeked at the tag. "Aaah. Peter. I knew it. Hmmm."

"My mom loved peonies," Jack said, and stared at the flowers.

"She took me to see *The Peony Pavilion*—the famous Chinese opera—at the Metropolitan Museum once. It was performed in the Chinese garden. An opera about a garden, performed in a garden." He half-smiled. "She wore red peony flowers in her hair when she married my dad."

His eyes lightened; I liked hearing him talk about his mom. His phone buzzed and he reached into his pocket. He read a text. "They just finished interviewing Edith. They're ready to talk to you in the library," he said to me.

My insides froze.

"You'll do fine," Mimsy said, hugging me.

"Just tell the truth," Dyna said.

Jack walked me down the corridor to the library and opened the door. Two men in suits sat in leather chairs in the corner. One was Jack's father, his giraffe-like neck looking even longer today. "I'll wait outside," Jack said. "I'm an intern, so I'm not supposed to be present during questioning."

I nodded, and he shut the door behind me. Both Jack's father and the other detective seemed bored out of their minds. The second detective's name was Detective Fairleigh, and he was completely bald and wore high-waisted pants. He looked like Humpty Dumpty.

I told them my name, age, and everything I'd seen. I tried to calm myself by focusing on reading the spines of the books on the shelves. My eyes settled on a row of gardening encyclopedias from the Royal Horticultural Society, a book called *Down the Garden Path*, and a few shelves above it, a thick blue book called *Home Arts: A Girl's Guide to Housekeeping* with a pink flower on its spine. It looked like a real pressed flower, and somehow that felt comforting.

The detectives looked me over. I could tell that they didn't believe me. Humpty said, "Are you a hundred percent certain of what you saw? Because it contradicts the statements from the workmen and all the available evidence. Officers investigated the building and they believe nobody was inside at the time. There were no other witnesses besides you."

The Giraffe picked up a cup of coffee. "It's an apartment undergoing renovations. The workmen said they locked the door when they left for the day, before the accident. Maybe what you saw was a trick of the light."

"I know I saw someone push it. They were wearing gloves. Probably because they didn't want to leave fingerprints." I remembered how in eighth grade we'd studied due process of law and the phenomenon of unreliable witnesses. Was my memory not really a memory at all, but something I'd imagined because Edith and Mimsy had convinced me someone was after Edith? My stomach churned.

"The doctors said you were hysterical after the accident." The Giraffe gazed at me. "As you said yourself, people often believe they've seen something that wasn't there."

"Lots of things fall out windows in New York, did you know that? Scary thing, being in a big city like this, after you come from Nebraska," Humpty said.

"Texas," I said.

"How old is she again?" Humpty asked the Giraffe, as if I wasn't even in the room and hadn't just told them that a few minutes before.

"Sixteen," I reminded them.

"Oh, right." Oh, right. Translation: How could a flighty, ridiculous sixteen-year-old girl ever say anything important, ever notice anything, ever have a reliable opinion?

"We studied unreliable witnesses in school, but I know what I saw. Someone pushed it. Someone is trying to kill Edith."

Humpty closed his eyes a little too long. "Thank you for giving us your story."

"I know you think Edith has dementia. But she doesn't. Someone's trying to kill her. You have to take it seriously," I said.

"We see homicides every day. Not like this—random poisonings, pushing air conditioners—that's not how killers behave," the Giraffe said. His mind seemed firmly made up. He checked his watch. "Thanks for your time."

He opened the door to the library for me. Jack was waiting in the hallway.

"They didn't believe me," I told Jack. "What kind of evidence do you and the police need? The killer to stick a knife in someone's neck in front of you and say, *I'm committing murder right now—please video record this so there's evidence, and make sure to focus the camera on my face!*"

He didn't laugh. "Look—I know it's—I do believe you. It's just—it's like trying to make sense of two opposite things at once."

"Did they even investigate properly? Did they scour the building where the air conditioner fell? I can't believe there wasn't any evidence."

"They searched it thoroughly. They didn't find anything. They're doing the best they can." He paused. "I know you're telling the truth. I want the same thing you do—to protect Edith."

Something clicked in my mind. "Did you know Edith has a heart condition—atrial fibrillation? That's what she takes digoxin for. The murderer knows that. So they knew that even if the air conditioner didn't kill her, the fright of it might. It could cause a heart attack."

"It's possible," he said. "My father won't believe it, and it wouldn't hold up in court, but you could be onto something."

I glanced at the wall beside us—a framed certificate from the Northeastern Dahlia Society was hung there, along with a giant white ribbon, awarded to two cowinners: Edith Fox and Wenli Zuo.

"Your mom." I touched the glass above her name. *Best in Show, Mandragora Moon*, the award said.

"That was a dahlia they bred together. Edith still grows it," he said.

"I planted it in Mimsy's garden yesterday," I said.

He was quiet for a moment, and then said, "She liked working with Edith to breed flowers, when she wasn't at the lab doing her bee research. She used to come back from Mandragora with armfuls of dahlias and fill our apartment with them."

"I loved planting them. It felt like caring for a kitten. Tucking them in and making sure they're safe." I paused. "You have your mom's last name, not your dad's?"

"She put it on the birth certificate when he wasn't looking. He was thrilled."

"I can imagine."

He stared at his mom's name, too, and the ribbon. "I'm sorry this has been so hard. I'm going to do what I can on my end to help. Also—I wanted to ask you—I don't know if it's true, but there's a rumor going around the building that you and Mimsy and your friend have been poking around in a way that's not exactly lawful."

I felt my face flush.

"Please—it's not worth the risk. You won't get involved, will you?"

"I won't," I lied, and looked away, wishing that I could tell him the truth.

twenty
SCOUTS FROM HELL

"There's only one thing to do," Mimsy said, back at her house. We'd visited Edith—she was in her bedroom doing well, with no significant injuries, and was resting now. We let her sleep while we tried to make a plan.

"Follow me," Mimsy said as she led Dyna and me up to the third floor, to a room she called her boudoir. It looked like a fancy boutique with racks of dresses, a row of pressed men's suits—"A woman should always wear traditional menswear sometimes," she said—and rainbows of sweaters stacked on glass shelves. A cupboard displayed hundreds of shoes and purses, like works of art.

"First, we need costumes," Mimsy said. Her hands swam

through the clothes on the racks above us. They'd been organized by size and color, a dancing wave of silk and wool and cotton. "Once we look and feel the part, the rest will fall into place."

I touched the sequin flowers on a black satin purse. "What parts do we need to feel?"

"The murderer can't know what we're doing," she said. "That would *not* be safe."

"What are we doing?" Dyna asked.

"Sneaking into the building down the street to search for clues. This time, in costume," Mimsy said. "Trust me. Everything important needs a costume."

"I think people will probably still recognize us, if we see someone we know." I told them how I'd just promised Jack that we wouldn't do any more rule breaking.

"We'll make sure he doesn't find out," Mimsy said. "The costumes will help. Here we go! I haven't seen you for years, but I knew you were waiting for me." She was speaking to two old Girl Scout uniforms, which she plucked from the racks to show us—forest-green skirts, white blouses, green neckties, and badge-covered green sashes. "Let's see if they fit you."

"Why do we need to dress up as Girl Scouts?" Dyna asked.

"When I walked by that building this morning, I saw workmen inside—what better way to have them buzz us inside than to sell them cookies? Who can say no to cookies?"

"But we don't have any cookies." Dyna sat on a blue velvet-cushioned chaise in the corner. Above it, a purple bookcase displayed antique classics, their navy and brown spines looking welcoming and well-loved. "I've never seen books in a closet before," Dyna said. "I like it."

"My decorating scheme is bordello meets indie bookshop," Mimsy said. "Existentialist meets *fille de joie*. And I always have Girl Scout cookies. I keep ten boxes on hand at all times. And we can print some order forms off the internet, too. Sell what I have and take orders for more."

An hour later, we headed out the door. Mimsy was dressed as our troop leader in a USO uniform she'd saved from an off-Broadway play.

We did look sort of official. If it was 1941.

"Normally I'd be embarrassed in this situation. But in times like this, you have to think, WWLED?" Dyna said as we walked down the street.

"Exactly," I said.

"What does that mean?" Mimsy asked.

"What Would Lucy and Ethel Do," Dyna explained. "This is the closest we'll ever get to being in an episode of *I Love Lucy*." Before she died, Dyna's mom had sent her the complete set of *I Love Lucy* episodes on ancient DVDs, which came in a heart-shaped box. It was a TV show from approximately a million years ago about a housewife and her best friend and their madcap adventures—Dyna's mom used to watch it with her mom. Uriah gave us a clunky old player from the library so we could binge-watch. I loved that Lucy was never afraid to look ridiculous—and I loved that I had Lucy's name.

Out on the street, nobody even blinked at us as we walked by in our costumes. One of my favorite things about New York was that you could stroll around with a monkey sitting on your head and nobody would stare.

We approached the building. A second-floor window was open. We pressed the main buzzer.

No answer. Mimsy tried the lock on the front door. It didn't budge. She pressed all the buzzers again, going up the row. A man poked his head out from the second-story window. Mimsy shouted to him, "Girl Scout cookie sales!"

"Ya got Thin Mints?"

"Of course."

He buzzed us through and we stepped inside the hallway. The man appeared on the landing. He wore jeans and a blue shirt with a logo that read "Charlie's Electric Service."

"That's sweet that you and your great-grandmother go around selling cookies together," he said to me and Dyna. "My great-gran loved Thin Mints. She ate them frozen. Helped her swollen gums. Let's see what you got there." He looked at the boxes in her tote bag and the order form.

I watched an expression of horror cross Mimsy's face at the words *great-grandmother*, but she bore it in silence.

"We heard about the accident that happened here yesterday," I said, glancing up the stairs.

"Unbelievable." He shook his head. "I'm in electric, I didn't install that AC window unit. The builders brought it in while they were working."

"Which floor was it?" Mimsy asked.

"Sixth floor."

"Our troop is working on our Safety and Accident Prevention Badges. Do you think it would be okay if we peeked upstairs?" I asked.

"Then we could explain to our troop how it was a normal window—how these things can happen anywhere, and we must be prepared? And take preventative measures?" Dyna asked. She was a natural actress.

He shrugged. "Sure. Went up there myself earlier, but there's nothing to see. No harm in you having a look. Good that you're talking about safety. Here's my card. Tell your friends to let their parents know that I specialize in updating old knob and tube wiring. Can do a consultation for a discount. For the Scouts."

Mimsy took his card. "We'll tell everyone. Thank you. Our troop takes safety very seriously."

We walked up to the sixth floor and Mimsy squeezed our shoulders. "I'm hiring you both immediately for the West Village Acting Troupe."

We reached the apartment. The door was open and it was empty with no furniture—just a stool and a ladder and two cans of white paint on the floor. It was still under construction, with unfinished drywall and plaster patches on the walls everywhere, and cans labeled Primo Paint and Yax Compound and Arnold Spackling, and brushes and tools.

"Shouldn't there be police tape here, or something?" Dyna asked. "Some signs of the investigation?"

"Jack said they finished investigating and found nothing. Case closed," I said.

I noticed dirty smudges on the wood floor—a lot of people had probably been in this room—but no visible footprints. I walked over to the window and looked down at the street below. A perfect view to the bus stop, a straight shot to where Edith and I had stood.

We surveyed everything, opening cabinets and checking wastebaskets. Nothing. I stood where the murderer must have waited, watching us. The window was perpendicular to a new wall the builders were making, adding an extra room to the tiny apartment. Whoever had pushed the air conditioner must've leaned against the drywall in this shadowy corner, waiting till we appeared below.

It would've been a long time to stand. I pulled a stool over from the corner and sat on it. I smelled something on the unfinished paper surface of the drywall.

A familiar cologne.

"Come here. Smell this. In this one spot. It's the cologne Cyrus wears. I know it is," I said.

Mimsy and Dyna smelled it also. It was faint, but certain.

"It must've come from someone who was sitting here on a stool for a long time. Waiting," Dyna said.

I took out my notebook and wrote down a description of the cologne. "I saw three bottles of it in his medicine cabinet—it's called Pure Man."

"Eww. Of course it is," Dyna said. "Should we tell the police?

What are the chances they'd see it as a clue?"

"Zero," I said. "They didn't believe me about the gloves. There's no way they'll take a scent clue seriously. It wouldn't hold up in court. I know what Jack's father would say: Thousands of people wear this cologne. It's not proof."

But it was still a clue for us.

"Hey, ya done in there?" the electrician called to us from the landing.

"Yes, almost, thank you!" Mimsy shouted. "Just a minute!"

The electrician appeared in the doorway, holding the cookie order form Mimsy had given him. "I want to try the S'mores, too," he said. "And a bulk order of Thin Mints. Can I pay on delivery?"

"Yes. The Girl Scouts thank you," Mimsy told him. We said goodbye and walked down the stairs.

"I feel a little bad we're being fake Girl Scouts," Dyna said when we were out of earshot. "He really seemed excited about those cookies."

"Don't worry. We won't commit complete fraud in the name of the Scouts," Mimsy said. "Just a tiny bit. I'll order his cookies and give them to him for free." She opened the front door. "Sometimes you have to shake things up a little for the sake of justice."

"Is that a Mimsy's Rule?" I asked.

"Yes."

We stepped onto the stoop. And there he was.

Jack—right in front of us. His floppy hair was tucked behind his ears neatly, and he wore a suit similar to his father's. He was probably on his way to his dad's office.

"Do what?" he asked. "For the sake of justice?" He took in our costumes. "What's going on?"

"How wonderful to see you!" Mimsy held up a red box of Tagalongs. "Dyna is a Girl Scout, and Lucy was in a troop back in Texas, and it's cookie sales time. I'm a former Scout myself. Always do what I can for the sisterhood. They earn prizes, you know. Would you like some?" She was in full actress mode. She opened her bag and showed him all the cookie varieties. She tapped my shoulder.

"Yes," I said. "If we sell enough boxes we can earn . . . tubers." It was the first word that came to mind.

"Tubers?" He raised his eyebrows.

Why did I say tubers? It had popped out of my mouth like a cough.

"Girl Scouts are really eco-friendly these days," Dyna said.

"Yes!" Mimsy said brightly. "Saving the earth, one tuber at a time! The girls have a choice—bulbs, plants . . ."

Jack was quiet for a few moments, glancing from me to Mimsy to Dyna and back again. "You're selling cookies at this building where the air conditioner fell, to earn tubers."

Mimsy turned around to face the front door. "Is this the same building? I didn't recognize it." Her face broadened with an expression that an acting coach might call "genuine surprise."

"How many cookies do you need to sell to earn a tuber?" he asked me.

"Ten boxes," I mumbled, not meeting his gaze. It was hard to lie to him. Maybe the police trained him to stare at people with those truth-boring eyes, like a heat-seeking missile.

When I finally did glance at him, he had an I'm-considering-arresting-you look. The same alarmed expression he'd had when he saw I didn't have a driver's license.

The window above us opened. "You know what? Add on two boxes of Do-si-dos, too, for my great-gran—I can mash them up for her if she can't chew them. Hey, and good luck with that accident badge!"

"You got it!" Mimsy said, and waved up at the window. She turned to give Jack an innocent smile.

"Accident badge?" he asked.

"Accident prevention," Mimsy said. "Important badge for all girls to achieve."

"Does that get you more prizes? More tubers?"

"Absolutely," she said cheerfully.

He stared intensely at Mimsy. "I know you've been in a lot of Hercule Poirot plays. But this isn't a play or a game. I don't mean to sound harsh. I just mean—we've got it covered. It's not safe for you three to be here."

"Why are you here?" I asked him. "I thought you said the investigation was finished?"

"After we spoke this morning, I wanted to take another look. I've been thinking about what you said. I want to make sure we have all our bases covered. But there's no need for the three of you to be Nancy Drew-ing around in costume."

"That's quite belittling, Jack," Mimsy said.

"I'm sorry—look, I know you want to help Edith," he said. "I know you have good intentions. But you don't see what I see, what my dad sees every day in this city. There are dark and terrible things out there. Horrible things. It's like—boiling a frog."

"What?" I asked.

"If you put a frog in boiling water, it jumps out. But if you keep a frog in hot water and slowly raise the temperature, it will boil to death. It doesn't realize what's happening," he said.

Dyna kept looking at him as if he were completely bonkers. Mimsy took a box out of her tote bag and held it out to him. "None of us will be boiled alive, I promise," she said. "Have a Thanks-A-Lot?"

He shook his head. "Please listen to me—please stay safe." He took a key out, unlocked the front door of the building, and went in.

The door closed behind him. "Figures he gets a key," Mimsy said. "And yet they still can't figure it out. His father's doing an awful job, but they don't want us to do it, either. There's only one thing to do."

"More costumes?" Dyna asked.

"Eat," she said. "All this talk of cookies—I'm starving."

twenty-one
SEA CHANGE

I t was warm out, but I shivered as we walked to Mimsy's house to change out of our clothes. I felt rattled from everything that had happened. Frogs in boiling water?

I could tell that Mimsy was rattled, too, because she started quoting Shakespeare again as we walked. *"Screw your courage to the sticking place, and we'll not fail. Lady Macbeth,"* she said. She called Edith, who'd woken up from her nap, and asked her to meet us for lunch. Dyna had a quick bite to eat and grabbed her viola—she was meeting her new musician group at Jane Street Garden to play—they'd formed a band, though they hadn't picked a name yet. We walked Dyna there down the winding West Village streets. Her face lit up when she saw her new friends—Julius with his giant bass and Ramona with her saxophone—and they passed out sheet music. Dyna beamed, and something lifted in me, too, at seeing her so happy.

Mimsy and I said goodbye to them and walked to a tiny café called Le Lutin. A red bicycle stood outside the front door; white miniature roses grew from its basket. We went inside, and the hostess seated us.

Edith arrived then, wearing a navy-blue scarf, looking like her old self again. We told her about the cologne clue, and how I was certain it was Cyrus's. "Of course it's possible someone hired Cyrus to push it for them—we need to figure out who," Mimsy said. "Or someone else wears the same cologne."

Edith frowned and pressed her lips together. "I've made a decision. I've been thinking this over, and I'm going to take a break from talking or thinking about this whole situation—who is after me and why. I decided I'm going to live my life without the fear or worry of it for a little while. I need time away from it, just to think."

Mimsy scrunched her forehead. "Is that wise? I mean—considering—"

"Absolutely," Edith said. "I don't want to talk about it any-more, starting now."

"I understand. Makes perfect sense," Mimsy said, giving me a look. Edith excused herself to use the restroom. When she was gone, Mimsy told me, "I think she's saying that because as it becomes clearer that the murderer is someone she knows, and not a stranger, it's too painful."

I thought of Jack's frog-in-hot-water story, and how all of this must feel for Edith. And I thought of what Thornton had felt like every day—like slowly being boiled.

I glanced around the café. Spindly poles made from birch trees lined the walls, twinkling with tiny lights like fireflies. There were rough-hewn wooden tables and cloth chairs the color of moss. This seemed like a place where you could leave the world behind and forget that awful things were happening outside its walls.

Mimsy opened the menu—the center of it had pictures of pastries—and ordered Edith's favorite things. White peony tea and three pink cakes with an upright rose petal balanced on top of each one, as if it were dancing. Dewdrops glistened on the petals like fairies' tears. And she ordered a trio of tiny white, tiered cakes that looked like they'd been made for a bunny's wedding.

"And let's get the allium, of course, and the cocoa butter gems," Mimsy said to the waiter. She turned to me. "Takes a while for them to prepare those, but wait till you see them." She sighed and leaned back in her seat. "A meal of dessert. Secret to a long life."

I gazed around at the twinkling lights and birch trees. I tried to focus on being here now. I didn't want to miss any of it.

Edith returned just as the rose petal cakes arrived, and she smiled. "My favorites."

Mimsy stood up and hugged her. "I thought we needed a Sea Change Day."

Edith squeezed Mimsy's hand and exhaled. "We do."

"A what?" I asked.

"It's a thing since we were teenagers," Mimsy said. "It's from one of Edith's favorite authors, M. F. K. Fisher. She started publishing books in the 1930s, and she wrote about ocean crossings to Europe—sea changes—and how your soul changes when you cross the sea. And she wrote about food and love."

If Edith and Mimsy wrote their own self-help book, it would be called: *How to Stay Sane and Happy in a Dark, Dark World.*

Our tea arrived, and Edith sipped hers slowly. "A Sea Change Day is when you say 'screw it' to everything that's expected of you, everything you're supposed to do. It's a way to turn around a blue day. A low day. To take a break and explore. Have dessert for lunch. Eat something beautiful."

Which was what we did. We ate the rose petal cakes first. Their dewdrops tasted like sugared snowflakes, and the pink cake burst with raspberries.

The plates kept arriving: a giant allium flower like a purple cloud. Mimsy instructed me to reach my spoon inside the flower to retrieve a vanilla-and-lavender pudding hidden inside it, dotted with violet pearls. The flower petals clung to the pudding like baby purple starfish.

The last course came: sweet green jasmine tea inside round spheres made of cocoa butter. We popped them in our mouths and they burst into a hundred flavors at once.

How was this possible? How did food like this exist? Mimsy explained something about liquid nitrogen and molecular gastronomy—I'd never even heard of that before.

Grown-ups made this, I thought. Grown-ups spent hours creating this magical food.

I thought back to when I'd first stepped in Mimsy's garden and time had stopped, and I felt that strange joy. A crack in the universe. A shift in reality. I felt that now, too, like someone had performed surgery on my soul and tucked this strange new thing deep inside me: this knowledge of the world and what mattered in it. How there were places where you could go to escape the dark, terrifying world, at least for a little while. How beautiful things—small beautiful things—food and plants and flowers—how they could change you. That food wasn't about numbers and calories and nutrition, but beauty. That these beautiful things could be a key to unlocking a world inside you, a place that you couldn't before reach.

It could be protection, an armor, a way to survive the darkness. A way to walk through the world when you wanted to hide in bed all day and night.

Mimsy sighed and relaxed into her seat.

Edith wiped her hands on her napkin. "Exactly what I needed."

I studied their faces, absorbing everything about them: Edith's cotton candy wisps of hair around her forehead, Mimsy's laugh lines like sunbursts.

"How are you feeling about New York?" Edith asked me. "I'm sure it's not what you imagined."

I thought of how I'd arrived with that emptiness in my chest, and it felt less hollow now, but the raw place was still there because Nanette's apartment was as far from a purple cottage as you could get.

I spoke slowly. "I think starting over wouldn't be as hard if I knew where I'd stay for good. Where I'd end up." It hurt to say it somehow, to talk of that feeling of not having a home, of not knowing how long I'd be here in New York, or if I'd be sent back to Texas, or finally live with my parents—to know when I'd stop feeling in-between. When would I feel like I belonged? When would I feel like I was home?

Edith stared at me. "It can also be wonderful when you don't know exactly where you'll end up. That's one of the loveliest things about growing old. You can see new endings to your stories, the stories of your life."

"What do you mean?" I asked.

"Well, look at the relationships I've had which ended. Losing Clifford. Those stories could seem like tragedies, depending where they stopped. If you wanted to finish the story when I was sixteen or twenty or even last year, having given him up and never found him, then it would have a different ending. I'd made too many mistakes. I'd screwed up. Or I thought maybe the problem was me, something was wrong with me."

Something was wrong with me. That was how I'd felt since Nana died: that I'd done something wrong, screwed everything up, and that was the real reason why I didn't have a home, a permanent place where I belonged, and why I'd felt so lost since she died—all my flaws and mistakes.

She paused. "Now, taking the long view, even after what happened these past few weeks, I'm optimistic. I think all those things were sort of rough turns along the way, detours to get here. Where I am now. I know there will be a good ending."

In the dim light of the café, she looked so young, all of a sudden.

I wanted to help Edith have a good ending—to keep her safe. She'd given me something in this short time I'd known her, she and Mimsy had, and I wanted to give them something back. If I could find who'd been doing this to her, then maybe it would prove there wasn't anything wrong with me, either. That people could trust me. That I could trust myself. Maybe it would undo the mistakes I'd made, the rules I'd broken, that look from the police officer in Austin, as if he'd stared into my soul and seen a bad person.

It would prove I wasn't bad. I could be trusted. I could find out the truth about myself. About who I really was. Who I would turn out to be. It would help my parents see that truth. I thought of how Edith said *new endings to your stories.* Our story hadn't ended yet, with my parents and me. It had barely even started. We had time, still.

Sitting in this woodland forest fairy café with the twinkling birch trees around us, I thought: There could be a good ending to my story, also.

The waiter brought glasses of champagne to Mimsy and Edith, and a flute of sparkling cider for me. "On the house, for the three young ladies," he said in a French accent. "Whose beauty lights up the room."

We laughed. No one had ever said anything like that to me before.

We raised our glasses.

"To writing our own endings," Edith said.

We spent the rest of our Sea Change Day at sea—literally. Dyna joined us later in the afternoon, and we rode the Staten Island Ferry just for fun.

I loved the wind and the views of the Statue of Liberty, and the faces of all the passengers, commuters, and tourists. At sundown, we walked from the ferry terminal around Battery Park and rode the SeaGlass Carousel, with glittery fish and seahorses and pink and aqua and purple lights.

The rattled feeling from earlier that day was gone, and in its place was this certainty that everything would be okay. Edith would be fine. We would all be fine. My new life would be okay. I would belong again—I belonged here, now, and that feeling could become permanent, someday.

It was a perfect Sea Change Day. When we left the carousel, we walked back to the pier. The wind died down and the harbor was quiet, and for a moment the glass sea seemed still and strong, as if nothing could ever crack it.

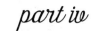

part iv

THE GARDEN OF SORROWS

Every flower holds the whole mystery in its short cycle,
and in the garden we are never far away from death.
—*May Sarton*

twenty-two
MANDRAGORA

Two stone columns framed the winding driveway to Mandragora, two hours away from the city, into New York State. Strings of paper lanterns swung between the trees. A stone mansion rose up on a hill in the distance. Mimsy drove Edith, Dyna, and me in her car. Dyna wore a black dress, and I wore a red velvet one, both from Mimsy's closet. Liliana was already at the garden with the dancers. Dyna brought her viola—Liliana had hired Dyna, Julius, and Ramona to play for the performance tonight.

Mimsy had packed a cooler with food and drinks for Edith— we weren't taking any chances. Our investigation plan was to observe all the suspects and check if anyone else was wearing the cologne, and to follow up on their alibis from when the air conditioner fell. Liliana had said she was at her dance rehearsal then, Clifford was working in the florist's shop, and Cyrus had gotten off work early that day, and attended a preview of a friend's play called *Easy Street*. Peter's alibi was that he was taking a walk on the High Line alone then, which was impossible to confirm, and Nanette refused to tell Mimsy when she asked her. Still, Nanette and Peter didn't have strong motives, like Liliana and Clifford did. They wouldn't inherit money or gain anything by hurting Edith. Peter still wanted to marry her. Though of course, as Mimsy said, "Love makes people stark raving mad."

Before we'd left for the party, when Mimsy, Dyna, and I were alone, getting dressed, Mimsy said, "The murderer has made attempts only in public, and always making it look accidental—possibly trying to scare Edith into having cardiac failure, like you said, Lucy—but if they try anything at Mandragora tonight, we'll catch them."

We saw Jack beside the entrance, on the path, his hands in his pockets. He wore a suit and carried a giant camera with a strap around his shoulder.

He stared at me. "I didn't recognize you." His tone was softer than usual. "All three of you look wonderful." He kissed Edith on the cheek, and then he kissed Mimsy and Dyna, like a gentleman in an old movie.

He kissed my cheek next, his face warm and smooth next to mine, and I thought about the investigation, and before I could help myself, I smelled him.

"Did you just sniff me?" he asked.

I shook my head. "No."

He squinted at me.

"You're not wearing cologne." I tried to sound nonchalant.

He tilted his head. "Am I supposed to?"

"Do you ever wear it?"

"No." He gave me a strange look.

"What's the camera for?" Dyna asked, changing the subject.

"I always bring it when I come here. Before my mom died, she saw a rusty-patched bumblebee here. *Bombus affinis.* They're endangered—they haven't been recorded in New York State in over fifteen years. She never got a photo or specimen, so I've been trying to confirm her sighting ever since, with no luck. Peter's cultivated all its favorite plants to feed on—hopefully, this will be the year when we find it again. And have a record of it."

People milled about in tuxedos and suits and long dresses. We walked down the path, which was lined with one-hundred-foot trees, and I thought of the short, scrubby trees of Austin. I'd never been anywhere like this. It seemed like Mimsy's garden, but a hundred times larger and more beautiful.

Waiters walked through the crowd, giving out drinks, but Mimsy poured Edith her drink from the flask she'd brought. The bodyguards Mimsy had hired were standing nearby, watching Edith. They wore suits and sunglasses and looked like the Secret Service.

Dyna checked the time. "I need to join the band—see you at intermission?"

I squeezed her hand. "Good luck."

She squeezed mine back.

Mimsy pointed at Cyrus in the crowd. We needed to get started on our plan. She waved at him, and he came over to say hello. He was wearing the hubcap suit again.

"Beautiful garden you've got here. We were exploring earlier," Cyrus said. "Nanette's networking. She saw someone she wants to profile for the magazine."

"You have lint on your jacket," I said to Cyrus, and I brushed his lapel, leaning in. He was wearing the cologne again. "I heard you saw the play *Easy Street*? How was it?" I asked him.

He wrinkled his nose. "What? Oh. Great play. Fantastic." He took a swig of his drink.

Mimsy and I exchanged looks. Was he lying?

Cyrus saw our expressions and held up his empty glass. "Off to get a refill. See you."

"I'm going to follow up on whether he was at the theater that day," Mimsy whispered to me.

I saw Clifford through the crowd, and I waved hello. Edith had provided a golf cart for him to go down the paths and see all sixty acres. Trish sat beside him. He drove toward us and stopped the cart. I asked what he thought of Mandragora.

"It's a special place," he said. The garden seemed to affect him, too—his shoulders relaxed, and he kept staring at the trees, drinking it all in. "Peter was right—it's different now from the

last time I was here. I'm hoping to see everything that's blooming before dark."

"I'm so glad you like it here," I said, and hugged him. His
arms stiffened. No cologne.

"Thanks," he said, giving me a strange look. "Um—good to
see you. Enjoy."

He drove off, and Jack whispered to me, "Did you just sniff
him, too?"

I shook my head.

Jack touched my elbow. "Excuse us for a second?" he said to
everyone. "Lucy, can I talk to you, please?"

"Sure."

Mimsy looked worried and gave me a concerned wave.
"Hurry back. The performance will start soon."

Jack and I walked down the garden path. We passed a grove
of lilacs. Their scent was sweet and addictive, like breathing in
sunlight. "What are you up to?" he asked me.

"What do you mean?"

"Why are you smelling everyone?"

"I'm not."

What would he say if I confessed that one of our investiga-
tive methods was smelling people for cologne? He'd laugh and
roll his eyes and scoff in ten different ways. I straightened my
spine. But what was wrong with it? If it got us closer to figuring
out who was after Edith, then why not look ridiculous? Why
not try anything we could?

The path opened onto a clearing above a rolling hill.

Daffodils and tulips stretched down the hill toward a large pond ringed with magnolias, flowering crabapples, and dogwoods, an explosion of petals and colors.

It felt like going through the wardrobe to Narnia, or wandering into Oz, or jumping into a sidewalk painting with Mary Poppins. But this was real.

He showed me secret spots in the garden that only Edith, his mother, and a few gardeners knew about—the olive trees that weren't olives at all, but were willows; the gardeners had braided the limbs and weighted them down as they grew to make them look twisted and ancient. And he showed me strange sculptures—a star stuck high in a tree, and a girl at the bottom of a tiny pond, fish nibbling her feet. An old cottonwood tree with a hollowed-out trunk you could sit inside. A stone with a bonsai tree growing around it; the stone was carved mysteriously with "February 1st." It was all so beautiful and odd. The art was woven into the garden so you couldn't tell what was made by nature alone—extraterrestrial flowers and heart-shaped leaves—and what was made by humans.

Jack pointed to a bench by the big pond. A man sat there, alone. Jack called out to him. "Peter!"

Perfect. He was next on my list to observe. Peter waved at us, and we walked toward him, down the hill. I took off my shoes and carried them. The grass felt silky under my toes.

"Well, hello there," Peter said when we'd reached him. He wore his wool vest again—his Peter Rabbit fashion. Of everyone I'd met, he still seemed the most harmless. He looked a bit forlorn, off in some kind of reverie.

"We didn't mean to interrupt you," Jack said.

"You didn't. It's lovely to have company—your company. Don't you two look marvelous, all dressed up. I just needed a bit of a rest from the crowd. I tried to talk to Edith, but some strange burly man in a suit wouldn't let me near her."

"He was probably one of the bodyguards Mimsy hired," I said. "She wanted to make sure Edith would be okay."

His face fell when he heard Edith's name, and he was silent for a while, then finally said, "Can't stay away from this corner." He pointed to the flower beds beside the pond—some had not been planted yet, with rich brown soil—and some were filled with alliums, phlox, and columbines.

I knew the names of these flowers now. It wasn't the kind of knowledge that would matter to Ms. Leery, but it mattered to me.

Peter frowned and kept nervously twisting his fingers. He looked worried.

"Are you all right?" Jack asked him.

"Fine, fine. This garden is a good place for thinking. Clearing one's head. Deep thoughts and such. I see Edith planted this giant patch of tricolor violas right here. Do you know what that means?"

He pointed at one bed that was bare except for a few recently planted flowers. I shook my head.

"She always loved their little teardrops in the petals. She plants them when she's deeply sad. It means—I think—well, it's almost May tenth, the day she was going to decide about the trip. I think she's sending a message to me in these flowers. I've been trying to accept that Edith and I"—he glanced my way—"it's not—it won't ever." His face looked weighted down like the willow trees.

"I think she's been overwhelmed with everything going on lately. She's—" I tried to explain, but I wasn't sure how. I also needed to check for the cologne. "I know Edith really likes you. This is a hard time for everybody. She's been uncertain about everything lately." He was a reserved English person, and I knew this would be awkward, but I went ahead and hugged him. I inhaled.

It was faint, but he was wearing the same cologne as Cyrus.

"Er . . . thank you for the hug. Americans. You know, I moved here in the first place loving the openness, the confessions, the American optimism. I've lived here forty years and I'm not quite used to all of the . . . er, warmth. The hugs. Very kind of you," he said.

"Your cologne—is it Pure Man?" I asked.

Jack looked at me as if I'd truly lost my mind.

"It is! It was on discount, bought it the other day. Around the corner from Edith's."

"It's great. It's very . . . manly." I didn't know what else to say. I smiled.

"Er . . . thank you," Peter said. "It's good to see you. Jack, it's been far too long since we've had you up here. I better head back to the party. You two young people enjoy this lovely night.

See you up at the circus on the hill." He waved goodbye, and he quickly made his way up the path. We watched as he paused at an old garden shed at the corner of the cut flower garden. The shed looked a hundred years old. Peter went inside for a few minutes, and then came out and walked toward the party.

Jack gave me a look. "Why are you harassing a septuagenarian?"

"I don't know what you're talking about."

"You smelled him. Pure Man? What are you up to?"

I thought for a while and then finally said, "Don't get mad," and I told him how we'd found the scent clue in the apartment.

He listened patiently, and then said, "That's—I'm sorry to say this again, but that's never going to hold up in court."

"I know. And that's exactly why I didn't tell you before. And please don't be angry that we're still trying to protect Edith."

"I'm not mad. My dad wears that cologne, too—he saw it on sale also—it doesn't make him a murderer. But I understand." He spoke more softly and gently here—the garden brought out the cat-walking side of him instead of the policeman side.

I looked at the flowers, where a bumblebee bobbed on a poppy. "Is that the bee we're looking for?"

"No, that's a common eastern. *Bombus impatiens*."

We heard orchestra music in the distance. "The performance is starting—let's hurry," he said. We headed back up the hill. "Can you please not smell anyone else while we're up there, though?"

"No promises."

Place cards had been arranged at different tables under a giant white tent; Edith's table was at the front with Liliana. Mimsy, Jack, and I were at a table in the middle. A buffet had been set up, and Jack offered to bring us back plates of food to eat during the performance. He walked toward the buffet line.

"Nothing herbal on mine, please," I said, and Mimsy said the same. We sat down at our places. The table was covered in a pale pink tablecloth and white napkins. "I'm sorry Jack waylaid you—I found out some things, though," she whispered. "Cyrus's alibi is a lie. He'd said that when the air conditioner was pushed, he was at a performance of *Easy Street* at the New Playwrights Theater off-Broadway, right? Well, my dear friend Lottie, who's here tonight, it turns out she knows the stage manager there, and she just called him and found out Cyrus's ticket was a no-show, so the seat was given to someone else."

"Really?"

She nodded. "He's hiding something."

"Peter is, too," I said. "He's wearing the cologne." I filled her in on how sad and nervous he seemed. "And Jack said his dad has the cologne also."

She put her hand on her chin. "Hmmm. Interesting." She glanced around. "I'm not sure where Clifford disappeared to. At least he's been far away from Edith all night. His coworker at Enchantments florist shop is here, too—Liliana invited him—he's the one who confirmed Clifford's alibi, that he was working there when the air conditioner was pushed. Well, that guy drinks so much, I don't think he'd remember anything. So that pokes a hole in Clifford's alibi. Let's see what else we can find out after the show."

Jack returned with plates of food piled high with pasta and steak. We ate while Liliana took the stage and gave a long speech. She mentioned all the generous donors to the Trillium Dance Company, and thanked everyone she'd ever met, and welcomed us all to the premiere of their new performance, *Natural Freedom*, which she'd choreographed. Finally, the dancers took the stage.

"I've hardly been to any dance performances," I told Mimsy and Jack. "My grandmother took me to see *The Nutcracker* in Austin once, and that's it."

"You're in for a treat. Liliana's company is very good," Mimsy said.

I was expecting ballet, or Broadway-style dancing. This was not what I imagined: they came out onstage completely naked.

Jack shifted beside me uncomfortably. His fingers touched his forehead. He looked at his lap, avoiding the stage.

I pretended to be a sophisticated New Yorker who went to naked dance performances all the time. Maybe they needed to save money on costumes. Maybe Liliana was inspired by Nanette's naked magazine cover. Maybe *oh my god that man is completely naked. And dancing.*

My entire body turned red.

Now Mimsy clapped. She grinned. "Bravo!"

The naked dancing continued for half an hour, and I kept glancing at Jack, who stared into the forest. Finally, it was intermission. The audience burst into applause.

"We survived," he said to me.

"I've never seen anyone stare at trees for so long," I said. "Studying every detail of all the different species?"

"Yes. I think I just wrote a whole new ecology paper in my head."

I watched Cyrus and Nanette walk down a garden path, talking. Mimsy whispered to me, "Can you follow them? I'm going to trail Peter."

I nodded and turned to Jack. "I'm going to explore the garden a little more," I told him.

"I'm coming," he said. "To keep you from your rogue sniffing."

We followed Nanette and Cyrus down the path. The sun was beginning to set, and lanterns glowed softly in the pinkish light. I was hoping I could overhear what they were talking about, but we were too far away. They walked into the woods, where there were no more lanterns. It was hard to see their figures in the darkness.

"Look—we're almost at the Ruin. I want to show it to you," Jack said.

"The what?" The path split into two, and I couldn't tell which way Nanette and Cyrus had gone.

"The maternity home that Edith went to—the Ruin is where it once stood. Most of the building was destroyed in a fire decades ago, and Edith had this built by an artist using the original foundation and some of the surviving rooms."

The Ruin looked like the decaying remains of an abandoned stone house, hugged by shaggy trees and dripping vines, with tiny lights on copper wire. It looked bewitched. It had a small locked bedroom; its roof had been planted with grass, like green hair. There was a dining room with a giant table like a sarcophagus, and a living room with a fountain in its center, its water dyed an inky black. Just under the surface of the water were faces carved from marble. It was spooky and strange and mysterious and beautiful.

I also felt a sort of sadness—almost like floating over the garden for a minute and seeing myself there, from far away. Not a bad sadness. It kind of seeped in over everything. I thought of our old purple cottage, and Gertrude, and how the Ruin seemed to whisper that what was sad was also beautiful, that you could feel sad and happy and a thousand different things at once, and that was okay.

I touched his arm. "This place is amazing."

"It's better than following Cyrus and Nanette." He smiled.

"You could tell?"

He nodded. He looked so different here—his hair was messier and his whole body relaxed.

We looked out over the garden beyond the Ruin. "My dad never understood why my mom loved this place so much," he said. "He never really saw the point in her research. Or mine. It's not saving lives, after all."

"It is, though," I said. "It does. I mean—Edith says it saved her life, working in the garden." Being in Mimsy's garden, and here now, it sort of felt like it was saving my life. "It changes you."

"I wish I could come here more often to work outside. At school I love the greenhouse and the bee room in the lab. But I wish I could be here more." He touched a leaf growing between the stones of the Ruin. "My father would say, 'Grow up. You can't play in the mud all day.'"

"There's nothing wrong with playing in the dirt all day. I love it, working for Edith. I love being outside and noticing the weather, and getting my clothes all messed up, and sticking my hands in the soil. Growing things."

Maybe gardens were my own sea change place. They helped me pick up those bits of soul that were leaking out all over the place, and put them back in.

"I always feel like myself here," he said. "More myself than any other place."

"What's your favorite spot here?" I asked.

"This," he said, and led me to a withered hemlock tree growing alongside the Ruin. Its limbs were arched and fanciful, like a hidden castle. It looked a thousand years old. "I've loved this tree since I was a kid." We sat on its lowest limb.

This whole garden seemed to say, in its weirdness and beauty, that of course you belonged: we all had a place in this world. And this world is connected to all the places you've loved—Nana's perfect weedy yard, the redbud tree, Mimsy's garden—they all seemed alive and present here now, too.

"I've come here since I was one year old. I used to sit here and watch my mom work." He touched the tree's rough bark.

I felt the bark also. "It's like your hands." I thought of the first day I'd met him, when he shook my hand and his had felt rough, earthen.

He opened his palm. "Gardener's hands, my mom used to say."

"That's what Edith calls her hands, too. She's proud of them. She said each line represents another year of experience."

"I was born with them like this, though. My hands as a five-year-old didn't look much different from this. Kids used to make fun of my hands at school. Grandpa hands, they called me. What's wrong with your hands, are you some kind of freak? Then my mom said I had gardener's hands. This is what they were meant to do."

His voice grew softer. Each word was careful and considered, with pauses between them.

I stared up at the branches. The cones dangled above us like ornaments. The tree felt comforting.

"You know how lots of gardens and fancy estates have names like this one does? My grandmother called ours Weeds Galore," I said. "She treasured each weed for landing there. I loved our yard. There was this redbud tree I worshipped—it had flowers that bloomed on the trunk."

"Cauliflory," he said.

"My grandmother called it that, too." The garden glowed; the light was dazzling. I told him about how I hid in the redbud, and about Nana and Gertrude—things began to pour out of me all of a sudden, things I hadn't spoken about since I'd come to New York. How Gertrude changed our days and nights, how she was a survivor, having been abandoned and homeless, and her gray fur and white paws, and the three-quarter moon on her back. "She was like the embodiment of pure love," I said.

"What happened to Gertrude?"

"She—we lost her." I left it at that.

"I'm sorry."

We were quiet for a while, and then he said, "I feel close to my mom here, too. Closer than anywhere else." He ran his fingers over a knot in the bark. "Maybe because death is everywhere here, plants and flowers dying all over the place."

I loved how it didn't feel like we needed to be fixed here. To be changed. To follow rules or do something to be valued and whole. Here, all you had to do was exist.

"What's your dream? To study bees, or keep working for your dad?" I asked.

"Those are both my parents' dreams. I want to work with plants. Like Edith does. I love how plants don't lie. They don't hide things. They're completely themselves. There's nothing fake or artificial with plants. When I'm working with them, I feel alive. Like I'm myself. More than anything else I do." He touched the frond of a giant fern. "I don't know if you noticed, but the Ruin is covered in ferns. Tree ferns and staghorn ferns, maidenhair ferns and ostrich ferns. My mom and I planted a lot of these ferns together." His voice changed when he talked about the ferns. "I really love . . . ferns. I want to study ferns. I want to learn more about them." He paused. "I can't believe I actually just told you that."

"They're beautiful," I said. "What's wrong with wanting to study them?"

"If my dad can't even accept my mom's world-renowned research on bees, how am I going to tell him I want to study ferns? When I was little I thought I could do it all—be a bee researcher, botanist, and crime-fighting hero like my dad. I think the truth is, what kind of crime-fighter could I really be—battling murderers by hitting them with ferns?"

"The best kind," I said. "The world doesn't have enough fern superheroes." I liked that he trusted me enough to tell me he loved ferns. I couldn't imagine saying, "I love . . . ferns" at school. They couldn't even handle loving a cat.

"This one is a *Pteridium aquilinum*—a bracken fern. My mom told me they eat it in China—you're supposed to soak the leaves in water, or it's toxic." He gazed at the ferns all around us. "Ferns don't play by the rules." He rattled their names off like poetry. *Adiantum pedatum, Pteridium feei, Pteris podophylla.* His voice grew softer, quietly urgent. "Ferns are some of the oldest plants, prehistoric. There's this one kind called a resurrection fern, *Pleopeltis polypodioides*—here it is, growing out of this rock—that looks dead. Then it rains or you pour water on it and it's alive, flourishing, like magic."

He showed it to me—it looked like a dried brown clump of lifeless leaves. That's how I felt sometimes.

"It's not dead," he said.

"It looks about as dead as can be," I said.

"It was only pretending. Pretending to be dead. It had to adapt to survive."

He touched the not-dead plant like it was a tiny baby, cradling it with an outpouring of love. He wanted so much to show it to me, to share it. "See?" His eyes lit up as if he were a resurrection fern himself that I'd just poured water on.

The darkening air hung heavily around us. He sat beside me on the wide branch. His hair fell into his eyes.

He sat so close to me that I could smell soap and his smell that was familiar now, faint and only him.

His fingers wound in mine. They felt rough and soft at once.

Then we heard the scream.

twenty-three

THE ARREST

Red and blue flashing lights.

The scream had come from Mimsy. She'd explained what had happened as Jack, Edith, and I stood by the steps of the stone mansion. Peter was in handcuffs by the front driveway, surrounded by three police officers. Edith looked pale. She leaned against the railing and cradled her face in her hands.

Mimsy said she'd discovered Peter beside my chair at our table, kneeling down, fiddling around in my bag. She approached him and saw he was putting a bottle in my bag—it looked like bourbon, she said. Then she realized its label read: "PARA-QUAT."

Jack froze when Mimsy said that word.

I touched his arm. "What's paraquat?"

"It's a weed killer. It's outlawed in many countries. It's tasteless—it's one of the deadliest poisons. All it would take is one drop to kill someone. How did this happen?" He turned to Edith. "Did you eat anything tonight? Drink anything at all?" he asked her, panic creeping into his voice.

"Only what we brought. I'm certain," she said. Her voice wavered as she watched Peter be led into the back seat of the police car.

"Edith's food has to be tested. Everything on her table. At once," Jack said. "Let's test all the food here tonight. Does anyone feel ill?"

Mimsy shook her head. "Everyone seems fine—just terrified. I think his plan was to poison her at the dessert service, since that hadn't been served yet."

"He was putting the bottle in my bag?" I asked her.

She nodded. "He was trying to frame you. Just like he did at the seder. I can't believe it was Peter all along. He wears the cologne. He was at the equinox party, he had no alibi when the air conditioner fell, and he comes here often, so he'd know the paraquat was in the shed, and how poisonous it is."

"We saw him go in the shed earlier tonight," I said.

Edith gripped the railing. "He said he went in the shed because he saw the door was ajar—someone had been in there already. Later, he saw a strange bottle poking out of your bag, and that's why he leaned in to look. He happened to be the one to find it. It was only bad luck."

Dyna came up to us, carrying her viola. "Are you okay?"

I nodded. "Are you?" I hugged her.

"Yes." She bit her lip. "Is anyone hurt?"

"We think everyone's okay," Jack said. He excused himself to talk to the police before they took Peter away.

The crowd of guests gathered nearby, and as word spread that the food may have been poisoned, someone in the crowd started crying.

Jack told me and Dyna, "Please, I need your help. Let's make sure there's not a mass panic here. Symptoms from paraquat poisoning are usually immediate, so if nobody is feeling symptoms, they should be fine. I texted my dad and more police are on their way to help us."

Dyna and I tried to calm everyone. There was a doctor in attendance among the guests, and he helped examine a man who felt faint. Trish helped also, holding the hand of a panicking woman, soothing her, and a guest who was also an off-duty nurse assisted her, too. Mimsy asked the bodyguards she'd hired to help keep everyone calm.

As the party guests began to leave, Jack said, "If that bottle is decades old, it's possible it's no longer potent." He touched my arm gently. "Are you sure you're feeling all right?"

"I'm okay," I said. "I think."

We checked on Edith. A police officer sat with her and Liliana on the stone steps, taking their statements. Liliana kept sobbing. "This was supposed to be my big night! My special night . . ."

"Peter did not do this," Edith kept saying. She stood up when she saw Jack. "Will Peter be okay? They'll release him, won't they?"

"I think they will, if you don't press charges," Jack said. "What's the motive? Peter has no real motive to hurt you—he won't inherit anything, or—"

"He would," Edith said. "You see—Peter and I were married three months ago."

twenty-four
A FOX'S CLUE

The trip Peter had kept talking about was to be their honeymoon. In late January, they'd attended a winter horticulture conference for one week in Maine, during a blizzard, and when the snow began to clear they impulsively found themselves signing a marriage license and standing under the moonlight on February first, exchanging vows, with a friend who was ordained. She'd never told Mimsy. "I couldn't believe we did it. I wanted to tell you—I'm so sorry I didn't. A few days after I got back to New York, Clifford and I met in person for the first time, and everything happened so fast—and I thought Peter and I had moved too quickly. I didn't want to tell everyone right away, and then—well, the equinox party happened, and things became so complicated . . . I'm sorry."

"I can't believe you didn't tell me," Mimsy said, trying to absorb it.

"The bonsai—with the rock by the tree in the garden we saw tonight—it said February first," I said.

She nodded. "Peter made it in honor of our wedding."

The steps of the stone mansion had cleared off as guests left the party. The officer added Edith's story of her marriage to her statement, and he took the bottle of paraquat to have it analyzed. The guest who was a doctor recommended that Edith go to the hospital to get checked out, just in case.

We stayed with Edith at the hospital for two hours until she got the all clear, and then drove back to the city. Mimsy wanted us to stay with her overnight at her place, but Edith said she wanted to sleep in her own bed. It was almost midnight then.

"Let's all try to get some sleep," Mimsy said. "So much has happened tonight. Everything will be clearer in the morning."

The next day, I woke up to the doorbell ringing nonstop. Then the phone. I glanced at the alarm clock. Almost seven. Nanette and Cyrus had already left. I put on a sweatshirt, and I walked through the empty apartment to the front door first.

I opened it.

Jack. He had dark circles under his eyes. It looked like he'd been up all night. "I have to talk to you."

"What happened? Is Peter still in jail?"

"It's Edith."

My heart stopped.

"She's missing."

"What?" I felt like my feet might fall out beneath me.

"Here—" He walked me to the couch and we sat down. Everything swam and swirled around me.

"I stopped by her apartment early this morning to check on her," he said, "to make sure she was okay after what happened last night. I rang the doorbell again and again, and nobody answered. I called her phone—also no answer. Then I noticed the door was unlocked. I went in and I looked for her, but she was gone. Her bed was empty. It wasn't slept in."

A chill ran down my neck. "I need to go look for her—"

"The search has started. The police are on it. There's no waiting period in New York—we look into disappearances right away." He stared at the floor. "She left the building alone—that's captured on the surveillance video. We've tracked her path to a certain point. We know she took a taxi to the Staten Island Ferry terminal. She boarded the ferry at four twenty-eight a.m. There's no record of her whereabouts after that. We're reviewing more surveillance tapes to see what we find out—if someone was with her, or—anything."

The room kept whirling. I felt sick. I thought I might throw up.

"Are you okay?" He put his hand on my shoulder.

"What happened to Peter?"

"After the arrest, Edith refused to press charges. He was let go. She hired one of New York's best lawyers for him, in case the police do proceed with charges after the evidence is analyzed."

"What time was he free to go?"

"Three o'clock in the morning," Jack said. "I know what you're thinking. I know it looks suspicious. But his release and Edith's disappearance aren't connected. Edith said there's no way he would harm her. I know she's right—I know Peter—I trust him. He'd never, ever hurt anyone."

I felt like someone had yanked my stomach out in one swoop. "Where were Clifford and Liliana last night? Do they have alibis?"

"Yes. Liliana was at her apartment, and Clifford didn't leave the building. Nobody left the building after midnight besides Edith—the surveillance video of the front door shows that she was the only one who left. And she left alone."

"Unless they used the fire escape," I said.

"Here—let me get you something—a glass of water? Are you okay?" he asked again.

Edith had asked me to do one thing: to protect her. And I didn't do it. Why had we left her alone last night?

He poured a glass of water for me in the kitchen. "Drink this," he said.

"This is my fault," I said.

"It's not your fault." His pant legs rode up as he sat down again. I gazed at his mismatched socks. One was white and one had little potted plants on it. He ran his hand over his face. "I didn't sleep much last night—I was worried about Peter and

Edith—bear with me if I seem a little out of it." He paused. "I thought of waking you up earlier, but we didn't have any information yet . . ."

"Maybe there's a simple explanation. Maybe she went to visit someone and didn't tell anybody," I said.

"Maybe so," he said. I could tell he didn't believe that.

I moved to the edge of my seat. "I need to go search for her now. Did you tell Mimsy?"

He nodded. "I called her just before I knocked on your door. She asked me to tell you to come to her house right away. Please—both of you—be careful."

"We will," I said.

"We won't stop searching," he told me. "There's one more thing I wanted to show you, to see if you know what it might mean."

He retrieved his bag, which he'd left by the door, and took out a piece of paper. "We found this on the dressing table in her bedroom. This is a photocopy. We're having the original analyzed."

A note in her tidy, elegant script.

I love you all and I am grateful for this blooming world.
Edith Fox

"That's her handwriting," I said. "But it doesn't make sense. Why would she write that?"

"This was under the note," he said.

A Fox's Rules for Living

1. TRUST. Plants want to live. . .

I'd read it before—it was a framed column, the same column that Mimsy had also hung on the wall of the folly. Scribbled on a Post-it stuck to the frame were the words:

Find the diary to show him

"What diary? Who is 'him'?" Jack asked.

"She must mean the diary she kept when she was in the maternity home." Was the "him" Clifford or Peter? I needed to talk to Mimsy and Dyna to hear what they thought.

"Why would she have left this?" Jack asked.

I shook my head.

He sighed. "I'm going to call my father and check on the search," he said. "My father believes—" He paused and frowned.

"What?"

"He's looking into it as a possible suicide."

My stomach flipped over. "There's no way—Edith would never do that."

"I know. I agree with you." He took a deep breath. "Let's focus on finding her."

I stood up. "I need to see Mimsy and Dyna."

We said goodbye, and I gathered my things and headed to Mimsy's house as fast as I could.

Mimsy couldn't stop pacing. "I just don't believe it. I can't. It's not possible. Not possible," she kept repeating.

Dyna looked frightened. She clutched her elbows. "I'm scared."

"Me too." I shivered even though it was warm outside, and I told them all about the note and the column.

"Why did she leave that?" Mimsy asked. She tried to calm herself by hugging a birch tree in her garden.

"What are you doing?" I asked her.

"I have a book that says birches can help you recover from any shock," Mimsy said. She hugged it even tighter.

"She was doing that earlier," Dyna whispered to me. "For like a half hour."

Mimsy let go of the tree and then placed her hand on it lovingly.

"I feel like we should leave the two of you alone," Dyna told her.

"I'm trying to calm myself. Oh hell. Edith never believed in tree energies, either. Okay. Forget the birch. Let's go look for Edith and see what we can find."

We designed MISSING posters on Mimsy's computer; we placed them at the Staten Island Ferry terminal and around lower Manhattan, and near Edith's favorite restaurants and shops. We asked around to see if anyone remembered seeing her, but no one did. Mimsy called every social media contact she knew and sent out online alerts. "Someone must've seen her," Dyna said. Dyna's musician friends helped distribute the posters in the subway.

We still had no luck.

The next morning, we sat in Mimsy's garden.

"I think our next step is to do what Edith told us to do. Find the diary," I said. "Maybe it holds a clue to where she is."

"And figure out why she left that column," Dyna said.

Mimsy took a photo of the framed Fox's Rules column in the folly, so we could study it closely in case it contained a clue. She thought for a moment. "The diary has to be in her apartment. Somewhere in the library or the storage room."

We headed to Edith's place.

twenty-five
THE MISSING DIARY

iliana opened Edith's door. Her eyes were red, and her fragile skin was splotchy. She squeezed our hands, and then led us into the living room, where Clifford sat on the sofa, looking crumpled and smaller than usual. Trish stood nearby, trying to get him to eat. She held a plate with a bagel toward him, but he shook his head. He stared at the floor.

"I can't stop my mind from thinking the worst," Liliana said, her voice cracking as she lowered herself into an armchair. Her phone buzzed on the coffee table, and I caught a glimpse of her text notifications—142 of them. Beside her phone was an old hardcover copy of *A Grief Observed*.

We told them how we'd been out searching. Liliana said,

"I've been spreading the word through all my social networks, to see if anyone might have seen Mother." Her phone buzzed again. "I've been in touch with everyone I know—I need support right now." She blew her nose into a pink handkerchief. "Mother left a cryptic note, the police said—why would she want us to find the diary now? What did she mean?" She kept biting her lip.

"I'm not sure," Mimsy said.

"I don't know why she would disappear and leave a note like that," Clifford said. His voice was low and quiet. "This is my fault."

Mimsy's eyes widened; she seemed to be bracing herself for Clifford to confess.

"Edith told me she wanted to find the diary she kept before I was born, to show me," he said. His hands turned into fists in his lap. "I never should have come into her life."

Trish touched his shoulder to calm him. "It's not your fault."

He shook her hand off. He kept gazing at the floor; he wouldn't meet our eyes.

"Please tell us—any information you have," Mimsy told Clifford. She leaned forward in her seat.

He opened his mouth, then closed it. "I keep thinking of Mandragora. The first time I went there, it was a rainy day, which fit my mood. I didn't stay there long—it was too painful, thinking of it. I wasn't ready. Then, this time, we saw all of it—the wildflower meadow, the cut flower garden, the old stone mansion, the hollowed-out cottonwood tree, the weighted-down willows, the little room off the Ruin with the green roof, the sculpture of the girl at the bottom of the pond. I kept thinking I finally understood that Edith built that place out of—love." His voice grew even lower, its tone darkening. "I've been working for ages on designing a living arrangement for her at Enchantments. I wanted it to be perfect. I never finished it." He stood up with his cane and walked slowly to the door. He flinched with each step; he seemed to be in more pain than he ever had before. Trish went to help him, but he waved her away. He left and closed the door behind him.

"Is there anything I can do for him?" Liliana asked Trish, in a voice that sounded a little too sweet.

Trish shook her head. "He needs to rest—his muscle strength has taken a turn for the worse."

Liliana arranged her hair so one wave swirled down each side of her neck. "As siblings, we need each other now. More than ever. Yet his instinct is to push me away."

Maybe because you give your hair more attention than you do anyone else, I thought, but didn't say.

Mimsy turned to Trish. "Do you think Clifford could be involved with Edith's disappearance in some way?"

Trish gazed at where Clifford had been sitting on the sofa, and there was a slight quiver to her arms, and a small flame of fear behind her eyes—it seemed, all of a sudden, that she might actually be afraid of him. Did she think he did something to Edith? She seemed to shake her fears away. "No," she said, though there was a sadness to her words. "I think he's overwhelmed by everything that's happened. I'll check that he's all right." She excused herself.

After she left Liliana said, "She's probably off to go sit at her craft table. Meanwhile, Mother is gone and there's no hope." She sniffled into her pink handkerchief. "I spoke to Mr. Hargenbach, Mother's estate lawyer, this morning."

"Why?" Mimsy asked.

"I'd called him to see if he might know anything about Mother's whereabouts. He said Mother called him two days ago to make sure all her financial affairs were in order. Almost as if—" Her voice cracked again. "As if she prepared for this. He said her priority was to leave her children well cared for. That's the kind of person Mother was—she always put others first."

Why was she using the past tense?

"Mr. Hargenbach said he's seen this situation many times before," Liliana said.

"What situation?" Dyna asked.

"Elderly people with dementia disappearing. Going missing. Sometimes even"—her voice lowered—"harming themselves. Scott—Detective McShea—he stopped by earlier, along with several others, to check on us. He said the continuous thread through all of the strange happenings lately was that Mother had become paranoid. Her eyes. Her poisoned drink. Someone following her—though nobody else ever saw that person. Saying someone stole plants. Then a plant appearing! Then the decades-old poison that only she knew was in the shed. Her behavior had become so strange and erratic. It's impossible to deny that," Liliana said.

"Scott is wrong," Mimsy said tightly. "He's been wrong since the beginning. Peter's arrest proves that—Lucy saw Peter go into the shed where the paraquat was. Even if Edith didn't believe Peter was responsible, Scott can't keep thinking Edith was paranoid."

"Scott said there's no evidence indicating that Peter did anything but find the paraquat in Lucy's bag. He had no malicious intent," Liliana said. She misted her face with a Trillium Botanicals spray labeled "Calm." "Mr. Hargenbach said something else—I can barely repeat it."

My chest tightened. "What?"

"He said if the search is unsuccessful, the best thing is to begin the process to have her declared deceased." Her voice cracked again. "I don't know what to believe. Everyone keeps telling me so many different things . . ." She blew her nose into her handkerchief again, then took out her compact to inspect her reflection. She sprayed "Calm" on her hands.

Mimsy sat up straight. "I've known Edith all my life, and she's the strongest, most resilient person I know. I have every faith that we're going to find her. Let's start by finding the diary. While you get some rest, we'll start looking in the library and the unused room."

"I tried to look for it myself this morning, but everything I touch of Mother's—it hurts to be here with all of her things, without her. It's like living with a thousand ghosts," Liliana said.

I glanced around the living room. It did feel so empty without Edith. Nothing looked right.

"Thank you," Liliana said. "Thank you for helping. I'm going to do my meditation app now. I'm of no use to anyone in this state. I want to believe you, that I should have hope."

She opened an app on her phone and sat cross-legged on the floor. Mimsy, Dyna, and I walked down the hall to the library to begin our search.

I gazed around the library—it seemed different now. Everywhere I turned, it didn't seem like Edith's home anymore, without her.

"Liliana wasted no time in calling the estate lawyer," Dyna said. "She's already thinking about her inheritance."

"Did you notice how Trish seemed a little afraid of Clifford?" I asked.

"I still suspect him," Mimsy said. "Maybe he and Liliana planned this together. Maybe their squabbling was all an act so we wouldn't suspect they were *both* behind this." She hesitated. "For now, though, let's focus on finding the diary."

We stared up at the shelves and shelves of books all around us. "Where do we start?" Dyna asked. "There must be thousands of books here."

"Edith left that column with her note, so there must be a connection to the column and where she hid the diary," Mimsy said. We studied the photo of the column Edith had left behind, from April 1956.

Trust. Dormancy Is Not Death. Record Everything. We All Stand on a Precipice

I read the end of the column again.

This month, design a bed of annuals in a perfect rainbow to shock the neighbors: red petunias, orange poppies, yellow pansies, blue ageratum, and violet snapdragons. Recommended reading this month: The American Gardener *by William Cobbett,* Down the Garden Path *by Beverley Nichols, and* The Gardener's Year *by Karel Čapek.*

"Maybe the diary is hidden in one of these books she recommends at the bottom," I said. "Though it seems like it can't be that simple—she would've looked in them already."

"It's possible she tried but couldn't find them," Dyna said, eyeing the endless shelves again.

"I saw *Down the Garden Path* when I was being interviewed in here by Jack's father," I said. I pointed to the shelf. We found the book and opened it, but it was still intact—no diary. After searching for an hour, we managed to find *The American Gardener* and *The Gardener's Year*, too, but they didn't hold the diary, either.

We thought for a while. "She grabbed this column off the wall of her bedroom," Dyna said. "But maybe she gave us this column as a general clue. Maybe she meant for us to look through all the books mentioned in other columns, also."

I felt something lift inside me. "Good idea."

Mimsy knotted her forehead. "That will take a long time, though. She wrote the column for over twenty years."

"But of all the columns, she most likely stashed it in a book mentioned around the time Clifford was born," I said. "She told us, when we were here in the library the night of the seder, that she stopped writing in it right after he was born and hid it then. When's his birthday?"

"June 1957," Mimsy said. "Edith was so traumatized that summer. I know that's why she couldn't remember where she'd hidden it."

"I saw a ton of old *American Housekeeping* magazines in the unused room," I said. We went there to collect as many 1957 copies of Edith's column as we could find.

In the unused room, Mimsy sighed as she looked around at the clutter, at the old silver kiddush cups, the seed boxes, and the grandfather clock leaning against the wall. "She kept planning to sort through all the stuff in here, but she never had the time. It's so hard to decide what to keep and what to throw away. At our age, it's like taking stock of your whole life. How do you make sense of all these things you've loved?" She touched an antique flowered teacup. "Edith's mother used to say, 'An immaculate home is a sign of a misspent life.'"

"I'd like to make a needlepoint of that and give it to Ms. Leery," Dyna said.

We continued hunting, sorting through all the dusty, yellowing *American Housekeeping* issues until we finally found all the 1957 ones. We brought them back to the library and laid them out on the floor. Almost all the columns recommended three gardening books each, and we searched for those books, too, which took almost two hours—and none of them held the diary. We were starting to lose hope.

We searched the shelves, and I kept thinking. "The book that Edith showed us she'd hollowed out before was *An Encyclopedia of Engineering*—do you remember?"

Mimsy nodded. "She didn't mind turning that into a hiding place. Edith loved books—they were sacred to her." She thought for a second. "Maybe Edith wouldn't destroy a gardening book she loved enough to recommend. She'd destroy a book she didn't care about."

I kept staring at the August 1957 column, which was different than all the other ones I'd seen.

A Fox's Rules for Living
AUGUST 1957

1. HEAL YOURSELF with flowers. They represent everything worth living for: beauty, gentleness, blooming despite the harsh conditions of the world.

2. ONLY YOU KNOW WHAT IS BEAUTIFUL. It's not what others tell you.

3. MESS IT UP. A garden is meant to be a chaotic mess, like life. Don't beat your garden into submission. Let go of trying to control it.

4. EVERYTHING IS TEMPORARY. Summer nights and first blooms, a new flower you've never grown before. What you see is different from what you know.

5. ANNUALS put all their energy into blooming and then die off. Learn from perennials. Bloom briefly and bloom well, and then go dormant and gather your energy. No one can bloom all year long.

6. REST is as important as work. We need time to be alone, to think, to build ourselves back up.

7. TEACH YOURSELF to listen to that small voice inside you, even when the world is blaring so loudly you can barely hear it.

8. SURVIVAL will surprise you. The perennials you thought had died were waiting patiently under the ground for their moment to soar.

"Look," I said. "It's the only column of all of them that has no recommended books at the bottom."

"It's much longer than the others, too," Dyna said. "Eight rules instead of four or five. There are no suggested flowers to plant, either."

"So if Edith stopped writing in that diary in June 1957, after Clifford was born, and she hid it then, maybe she put a clue in the column she wrote at the time. Except there was probably a lag time from when she wrote it till the magazine printed it, right?" I asked.

Dyna raised her eyebrows. "This is a question for Uriah. He's a librarian superhero." She texted him and asked him how long magazines took to print a submitted article back then, and he got back to her in ten minutes. "He says the lead time would probably have been two months then. So a column she wrote in June would probably have been published in August. It would be this one."

I kept staring at the column until my eyes began to swim.

And then I saw it.

I touched Dyna's hand. "Do you remember when you sent me that note with the chocolates hidden in the hedgehog back at Thornton? You'd sent me a letter that had a code—the first word of each sentence spelled out Look Inside This Animal."

She nodded. "I was proud of that. Leery didn't confiscate it."

I pointed to the first letter of each rule. "They spell something."

"Heal, Only, Mess, Everything, Annual, Rest, Teach, Survival," Mimsy read. "What?"

"Read just the first letter of each rule—H-O-M-E-A-R-T-S. *Home Arts*. I saw a book with that title when Jack's father interviewed me—I remember it was a thick blue book with a flower on its spine. It looked like a real flower—a pressed flower that had been taped on it."

I walked over to the shelves to search for it. "It was over here," I said.

"Maybe Edith put the flower on it herself," Mimsy said. "That would be a very Edith thing to do. Back then, neighbors and teachers used to always give young women housekeeping books. She'd be happy to destroy a home arts book—lessons on cleaning up and housework and women's place in the home,"

Mimsy said with a roll of her eyes. "Also, she didn't want her father to find it, and I doubt he'd look in a book about house-keeping."

"When I saw it, it was over there." I pointed to the top of a bookcase. The shelf looked empty now.

We pulled over the rickety ladder, and I climbed up to check. "It's not here." I noticed something strange. "There's an outline in the dust. And no new dust has settled in the space. It must've been taken recently."

"Maybe someone else found it before us?" Dyna asked.

"Let's find out exactly who else has been here this morning, among those visitors Liliana mentioned," Mimsy said.

We approached Liliana, who was lying on the couch scrolling through her phone. She looked up when she saw us. "Have you found it?" she asked us. "Any luck?"

"Not yet," Mimsy said. "Though we're getting close. Sorry to interrupt, but—you mentioned visitors this morning—did anyone come in the library?"

"Oh, a few people. Scott, Jack, the police, and Cyrus."

"*Cyrus?*" I asked.

"It was so kind of him. He wanted to see how I was doing. He even said that he'd seen a book about grief in the library and he wanted to get it for me. It was so thoughtful. He gave me *A Grief Observed*. He'd also left his coat here before, and he was looking for it. We couldn't find it."

"He'd lost his coat? What's it look like?" Suddenly, all his gray and silver clothes became clear, his hubcap aesthetic. My blood pounded. *The man following me wore a gray hooded coat.*

"It was gray. With a hood. He's very forgetful, leaving things here."

"Did he have any other books with him, by any chance?" Mimsy asked.

"Yes, he asked to borrow a few books from the library—I forget which ones. Nothing I'd ever read."

"Was one a big blue book about housekeeping?" I asked.

"Yes! One was called home something," she said.

He'd taken it.

twenty-six
THE PINK ROOM

We decided to go to the auction house where Cyrus worked, to pay him a visit and get *Home Arts* back—hopefully the diary would still be inside it.

"Why would Cyrus take that book?" Dyna asked.

"Liliana said he took several—maybe he thought it was valuable," Mimsy said. "His motive could be that he's been stealing Edith's books and possessions and reselling them through the auction house—but then why would he want to harm her? It's a big leap between stealing and hurting her."

Mimsy's phone rang just as we were trying to hail a taxi to the auction house. She handed it to me. *Todd Clark*, it said.

"Cricket! We heard what happened! Edith Fox is missing?

And a man was arrested? You didn't know him, did you?" my father asked.

"Not really. No . . ."

"I'm so sorry you were in danger." My mother's voice. "If we knew—we never would've—we're so relieved you're safe. That's what matters. We have a break from filming, so we're going to buy you a ticket—we want you to come home as soon as possible."

"Home?"

"Here. To Hawai'i. We don't want you to be there anymore. It's too dangerous. I know you've done your best there and worked hard. Your safety is what's most important to us," she said.

"I am safe—"

"And we have big news we've been wanting to tell you," my father said.

"Where are you right now—do you have internet access?" my mother asked. "You have our permission to use it. There's something you need to see right away. I just sent a link to your email address."

"Yes." I took out my phone and clicked on the link they'd sent me. It was to a website called Your Perfect Place: Home Design for Everyone.

"It's a famous design website. Can you see it? And look what's featured!" my mom said.

On the front page: The Clarks at Home.

The website talked about their upcoming TV show, and it

showcased their yellow house in Hawai'i. Their purchase had gone through.

"The publicist for the TV network helped place the article," my dad said. "It's quite a spread."

"Look at the pink room," my mother said.

One photo was captioned: *The Clarks' daughter's room.* My heart nearly stopped. *The Clarks' daughter, Lucy, is sixteen years old.*

A white fluffy comforter and a bright pink pillow. A swinging basket chair for reading.

"We only let them take that one photo because the rest of the room isn't ready yet—but when it is, you're going to love it. This is just a glimpse—the rest will be such a surprise."

The paint color was called Peaceful Pink, the website said.

"Well? What do you think?" my father asked.

My chest hurt. I felt so many different feelings that I couldn't find words for what to say. "I—"

"I know," my mom said. "You love it. I can hear it in your voice. We know you'll be happy here, when it's ready."

"I'd love to come see it. It's just—I can't leave right away. There's something I need to finish here first."

"What?" my dad asked. "Nonsense. You're coming back as soon as we get your ticket. I won't hear a word otherwise."

I didn't know what to tell him, so I said nothing. They went on about how the producers expected to renew the TV show for multiple seasons, and then we said goodbye.

Mimsy hailed a taxi, and the three of us climbed in the back.

We bumped down the streets to Tribeca, and I kept thinking about my parents and the pink room. I told myself to think about it later, after we made progress finding Edith. Yet my mind kept looping back to it.

I thought of my parents' visit in January, the last time I saw them before the Incident and everything that had happened after, when my father came to Austin to give a workshop and accept an award at the Innovators Conference. He and I ate lunch alone one afternoon at Veggie City while my mother and Nanette had their hair styled and blown out before the ceremony.

My father had this coldness—a reserve, Flo once called it after she met him. He had a different personality in his workshops—the cameras, audience, stage, and adulation of the crowd seemed to fill up his body and make him appear larger than life. In the real world, when he was alone with just one person— me—he deflated. As the Veggie City waiter placed our water glasses and menus down, he never looked up from his texts.

I tapped his arm. "After I graduate, I was thinking maybe I could go to college in Hawai'i?" I'd rehearsed those words, practiced them in my head. I felt like Dyna playing her notes on the viola strings, the careful position of bow and fingers. I'd wanted to say it for so long, and I had to get it out of me.

He put down his phone. "What?"

"When I finish high school—I'd like to apply—Hawai'i colleges?" I didn't know how I managed to mangle it the second time.

His fingers smoothed his paper napkin into a wrinkle-free rectangle. "That would be wonderful, except Hawai'i doesn't have the best colleges. The best colleges are on the East Coast. Have you taken advantage of Beverly's career guidance program?"

"I might want to go into art," I said.

He laughed. "That'll make money. If you keep your nose down and listen to Beverly, she'll point you in the right direction. She taught me Reinvention when she was my teacher at the military academy. Change your Story, Change your Life, Change your Future. My father, bless his soul, saved all his money to send me to that prestigious school. He invested in me, just as Beverly invested in my Future, too. They both taught me that you can't let anything hold you back. That you can make anyplace your home. Now we're investing in your Future."

He picked up his phone and scrolled through his messages again. There was always a curtain in his mind; he'd let it rise for a second to focus on you, and then drop it down and shut you out. Any challenge to him or uncomfortable statement could bring it down, crashing, ending the play all too soon.

I thought of how Nana had left her husband, Charles, my grandfather, when my dad was only a year old. Nana said Charles was a pragmatic, moralistic, angry man; he was also a lawyer, and he sued her for custody and won. I knew to never bring it up with my dad. He couldn't stand to talk about it. But I felt like I had to now. "Nana always said not getting to raise you was the most painful thing to happen to her in her life."

More scrolling.

"It wasn't her fault that she lost custody. She wanted more than anything to raise you like she did me. She said the best thing to ever happen to her was getting to raise me."

My dad was silent. This conversation wasn't allowed; I knew that.

"With the Path—" he began.

I exhaled. "I don't want to talk about the Path. I'm your daughter. Not one of your fans or workshop participants."

His eyes darted to the menu, the napkin holder, the window, his phone. The curtain began to fall, about to close on me.

"Of course you're my daughter. Who else would you be?"

"Am I a disappointment to you?" I asked him.

He made a huffing nose.

"I mean—I want to feel like your daughter. For us to be close. Mom, you, and me. To live together. Finally. Once and for all. If not now, then in college I can live on campus, but stay with you on weekends or in the summer."

He morphed, again, into the famous person who'd helped millions. "You've helped your mother and me by your sacrifices—we've helped people around the world, and you've played a part in that whether you embrace your role or not. When this TV show moves forward, you'll see. You'll understand your impact." He gulped his water. "Onward! Let's not dwell in the Past. It's gone. That is the Key," he said. "Home is what you make it, you know. Home is what you carry with you in your heart." He touched my hand for a moment, and then let it go. His phone rang, the curtain crashed down, and the conversation was over.

twenty-seven
SAD DOG PAINTINGS

The taxi arrived at the auction house, an old limestone mansion with gold front doors. I shook off my father's words and the images of the pink room, and tried to focus on the present. The most important thing was to track down the diary and find Edith.

Inside, the walls were covered in framed art—but it wasn't like the free-spirited paintings we made in the art room at Thornton. A sign proclaimed, "Currently Showing: The Art of the Wallingford Estate," and apparently the Wallingfords owned many unhappy dogs. Portraits of surly bulldogs, growling collies, and depressed-looking poodles covered every wall.

We stared at a painting of a Yorkshire terrier wearing a pearl necklace and sitting on a velvet cushion. A price tag in tiny print read: *$160,000.*

"Good lord," Dyna said. "Is that for real?"

We walked down a hallway and past more dog paintings, and followed a sign to the reception desk. The receptionist wore giant gold earrings shaped like turtles.

Mimsy cleared her throat. "Excuse me, we'd like to see Cyrus Shaw, please."

"Who may I say is here?" the receptionist asked.

"His . . . neighbors."

The receptionist buzzed his number, but there was no answer. She glanced at a schedule book in front of her. "He's not answering because he's in a meeting with a client right now."

"We'll wait," Mimsy said.

"It might be a while."

"We'll wait," Mimsy repeated. The walls were covered in green fabric wallpaper. I couldn't stop touching it—I'd never seen fabric on the walls before. Heavy drapes covered the giant windows.

I asked the receptionist what Cyrus did exactly.

"As our head cataloger, Cyrus's job is to label everything that comes in, tag it, photograph it, and create a record of it for the auctions. He works in the basement—it's attached to the warehouse, so when the shipments come in he can receive them and catalog them right away."

I had an idea. I whispered to Dyna and Mimsy, "Will you ask the receptionist a question about one of the dog paintings, so I can get a look at the schedule book on her desk?"

They nodded. Mimsy went into full actress mode, and said, "My dear, that painting of the beagle over there reminds me so much of my dear Fluffles, and I have a question about something. I can't tell if what I'm seeing is a scratch in the actual paint, or perhaps just dust from a lack of cleaning."

The receptionist stood up from her desk and followed Mimsy to the painting.

I glanced at the receptionist's schedule book.

Time	Employee	Visitor
11 a.m.	Cyrus Shaw	Peter Lloyd

It was almost noon now. "Peter was here," I whispered to Dyna. "Maybe he's still here." My heart thumped. I slid the schedule book back into place. Mimsy and the receptionist were still squinting at an invisible spot on the painting.

"I just don't see what you're talking about," the receptionist said. I squeezed Mimsy's arm and pointed toward the door.

"Oops! My mistake!" Mimsy said. "I must've imagined it, my eyesight isn't what it used to be." She touched her stomach. "I'm suddenly ravenous. Lunchtime! I don't think we're going to wait after all."

The receptionist shrugged. "Suit yourself." We thanked her and hurried out and down the hallway.

We rode the gold elevator down to the basement floor, and I told Mimsy what the schedule book said.

The basement and warehouse were dark and gloomy, with cement floors and a warren of little offices on one side of the hallway. On the opposite side were stacks of boxes, and shelves and shelves of objects, and giant doors where a truck was lined up to unload. A security guard approached us, and we said we were there to meet Cyrus Shaw, but couldn't find his office.

"I think you just missed him. You can leave him a note," the guard said. He pointed to a tiny, cramped, dark office. He switched the light on for us. I held my breath, hoping to see *Home Arts*—but there was only a desktop computer, pens, and an inbox tray that contained nothing but a jumble of different business cards.

Someone called the guard to the loading dock, and we searched the rest of the office as quickly as we could. Under the desk, against the wall, was a big cardboard box. We opened it. It was filled with stacks of vintage books.

"I think these are Edith's," I said. I saw books from the 1800s and first editions of classic novels. We looked through them all, but there was no *Home Arts*. None had been hollowed out with a secret compartment.

I picked up the business cards out of his inbox tray. They were for estate resellers, auctioneers, and then one caught my eye.

PETER LLOYD

Professor of Botany and Ecology

232 Langdon Hall

Greenwich University

(917) 555-2470

Written on the back of the card in blue ink was: *Home Arts,* *$1,000.*

twenty-eight
THE BEE ROOM

Mimsy called the number on Peter's business card; his administrative assistant at Greenwich University picked up, and Mimsy asked if Peter was there. The assistant said yes, Peter had just arrived at his office. She added our names to the visitor list.

We hopped in a taxi to the university, fifteen blocks north, to try to track down Peter and the diary.

"What would Peter want with Edith's diary?" Dyna asked.

"Maybe it's like those serial killer obsessions you read about," Mimsy said. "Saving trinkets of their victims. I think every person has a dark side. You just don't know what they're capable of. Some people hide their darkness. They seem like normal people, but underneath they have evil, twisted souls."

"So Cyrus was stealing and re-selling Edith's books. But maybe Peter had more sinister intentions?" Dyna asked.

"It still doesn't seem like the whole story to me," I said. "Let's try to get the diary from him and see what it can tell us."

Our taxi reached the university's front entrance. The botany and ecology department was located at the top of the sciences building. We could see a dome-shaped greenhouse on the roof.

We gave our IDs to the security guard on the ground floor and stepped in the elevator. When we reached the department, the assistant's desk was empty. A sign read:

WELCOME TO THE LLOYD LAB

Outside Peter's office, a student was at the communal lab tables, looking into a microscope.

Jack. He looked up.

I noticed it then: ferns everywhere. Hanging in baskets, on the shelves along the wall, all around the room.

"I thought you were out looking for Edith?" I asked him.

"I was. I had to come back for a meeting here. I also wanted to check on Peter. He took the news about Edith's disappearance hard. He blames himself."

As he should, I wanted to say. Because he probably caused it.

He looked at the three of us. "I wish I had some more news on Edith, but I haven't heard anything. I'm meeting my father in an hour, though, so he should have an update then. I'll tell you everything I know."

"We'd love to hear whatever news you have," Mimsy said. "I spoke with Peter's assistant earlier. We just wanted to check on him also. To say hello. To see how he's doing. Difficult times for all of us, right now."

"He just left—he's teaching a lecture on the first floor. He'll be back in about an hour. He didn't mention that you were coming. Did you want to wait?"

"Yes," I lied. We didn't want to wait—we just wanted to search his office for the missing book and Edith's diary. We had to figure out how to distract Jack and get in there.

I squinted through the glass window into Peter's office and saw something on the shelf. "Is that a *Pleopeltis polypodioides* fern?" I recognized it from the Ruin at Mandragora.

Jack's eyes lit up. "Yes! Peter collects them. Here—I'll show you." He opened the door.

Dyna gave me a look. "What language was that? Martian?" she whispered.

Peter's office was beautiful. Air plants hung from the ceiling in terrariums, and ivy and spider plants trailed down along the window. An antique apothecary's cabinet held little glass jars. An antique typewriter sat on his desk; tiny ceramic toadstools had been glued to the top of it. Glass domes protected baby succulents, an ancient scale held a bowl of moss, and one shelf displayed miniature clocks. Stone owls were perched everywhere, on bookshelves and on the edges of plant pots; they gazed at us intently. A baby bonsai grew beside an owl—it looked just like the bonsai on their wedding stone at Mandragora.

If offices had souls, this would be the soul mate of Edith's.

Then I saw it, behind the typewriter: a large blue book, nestled against a stack of papers, with a flower on its spine.

Home Arts.

I gave Mimsy a look. She nodded—she saw it, too.

"I love this office," I told Jack. "It reminds me so much of Edith." What we needed was to get Jack to leave the room for a minute, so one of us could take the book.

I had an idea.

"I'd love to see the bee room," I said. "You mentioned it to me at Mandragora? I think you said it was here, in the lab?"

"Sure, I'd be happy to show it to all of you."

"Oh god no, I'm deathly afraid of bees," Mimsy said. "I'll just wait here, if you don't mind."

"Are you sure?" Jack asked. "It's really amazing."

"I'm sure," Mimsy said.

"I'll stay with Mimsy," Dyna said. "To keep her company. I'm scared of bees, too. Terrified of being stung."

"It's safe, I promise," Jack said, but she shook her head. He shrugged and turned to me. "I guess you're my only customer."

He led me down the hall to a sink where we washed our hands, and then into the bee room. It was the size of a small office, and dark inside, with a dim red light. It was warm and humid and smelled faintly sweet. It took a few moments for my eyes to adjust. The bees seemed to be going about their own business in their colonies, which looked like shoeboxes stacked on top of each other.

"So this is where it all happens," I said. "Bees." Why did I sound so awkward sometimes?

"A lot of our research takes place outside, but here in the lab we're experimenting. We study what might be causing the decline of populations and even extinctions. Then we analyze and compile the data."

His entire body changed in the bee room—he became the person from Mandragora again. Passion seeped out of his pores, and he seemed to vibrate with it—a passion for flowers, and bees, and ferns, and green growing things—the opposite of the person he seemed to be when doing his police work, when he seemed crushed by the realities of that world.

"I'm worried about Edith," I said.

"Me too. I needed a break from worrying. To think. That's why I came here today and didn't cancel my meeting. I keep thinking there must be something I'm not seeing—some way to find where she is. I feel better when I'm working here."

He picked up a big pair of forceps, opened a colony box, and pulled out a bumblebee. "This one's a male—they don't sting," he said. "Do you want to touch it?"

I nodded, and he showed me how to hold it between my thumb and two fingers, firmly and carefully. I felt the fuzz on its back, and it made strange clicking noises.

"They're gentle creatures, generally speaking," he said. "This is a *Bombus perplexus*. We started this colony from a wild-caught queen."

The buzz of it, the warmth, the smell of honey—I could see what he loved about being here.

The bee suddenly flew out of my fingers and I winced, still afraid I could get stung. He put a hand on my shoulder. "It's safe," he said.

"I think you like bees better than humans," I said.

"Maybe I do. I like being in the greenhouse here, too—I can show that to all of you after this. If you want. We have over a hundred species of ferns in there."

"That would be great." I paused. "You always seem happier in the natural world."

"The natural world can be brutal, though, too," he said. "There's a type of bee called cuckoo bumblebees, who are parasitic. They invade the nests of other bumblebees, sting the queen to death, steal her nest site and her pollen, enslave her daughters—the worker bees—then kill her larvae and eggs and replace them with her own."

"There are no cuckoo bumblebees in here, are there?" I asked.

He laughed. "No."

"Good."

The room was so humid that I began to sweat.

"I've been wanting to ask you something," he said.

"What?"

His shoulders stiffened, as if he was turning back into his

aspiring-homicide-detective self.

My heart beat so strongly I could practically hear it. Could he tell that we were lying, that we really were here to find Edith's diary?

He kept pausing, mulling something over in his mind.

He finally spoke. "At Passover—when Nanette brought out the shakes—is that really all she's been feeding you?"

"What do you mean?"

"Is that all she's been giving you? Shakes? Every day?"

"Oh. That. It's my dad's business. It's part of the deal, me living here. To eat a certain way. So far I'm not—"

"That's insane. That's crazy. That's—child abuse." He ran his hand through his hair.

"It's not a big deal. I never even have them because I eat with Mimsy and Dyna, and with Edith, until—"

"So your parents decided that was healthy, to try to control all your food? All your meals?" He looked angry.

"Why are you taking it so seriously? It's just kind of—it's ridiculous really, kind of a joke, and I don't take it seriously—"

"It is a big deal," he said. "It's not okay."

"They want me to be healthy, I guess." I felt ashamed saying it, for some reason. "To change."

"You don't need to change."

The words seemed so simple, words I'd heard before, of course. *Don't change*—Dyna had written that in my yearbook once—yet he said it so slowly and urgently. He was right next to my face. I could see tiny beads of sweat on his neck. I smelled a sweet soap smell, the laundry soap on his shirt, and I could see the stubble on his face, the tiny dark hair coming through, and his dark eyes right in front of me. His gaze searched mine, like he wanted to tell me something else.

I didn't know what to say or to do.

There was a loud knock on the door.

"Hello? Are you all right in there?" Mimsy's voice.

"Fine!" I said.

Jack opened the door. We came out of the bee room and into the hall. We blinked in the bright light.

"Just wanted to make sure you were okay," Mimsy said. "Not attacked by killer bees or anything."

I turned to Jack. "Thank you for showing the bee room to me."

"You're welcome," he said with a sudden formality and politeness, as if we'd turned into eighteenth-century acquaintances. He led us back down the hall to the lab tables. I shot a quick glance into Peter's office—the book was no longer there. I looked at Mimsy and Dyna. They were smiling. Where had they put it? Mimsy had a small purse, and we weren't wearing coats. Then Mimsy moved slightly to the side, and I saw where she'd hidden it.

Her bottom was enormous. Moon-like, fluffy, as if it had grown three sizes in the last fifteen minutes. It ballooned out from the back of her skirt like an ancient bustle, a giant mound of flesh.

She must've stashed the book on her butt, then padded it

with something lumpy.

Mimsy glanced at her watch. "We should be going! I just realized I need to rush back for a doctor's appointment. Please tell Peter we're so sorry we missed him. And please tell us as soon as you hear news about Edith."

"I'm sorry we have to run out," I said. I really hoped Jack wouldn't notice her bottom.

But Mimsy turned around, and he did notice. His eyes bulged. Then he must've realized it wasn't appropriate to stare at it, so he kept looking away, at the plants by the windows, then the ceiling, and then quickly glancing back at it.

"Mimsy's been eating a lot lately," Dyna said, apparently feeling the need to explain the gargantuan tush. "Stress."

"So much stress. Nothing like a good pastry to help calm yourself. Or ten pastries. Twenty. More the better, I always say." Mimsy smiled.

Jack must've decided he was too polite to discuss a septuagenarian's bottom, because I'd never seen him so uncomfortable. He shepherded us to the elevator quickly.

He gazed at me. "Thanks for coming by," he said. "It means a lot that you were concerned about Peter. I'll tell him."

He seemed so sincere that I felt a little guilty. "Thanks," I said. "Thank you again for the bee room tour."

"Anytime."

The elevator pinged. Down we went.

Mimsy tapped her bottom. It was the dull sound of a book. "You did it!" I said. "What else is in there?"

"Wadded-up paper towels," Dyna said. "And we saw a 'Lost and Found' box in the corner with a few old sweatshirts in there, so we stuffed those in, too."

"I like it," Mimsy said. "I haven't had a prosthetic rear since my performing days, but it's actually quite nice. I feel fuller. More complete."

Dyna carefully removed the book from Mimsy's false butt so that the paper towels and sweatshirts wouldn't fall out on the floor. "Here it is." She cradled the book in her hands. *Home Arts.* I touched the pink pressed flower.

The elevator reached the ground floor. "Let's go back to my place and look through it," Mimsy said. We hailed a taxi back to her house, then went through the gate to the garden. Mimsy sat on the stone bench next to the fairy garden, and Dyna and I stood beside her as she took out the book.

Mimsy opened the cover slowly, her hands slightly trembling.

twenty-nine
FOXES AND KESTRELS

nside, the middle of the book had been hollowed out and covered with a cardboard rectangle. The cardboard was stuck closed and hardened with brownish glue. Mimsy got a kitchen knife, and she carefully pried the cardboard cover off the secret compartment.

A red leather-covered diary with gold edges was hidden inside it.

We opened the cover. The delicate pages were tinged with brown.

This diary belongs to:
May 1957

No name. Just a little drawing of a fox.

I turned to the first page.

May 21, 1957

We're about to leave for the home. I feel sick. 'You'll like it,' he says. 'It's a beautiful setting.' He doesn't even look me in the eye when he speaks now, he's so ashamed of me.

Mimsy glanced over my shoulder. "Her father," she said as she touched the page.

"Is it okay for us to read this?" It felt suddenly like breaking a vow, invading her privacy. "It's her secret thoughts. Her sacred space." I thought of how, as soon as I started writing in my diary, something took over. The knots began to loosen. Things started to become clearer and make sense. Something we never learned how to do in school. They didn't have classes in making sense of things.

Mimsy touched the diary's gold spine. "She asked us to find it, though—I think she'd understand."

"Maybe it's best if only one of us reads it, instead of all three of us," Dyna said. "Then they can share the important things— why Edith wanted us to find it and if there's a clue to where she might be."

"Brilliant idea," Mimsy said, and clasped her hands together. "If someone is going to read it, I think it should be Lucy."

"Me?" I asked.

"You remind me of Edith so much, when she was your age.

Also, Edith trusts you."

"She trusts you, too," I said.

"Well, she knows me better than anyone. She knows I'm not so great at keeping secrets. You keep a diary, Lucy—you'd know what she might want to keep private, and what she'd be okay with us knowing. I'm an actress—we lay it all out on the table. But you're a private person," Mimsy said. "You're the writer."

They both smiled at me encouragingly.

You're the writer. No one had ever said that to me before, that I had a thing that I did, something of value. *A writer.* Was that me?

"Music makes me feel like I'm home," Dyna said. "Playing Rosie keeps me sane. It makes everything in the world feel better, feel okay. I think maybe writing and drawing in your diary—it's your Rosie."

I nodded. I loved how my diary felt like a hiding place, its own universe, a world where you could unravel your deepest feelings. It wasn't just pen on paper. It was like a living, breathing being.

I glanced down at Edith's diary again.

May 22, 1957

We're all given fake names here since our families are so embarrassed by us that they don't want us to be recognized. They gave us simple names like Mary and Alice and Ann, but the girls on our floor have changed them with nicknames for ourselves. Animal names. Raven, Kitty, Lark, Kestrel, Robin. I chose Fox of course. I don't care if I am recognized.

Mimsy and Dyna watched me closely as I read, as if those first few pages might say, *Almost sixty years from now, I'm going to disappear and leave a cryptic note to you about this diary, and this is why, and here's where you can find me.* I wanted it to say that, too. The pages were filled with her looping handwriting on the narrow lines, the first entries filled with descriptions of the maternity home, the other girls there, and the land around it. "I think this is going to take a while to read," I said. I took out my own diary. "I'll take notes on any entry that seems relevant—that might have any clues."

"We'll give you some space to read it," Mimsy said. "I'll be in the house—I'm going to send out more emails and alerts to search for Edith. Yell for me if you find a clue."

"I will."

"I'm going to practice," Dyna said. "For a mental health break and to think through how all these clues add up. Yell for me, too, if you find anything. Or if you need a break."

I nodded, and she fetched Rosie and went to the folly to practice and to think.

May 23, 1957

Peonies are blooming here—giant plants, someone must have planted them ages ago—puffballs of white and pink and purplish ones that smell like sugar. I found an old cottonwood tree with a hollow in its trunk near the peony patch, and I love to hide inside it and write in here. This tree and the flowers are the only things keeping me sane. I hide inside this tree and I hold my fox necklace and I feel like my mother is here, telling me it will be okay. Have faith in the natural world, she'd say.

May 24, 1957

We got to go to an ice cream shop today, but several townspeople saw us and made a scene. They called us names and shouted, 'You should be ashamed of yourselves. If you were my daughter, I'd kill you.' I yelled back at them, 'Go to hell.' Mrs. Smith, who runs the home, said she was going to call my father and tell him about my misbehavior. I'm sure he won't be surprised. I wasn't allowed the ice cream.

May 25, 1957

I think I've made a friend. Her nickname is Kestrel—she came and found me by the peony patch. She asked about my fox necklace—she said I'm always holding the necklace and pressing it to my lips. I told her about my mother, how I feel she's with me here in the garden. I showed her the hollowed-out tree and we hid inside it and felt safe from the world.

I told Kestrel how my mother would send a message to me in flower colors. Our own language. Yellow sunflowers were her favorite flower—a symbol of herself. Red flowers meant love. Orange flowers were me—her little fox. Sometimes when I came home from school she'd have them on the table that way, as a comfort: I love you. In flowers.

May 26, 1957

Kestrel told me about her mother today.

She said the shaming from the townspeople at the ice cream shop was nothing new for her. The shaming from her mother was even worse. "You're huge," her mother told her. "You gained too much weight. You ruined your body. You ruined your life. Nobody will ever want you now."

The father of Kestrel's baby was a football player at her high school. She thought they'd get married, but after she got pregnant he said the baby wasn't his. He never spoke to her again.

She told me that since she turned thirteen, she and her sister have supported the family with different jobs—housemaids, cooking, cleaning rooms at the local hospital, babysitting, anything they can find.

She told me she has no father—he abandoned them soon after she was born.

The last thing her mother told her before she dropped her off was: "You're not my daughter anymore."

An hour later, Mimsy looked for me in the garden. She yelled for Dyna to come, also. She had her phone on speaker.

It was Liliana. She was crying.

"What happened?" Mimsy asked her.

"Come to Summer Street. Right now. The police are here. The ambulance came and left. It's Cyrus Shaw. There's been an accident."

A line of police cars flashed all the way down Summer Street. We told the officers that I lived there, and they allowed us to walk into the lobby. Jack stood beside Nanette, whose face was red. Clifford and Liliana were there, too, talking to the police.

Jack came over to us. "Cyrus was found at the bottom of the stairs. The big steep flight from the second floor to the first. Nanette found him. He was facedown and bleeding."

"Is he— Will he recover?" Mimsy asked.

"He's unconscious," Jack said. "He has a head injury. The ambulance took him to the ER."

"Was it an accident?" Mimsy asked. "Did he slip and fall?"

Jack shook his head. "They think someone pushed him, judging from the position he was found in."

Nanette saw me. She raised a manicured finger with silver nail polish. She pointed at me. "You did this. I know you did." Her voice was high and strange.

I froze. "She's lost her mind," Dyna whispered to me.

"She was with us the whole day," Mimsy said as she and Dyna moved closer to me, like two shields.

Nanette kept pointing at me. "Ever since you came here, it's been nothing but trouble. I learned about your history today. Hurting that poor girl. Pushed down the stairs. Violent. Disgusting. Now Cyrus, too."

My blood pounded. My head hurt. Dyna and Mimsy stood on either side of me, holding my arms tightly. Mimsy said, "Let's get out of here." We turned to leave.

"Don't come back here—ever," Nanette said. Jack flinched as she spoke.

Mimsy, Dyna, and I made our way outside. A crowd had gathered behind the police tape. We burrowed through the throng of onlookers and walked down the block as fast as we could. On the corner, we hailed a taxi back to Mimsy's place.

As we drove down the street, I told Mimsy about the Incident and how I was suspended. I braced myself for her reaction. I was afraid that once she heard the whole story, she wouldn't want me staying in her house, either, but she waved her hand and said, "I was suspended from boarding school so many times, I can barely count. Once for smoking cigarettes—they didn't like that back in the day—once for kissing four boys—they didn't like that, either. And once for kissing two girls—they *really* didn't like that one. And once for running naked through campus."

I exhaled, relieved that the story of the Incident didn't change the way she thought of me. I realized I'd barely been breathing.

"You ran naked through campus?" Dyna asked her.

"It was a dare from another girl. I ran around the center of the quad once, and it felt so freeing that I couldn't help but run through the campus chapel, too. That felt *really* freeing." She shook herself back to the present. Dyna told her more about the Things and the whole soul-crushing feeling of being at Thornton.

"I'm so sorry you had to go through that," Mimsy said. "Humans. Not the best species in the world."

"A Mimsy's Rule?" Dyna asked.

"Yes."

We tried to absorb everything that happened. "We have to get your stuff from Nanette's place," Dyna said.

I shook my head. "I can't go back there."

We reached Mimsy's house, and she paid the driver. "You'll stay here with us," she said as she shut the taxi door. "I'll get your things from Nanette's after she calms down."

I thanked her, and she unlocked the side gate to the garden. I sat down on a stone bench and tried not to think about how I'd explain this to my parents.

"Who pushed Cyrus? And why?" Dyna asked, and sat down beside me.

"Maybe someone else is after the diary, too," I said. "Maybe Peter wants it back. Or another suspect."

A little while later, the doorbell at the garden gate rang. Mimsy opened it.

It was Jack. The corners of his mouth turned downward. He carried a rolling suitcase—my suitcase.

"Nanette left this on the curb by the trash cans. She's so upset, she's not thinking clearly. I'm sorry it got dirty. I tried to clean it off."

"Thank you for bringing it." I turned the suitcase over on the stone pathway and unzipped it. I hadn't brought much to New York in the first place, but everything seemed to be there—all my T-shirts and yoga pants and clothes were jumbled up inside, and all my stuffed hedgehogs. I saw a tiny flash of pale green flannel peeking out beneath them. Nana's nightgown. I'd never even unpacked her nightgown or my hedgehogs—I'd wanted to keep those things I loved safe and secret. I hated the thought of Nanette touching the suitcase, putting my clothes inside it. Throwing it out.

"Cyrus is still unconscious, but stabilized," Jack said. He sat down on the edge of the wooden chair across from me, leaning forward, twisting his hands.

"Nanette was completely out of line to blame Lucy again," Mimsy said. "We were together the whole time. Of course Lucy had nothing to do with what happened to Cyrus."

He nodded. "I know." He gripped his forehead. "It doesn't add up. Who pushed him? Why?" He glanced at the fairy village on the grass beside him, and he picked up a tiny red bicycle and spun the wheel, as if that might make everything come clear.

He put the bicycle back down. "I have news about the search for Edith. I just spoke to my father on the way over—they finished reviewing all the surveillance tapes from the ferry, and there's a video of Edith getting on the ferry, but there's no sign that she got off of it. They searched the ferry ship itself and interviewed workers and fellow passengers. My father said the police department plans to rule it a suicide."

Mimsy put her hand to her mouth. "That's wrong. That's a mistake."

My chest ached and my throat felt dry.

"I know it is," Jack said. "I'm not sure what else to do." He twisted his hands again.

I wished we could be honest with him and tell him about the diary—I wished he wasn't always halfway torn between our version of events and his father's. *Which side are you on?* I wanted to ask. *Which will you choose?*

His phone buzzed. He took it out of his pocket. "Nanette. She keeps texting and calling me and my father, too."

"What does she want?" Dyna asked.

"I'm sorry, but—she wants us to investigate you," Jack said to me.

"She's lost her mind," Dyna said.

"My father's going to ask you—were the three of you within each other's sight between four p.m. and five p.m., when Cyrus was pushed? Nanette's saying you could've slipped out and gotten back within an hour—I know it's impossible. I just wanted to warn you what she's saying."

I told him how Mimsy was in the house, and Dyna was in the folly, and I was alone in the garden.

"Of course Lucy didn't do it," Mimsy said.

"I know." He opened his mouth as if to say something else, then closed it. He glanced at the fairy garden again and picked up a tiny teahouse. He looked awkward holding it, like a giant who'd wandered into the wrong story. He put the teahouse down, and then took a brown envelope out of his bag. "Nanette handed this to me right before she left. She said someone put it under her door, anonymously."

The envelope was torn open. I saw the return address: Austin School Police.

"It's something you were involved in at your boarding school? Nanette said there's a similarity with Cyrus." His voice sounded different—lower, more serious.

My stomach dropped. My records from the Incident.

"I thought it was confidential?" Dyna asked. "How did Nanette get that—who gave it to her?"

"I'm not sure," Jack said.

My face felt hot. The envelope was open. He'd already read it. "Can I talk to Jack alone?" I asked Dyna and Mimsy. I wanted to explain it to him, to tell him the real story. He wouldn't be as cavalier as Mimsy was, with his policeman side, but maybe if I explained it in the right way, he'd understand.

"Are you sure?" Dyna asked me.

I nodded. "We can talk in the folly." Jack followed me down the stone path through the garden, and as we walked I noticed the deadheading we needed to do, the work that Edith would want us to accomplish. I opened the heavy door to the folly.

"Of course I don't believe Nanette," he said. But he had a strange expression as he gripped the envelope. I took it from him and removed the documents and photos and laid them on the small wooden table.

It was the preliminary report, before the charges were dropped and the records were supposedly sealed. I stared at the photos. Pictures of Victoria's injuries, taken over days. Bruises. Dried blood around her nose and down her shirt. Marks that were red and then black and blue and purple. My palms watered, and my throat started to close up, and a crater reopened inside me. This was different than telling Mimsy my version of the story—this was its own story. Jack saw it for himself.

He kept staring at the photos. In my mind I saw the Texas policeman's expression from months ago: *Who are you?*

All the cells in my body seemed to race and freeze at the same time. I didn't know how to explain. *It was an accident. I'm not a person who would do that. That's not really me.* None of that sounded right. What had I done? Who was I?

"I didn't mean to upset you," Jack said. "I didn't know—"

The policeman's eyes: *You are a bad person.*

I could see her on the stairs again, hear her voice. *They never wanted you.*

She was right. I remembered how when my parents dropped me off at Thornton for the first time, with this same rolling suitcase, how I sat on the twin bed in 302 Thornton East, alone, for the first time, and I felt I'd done something wrong. That I must've made a mistake to end up in this place. There was something fundamentally flawed with me. Ms. Leery had said in her kind-sweet-fake-talking-to-parents voice that the best thing was for my parents to leave quickly because kids bounced back immediately once they left, it always happened that way, they'd be so happy to see.

You're a bad person.

My dad was always saying Reinvention! Change yourself! Change your Path! But you couldn't. Edith was gone and we'd found the diary, but we were no closer to finding her, or to figuring out who was after her. I was kicked out of Nanette's. My parents wouldn't want me to live in that pink room in their yellow house, not now, not ever.

My father was wrong about reinventing and changing yourself. I'd always be a person with a hole inside me. You couldn't fix that. The hole never completely went away.

Maybe the world was saying, would continue to say, as it had for years: You're not on solid ground, and you never will be—there's no such thing—because at any moment a landslide will come through, again and again, all your life.

Staring at Jack, I felt this strange, deep envy of him, suddenly, too—of his apartment he'd lived in since he was two, on Summer Street, always, of what that must feel like. A home that was not a rolling suitcase. And I envied his cherry tree that wasn't chopped up and gone like the redbud. It continued to bloom every year. How that must make the hole you carry around bearable. It would slowly fill it up.

Jack's face seemed gnarled with confusion. He looked torn between wanting to believe two opposite things at the same time. His initial idea of me and this new information.

He blinked and waited for me to say more.

The words wouldn't come. What could I say? *I've been trying so hard to make a new life, but I did that. I hurt her. I am a bad person inside.* Now I understood why Uriah never spoke.

We heard a rustling outside. I glanced at the window. Eyes peered over a hedge, behind the window screen. "This really needs a good pruning," Mimsy said loudly, and gazed at us.

Dyna knocked on the glass pane above the open window. "Are you okay?" she asked through the screen when she saw my face. "What did you say to her?" she asked Jack.

Jack opened the door and let them inside. "I didn't mean to upset her—"

"Well, you did," Mimsy said, angry, too.

"It's not his fault," I said.

Dyna touched my shoulder.

"I'm sorry if I caused trouble," he said in his formal tone. "I shouldn't have shown that to you. I thought you'd want to know what Nanette was telling everyone—"

"I think you should go," Dyna said protectively.

He turned toward the door. "I'm sorry."

I sat in the folly as they walked him to the gate.

When he was gone, Mimsy and Dyna returned and sat down across from me.

"Are you all right?" Dyna asked.

I squeezed the chair until my fingers turned white. The thing I wanted then was my diary, to write down what had happened. These feelings inside me, a thousand different ones in an hour. "I need to be alone for a little while, I think," I said. "To finish reading Edith's diary, and to write in mine."

They hugged me, and said they'd check on me again in an hour. I went to get my diary and I poured everything out, and I began to feel better. I'd never before had a place where I could tell the complete truth, where I could be me—whoever that was—a place where I could say the sometimes ugly and scary things that I felt. Things that I'd been too scared to even think until I put them down on paper.

Writing in my diary was the first time, I realized, I got to tell my own story, my true story. I flipped through the pages filled with my drawings and writing since I'd come to New York. In here I had all the things Edith and Mimsy and Dyna had taught me—Sea Change Days, planting Popsicle Toes, Fox's Rules, *writing and drawing is your Rosie. You are not bad*, I wrote. *There's nothing wrong with you.*

I was trying to figure out my own rules.

Lucy's Rules for Living. Ms. Leery would say, *Who do you think you are?*

I picked up Edith's diary and I started reading her story again.

June 2, 1957

I found packets of seeds in the old rickety garden shed on the property, and I showed Kestrel how to plant them. Sunflowers, zinnias, cosmos, and herbs. She'd never planted a seed. I've been writing next month's column and she likes to hear about how to grow things—she says it soothes her.

I showed her the plants in the garden to be careful of—the poison ivy and stinging nettles—and also the bottle of paraquat I saw in the shed—my mother told me it's one of the deadliest poisons. Even to look at it makes me shiver. And I showed her the edible flowers— pansies and nasturtiums and dandelions—and how my mother called pansies 'heart's ease'—how plants can cure sadness, too.

I read for two hours. Mimsy and Dyna stopped by the folly to check in. I showed them the passages I'd taken notes on.

"Any clues yet?" Mimsy asked.

"She mentions the paraquat in the shed, but it's not a clue to who's after her or where she could be. I'll keep reading."

We ordered dinner, though none of us were hungry.

We sat in the living room before we went upstairs to sleep. We all were going to sleep in Mimsy's house that night.

Or not sleep.

Mimsy's armor of faith and hope seemed to be cracking. She practiced her deep breathing. She chanted a mantra. "All will be okay," she said in a throaty voice. "You are well. You are loved and whole. Every human is perfect. A perfect being worthy of love," she croaked.

"That mantra is kinda freaking me out," Dyna said. "Isn't it supposed to be calming?"

"It is. I would go hug some birch trees, but it's dark outside and I'm in my pajamas," Mimsy said. "So the mantra will have to do."

"I'm going to stay up and finish reading," I said. Eventually, Dyna and Mimsy both fell asleep on the couch in the living room.

> *June 15, 1957*
>
> *Sometimes Kestrel looks at me with envy. 'I wonder what it would be like to be you. To have your life,' she said today in the hollowed-out tree. 'One of the girls told me who your father is. You're rich. You have everything.'*
>
> *'I don't,' I said. But I knew having a mother who loved you was everything. 'I'm sorry,' I said.*

The most dramatic part of the diary was about Kestrel's mother.

> *June 16, 1957*
>
> *Kestrel told me that the morning her mother dropped her off here—they live not far away—her mother handed her a letter. It was an accounting.*
>
> *Schoolbooks $288*
> *Bread $519*
> *Milk $224*

Eggs $282

Clothing, medicines, rent—it went on and on.

At first she didn't understand what it was. Then she realized: it was the amount that she and her sister owed their mother for their upbringing. Kestrel showed the letter to me. She expected it would take them years to pay her back.

Her mother said to her, "What have you given me for all this? Nothing."

The total they owed their mother was $25,758.

Kestrel said it felt good to tell me about it, that it felt like unburdening herself. She showed me a photo of her mother, too, and even holding the photo, she said she felt sick. She couldn't stop thinking of the words "You're not my daughter anymore."

"Let's burn it," I said. Her eyes lit up. We decided that later tonight, in the garden, after everyone's asleep, we're going to sneak out and burn it in a ceremony. She asked me to hide the letter and photo for her until tonight—she can't stand to look at them anymore.

June 16, 1957, before dinner

I keep thinking about Kestrel's mother, how even if your mother is alive, it can be worse. It can be worse than having a mother who is dead.

Unconditional love has its own rules, its own solar system. I would die for this baby. Even that doesn't capture it. This love is the biggest, maddest, craziest love I've ever felt. Like my soul wants to cover this baby, protect and care for it always—bound *together, no matter what—it's indestructible. It's constant. It exists apart from all other kinds of love in the world. It's ever present—it's immortal—it's ever-everything.*

She wrote pages and pages about her love for her baby that night—twenty pages of it—and I knew why she wanted Clifford to read this—she needed him to understand. Reading her words felt like time traveling to when she was sixteen. She wanted Clifford to understand how she felt at that moment, and what her unconditional love meant—that her love for him was stronger than anything else in the world. That she would never stop feeling that love for him.

She and Kestrel never got to have their photo-burning ceremony—the diary entries stopped that evening. Edith's water broke and she went into labor that night, on June 16.

I have to go to the hospital now. I hope I survive this.
A life grew in me.
And now I'm going to lose that life.

That was the last entry. Blank pages after that, a dozen of them.

I closed the back cover. Something sank inside me—the grief that Edith felt over leaving her baby, and knowing that she'd keep feeling it for decades—and also I'd read every word so carefully, and didn't find anything that would help us find her. I sat forward and put my head in my hands. The diary fell off my lap and onto the floor.

I stared at its gold edges, its red leather cover.

I thought of how we'd stood in the library on Passover, and she said she longed to find this diary. I picked it up again. I turned it over. She'd said, *My diaries had little pockets in the back where I could stash photos and things.*

I touched the inside of the back cover. There was a bump under the endpaper. I ran my fingernail along its edge—there was a pocket, an opening by the side of the binding. I reached in and I saw a serrated corner—a photo. I pulled it out. Behind it was a small, yellowed handwritten letter.

Schoolbooks *$288*
Bread *$519*
Milk *$224*

My heart banged in my chest. I stared at the photo—it was an old black-and-white photo of a woman. The photo Kestrel had given her, that they had planned to burn, of her mother smiling at the camera in a cardigan with a tiger brooch.

I'd seen this photo before. On Ms. Leery's photo wall. A photo Ms. Leery said was of Willa Thornton.

I woke up Dyna and Mimsy.

"What? What's happening? Am I dead?" Mimsy asked.

"You're not dead," I said.

"What's going on?" Dyna asked.

"Look." I showed them the small, very old photo. Black and

white, rectangular, with a serrated white border. "This was in Edith's diary."

Dyna froze.

"You've seen that before, haven't you?" I asked.

Her eyes widened. "Yes."

"Where?" Mimsy asked. "I've never seen that photo. That's not even Edith."

"It's a photo of Willa Thornton. Ms. Leery's mother," I said.

She taught me Reinvention, my father said. *Change your Story. Change your Life. Change your Future.*

I pictured Ms. Leery. Was it possible? Was she Kestrel? I remembered her office, the photo wall, the bird paintings behind her desk with their striped bodies and speckled heads. "What does a kestrel look like?" I asked Dyna.

"I'm not sure." She googled it on her phone and showed the picture to me. Striped body. Speckled head.

When I spoke to your headmistress, Nanette said, *she was so kind, she said I was a perfect role model for you, that I came to mind immediately when she sent you here to change your life.* Was it Ms. Leery's idea to send me here—had she convinced my parents to do it? Had she arranged for Nanette to move in, told Nanette to place the plant on my fire escape, asked Nanette to help execute her plan?

I thought back to my last day at Thornton. Her canceled conference due to thunderstorms in Oklahoma City. I took out my phone and looked up the weather in Oklahoma City that day.

Crystal clear skies. No storms at all.

"Mimsy, did anything happen here on April twelfth? That was the day Ms. Leery told me she was sending me here." I had a strange, cottony feeling in my stomach.

"I'm not sure—let me check my calendar." Mimsy took out her phone. "That was the day I visited Clifford and told him Edith's blood test revealed traces of *Brugmansia*. He knew I suspected him. Do you think that spooked your headmistress somehow? That's why she decided to send you here?"

"Maybe."

I thought of calling my parents. What if they didn't believe me? *That doesn't sound like Beverly. I don't believe that Beverly would ever do that,* my father would say. *That's not Beverly's mother in the photo. You must be mistaken. Beverly is a good and trustworthy person.* I couldn't bear to hear that right now. I couldn't tell them until we had proof—for the police and for my parents. We could find the matching photo on Ms. Leery's photo wall, and maybe even something better in her file room. I thought of Jack clutching the document from the Incident. A file, a document—more than a coincidental photo—that was what we needed to prove Ms. Leery was involved in this.

"We need proof," I said. Proof that Ms. Leery was Kestrel, that she'd known Edith and was involved in this.

Dyna and I exchanged looks. We knew where that proof would be.

"Ms. Leery's whole life and history is in that file room. All her secrets," I said. I kept thinking back to the day she sent me to New York. "She had two file folders on her desk that day that she kept clutching. One had my name on it, and the other one read 'Willa Thornton History.' Maybe there's proof in that file, or somewhere in her file room."

"We're going back to Texas," Dyna said.

"As soon as possible," I said.

Mimsy hesitated at first—she wasn't sure if the trip was too risky—but we promised her we'd be careful, and Flo and Uriah would surely help us. We looked into plane tickets. Mimsy offered her frequent flyer miles to us, but I had enough money saved from my salary from Edith to pay for both our tickets. Mimsy wanted to come with us, but we decided she should stay in New York, in case there was more information here, or a lead to Edith's whereabouts while we were gone.

Dyna said, "We'll investigate as quickly as we can, and then fly back home."

I touched Dyna's elbow. "Home. You called it home here."

"It is home," she said. "I want it to be home."

The next morning, we called Flo and told her everything. She checked the school calendar and Ms. Leery's schedule, and told us that Tuesday Ms. Leery would be off campus at a fundraising event, and the girls had a field trip to a baseball game, so the campus would be empty. Flo insisted on picking us up at the airport, and that we stay with her in her house overnight. We booked our return flight for noon the day after. Dyna texted Uriah, too, and told him what had happened, and that we were coming. He said he'd do everything he could to help us, also.

We started packing for Texas.

part v

MESSENGERS

To create a garden is to search for a better world.
—Marina Schinz

thirty-one

UP IN THE AIR AND IN BETWEEN

The sky seemed to break open and grow wider as we careened toward Texas. The sun shone through the plane windows, bright and blinding. My insides felt the way they did during tornado warnings in Austin—that ballooning dread as the sky turned an orangey color and the clouds darkened.

I kept glancing out the window. My mind floated back to everything that had happened since I'd left Texas, and everyone I'd met. And my brain kept getting stuck on Jack and his two personalities, and how confused I felt around him.

"What are you thinking about?" Dyna asked me.

I shrugged. "Everything."

"Jack?"

"How can you tell?"

"There's a vibe."

I shook my head. "There's no vibe."

"Even as you're saying that now, there's a vibe. Your hands are literally kind of shaking."

"He makes me nervous."

"He's just an old dude with father issues, like us, and paranoid suspicions. No reason to be scared of him."

"He's not that old," I said. "He's nineteen."

"Grandpa old," Dyna said.

"I can't even tell him about the connection between Edith and Ms. Leery because he probably won't believe me, or he'll tell his father. There's that weird policeman part of him, and then this other part of him, the gentle part. I don't know which one he really is."

She touched my arm. "It's okay to like him. It's okay to have a crush. Even if you don't totally get him or understand him. It's all okay—that's what my mom used to say."

This was a crush? It felt like gum stuck in my throat. Gum stuck in my heart. Mucking everything up. *Crush.* It felt crushing. Not in a good way. In an eating-too-much-cookie-dough-and-getting-a-stomachache way. Too overwhelming. "How do I make it go away?"

"Why do you want it to go away?"

"It's distracting me from what matters—finding Edith. And it sort of hurts when I think about him."

"That's love," she said. "It's totally screwed up."

"It's not love. It can't be. It feels like carrying some useless bag around. Some jumbled bag and I don't even know what's inside of it, or what the point of it is. It's just there and I can't let go of it, because it feels important. But I'm not even sure why or how yet."

"Yep. That's love," she said. "If I had my viola here, I'd play you one crazy tune right now."

thirty-two
NOT HOME

Our plane touched down in Texas, and my stomach dropped as the landscape came into view. I felt like I'd been away for a million years.

Flo waited for us at the bottom of the big escalators beside baggage claim. She whooped when she saw us and gathered us into her arms and kissed us. "Lord, I've missed you two. Tell me about New York City! Tell me everything! I didn't know if you'd ever come back." It was lunchtime, and she gave us a bag filled with breakfast tacos from Taco Deli to eat, and another bag filled with a Violet Crumble, Crunchie, and Marabou candy bars. We thanked her, and she surveyed us. "Look at you. You look healthier. Happier. You've been getting enough to eat in New York?"

"Plenty." I nodded and hugged her again. Dyna told her about the food in New York, how Mimsy ordered delivery of cheese pupusas and pan con chumpe, the turkey sandwiches Dyna's mom used to make on Thanksgiving. "Matzo ball soup, too," she said. "Anytime of year. And you can get it delivered at midnight."

"To your door? At midnight? Maybe I'll move there, too," Flo said. "Thornton hasn't been the same place with you gone. Ms. Leery's been in a state. She's freaked out about finances. There's a hiring freeze and a salary freeze and 'austerity measures.' I double-checked her schedule today, just like you asked. She'll be out the whole day in fundraising meetings till six o'clock," Flo said.

"Thanks for checking," Dyna said. "Now we just need to break into her file room. No problem."

Flo exhaled. "You said that on the phone. Are you sure about that? Seems like you'd be safer just jumping off a bridge and ending your lives more quickly." She tried to talk us out of it for a few more minutes, then finally said, "I don't want to see you two dead, so I'll help you as best I can. But I can't go in there with you. Sneaking chocolate and kitties is one thing, but if she caught me in there, she'd not only fire me in half a second, she'd *kill* me. You know there are rumors about people who've crossed Ms. Leery. They're no longer with us. I don't care about myself, but I've got four cats, two dogs, six chickens, and three bunnies to support."

"That's exactly why we need proof. Evidence." My insides whirred.

"I texted Uriah, and he said he'd meet us in the library when we arrived, to give us the keys—he stole a key ring from his dad," Dyna said. "I caught him up on everything that's happened."

Flo glanced upward. "Please don't let Leery kill him, too."

It felt strange to drive through Austin—there were new buildings going up everywhere, and there were shops and restaurants I didn't recognize. I thought about how you leave little bits of your soul everywhere you go. I'd left these tiny scraps of myself here in Austin, even in the airport, on its shiny floors and giant windows, and on these streets and in the scrub trees and Town Lake and the skyline. But I was someone new now, and those parts didn't completely fit back inside me anymore.

We reached the campus. I'd forgotten how ugly Thornton was. Its office-park, cinder-block-utilitarian buildings. The architecture seemed like a giant *screw you* to humanity. The opposite of the brownstones of New York.

No beauty here, you jerks, the buildings seemed to be saying.

Dyna narrated a campus tour in a cruise director's voice. "Note the beautiful grounds, carefully gardened so everything looks extra dead. Turning horticulture into morticulture one dead plant at a time, folks. At Thornton, we like to keep the soil bare in case we need to make an impromptu grave for unruly students."

"I really have missed you," Flo said. She told us we wouldn't recognize the library, since Ms. Leery had made some changes.

"Half of our library doesn't have books anymore—everything's going digital."

"That's just sad," Dyna said.

The campus was eerily quiet. We passed the herb garden—now mostly dead—and I thought of Gertrude. I felt a knot in my throat, missing her.

We arrived at the main building, and texted Uriah, who met us in the parking lot behind the administrative building. He wore a dark green hoodie, and his eyes lit up as he approached us. He always managed to say a thousand words with his eyes.

He held up a giant set of keys.

"You're the best," Dyna said, and hugged him.

"Well, I'm pretending I haven't seen any of this," Flo said. "I have to get back to the kitchen and place the food orders for next week. If I can concentrate." She hugged us again. "Just whatever you do, don't get caught. I'll keep an eye out on the parking lot so I can tell you if I see Leery or anyone returning, and give you a good warning to get out of there. Be safe, okay? Call me if you need anything."

We nodded and thanked her and followed Uriah into the administrative building. He bounced as he walked, happy to see us. We followed him up three flights of stairs and down a long hallway. The giant key chain kept jingling.

We reached Ms. Leery's office door, with its "Headmistress" sign on the thick gold plaque.

Uriah unlocked it for us.

We stepped inside.

It looked almost the same as the last time I'd seen it—the giant drapes and her huge black wooden desk—but this time, the closer I looked, I noticed how everything was plastic and particle board. The fake tree next to her desk looked extra forlorn. Only the top leaves had been dusted, so the bottom ones were coated in an even thicker layer of dusty fur. She'd taken the bird paintings down. Did she know we suspected her?

We walked across the room to the photo wall. "Look," Dyna said, and pointed. The matching photo from the diary was gone, too. She'd replaced the space on the wall with a generic picture of Thornton's campus, cut from a brochure.

"She took it off the wall," Dyna said. "She must've known we were close to finding the diary. Nanette or Clifford—or someone—must have told her."

The skin on my neck prickled. Dyna sat at the giant black desk. She picked up a pair of glasses—Ms. Leery's spare reading glasses—and put them on her nose, cleared her throat, and pretended to address an invisible audience. "Good afternoon, losers," she said in a gravelly voice. "I hope you're having a truly awful day."

I laughed—I needed to laugh. "We better hurry," I said. "Let's search the file room."

Uriah unlocked the door to the file room for us. His eyes were wider than usual. He looked nervous.

"Have you been in there before?" I asked him.

He shook his head. The door creaked open.

thirty-three
THE ROOM OF SECRETS

The smell wafted up in a cloud, redolent of cake and cream and coffee, doughnuts and something slightly rancid. In the center of the room, a large metal table was covered with bakery boxes and potato chip bags, a box of Swiss Rolls, and empty candy wrappers everywhere. So this was where all the confiscated care packages went.

And laundry. Piles of laundry—heaps of sweatshirts and ratty old clothes covered every chair and the small sofa, and mountains of fleece blankets lay in the corners, as if someone liked to sleep here.

Was that a bottle of gin?

There was a giant stack of advance copies of her book, *Top of the Class*, too. Uriah pointed at the gray metal file drawers—rows and rows of them, covering two whole walls of the room. He moved to the doorway and motioned that he'd stand guard for us outside.

"Thank you," Dyna said. "Knock three times if she's coming, okay? Or call my phone? Or just bang on the wall or something?"

He nodded. He stood with his legs still, glancing around like a gentle soldier.

I surveyed the towering walls of files. "We'd better start." They were organized by category—faculty, curriculum, grades—I looked in each file drawer, but I couldn't find the "Lucy Clark" or "Willa Thornton History" files I'd seen before.

"They must be here somewhere," Dyna said.

We searched drawer after drawer. There were files marked "Building Renovations," "Educational Philosophies and Pedagogy," and files about every teacher who'd ever been in the school. I opened another drawer.

Files marked "Students: Past" and "Students: Present."

"I found current students," I said.

I saw Dyna's name first. Her file was thin, and she ran over and pulled it out. Then I found mine—the "Lucy Clark" file. It was one of the thickest. I opened it. There was my admissions application, and the report from the Incident—a copy of the one that had been given to Nanette—and all my grades, and my artwork.

I touched my old narwhal cat and hedgehog unicorn drawings and took them out of the file. It felt like finding a part of me.

I remembered how I used to feel at Thornton all the time, like I was swimming in a radioactive stew, but it became so normal. A constant feeling of walking on eggshells, of not really understanding how to let your soul survive, of feeling scared all the time—like I felt now.

I glanced at the clock on the wall. Time was running out. "We should hurry. She could come back early."

I put the file back in the drawer, and we spent a half hour combing through file after file, drawer after drawer, looking for anything under Willa Thornton, Family, and History, until finally, on the top row, in the very back, was an unmarked category—the only cabinet without a label. I opened it. In it was one file folder with "Willa Thornton History" in the corner.

I pulled it out. Inside the file were more photos of Willa Thornton, and there it was—Willa smiling at the camera in her tiger brooch. The photo Ms. Leery had taken off the wall.

Next to the photo were four pieces of paper. The first was a birth certificate. For a baby boy born on June 17, 1957. The birth certificate was Clifford's.

Mother: B. Leery
Father: Unknown

"Look at this." I showed it to Dyna.

"Oh my god. She's Clifford's mother. But what about the

DNA test?" Dyna asked.

"They said it was a mail-in one. If Clifford and Beverly planned this together, then he could've switched the sample with Beverly's."

The next piece of paper was a note in Ms. Leery's neat, exacting handwriting, each line in a different color of ink. Another accounting:

Diamond, June 1957, payment wired, $6,000.

Emerald, July 1957, payment wired, $1,000.

Pink diamond, December 1957, payment wired, $37,000.

Blue diamond, 1962, payment wired, $120,000.

Red diamond, 1964, payment wired, $100,000.

The sales continued. I thought of something. I picked up a copy of *Top of the Class* from the table and glanced at the biography on the back. *Beverly Leery is a self-made business leader and award-winning educator who has held jobs ranging from teacher, member of the Texas Ethics Commission, field hockey coach, hospital administrator, coveted speaker, philanthropist, and writer.* Hospital administrator. Edith had written in her diary that Kestrel had different jobs, including cleaning rooms at the local hospital. *Administrator* was her "reinvented" code.

She wasn't self-made. Her money came from Edith.

I looked through the rest of the papers in the file. In 1957, there was another handwritten receipt, to Willa, her mother, for $25,758.

"That debt to her mother was in the diary. She paid it back by selling the jewels from Edith's watch," I said. "And there's a notation here for selling a pink diamond in 2001—that was the year she started this school. Started it from 'nothing.'"

The money she invested in my father's career—for him to reinvent himself—must have been to make him feel he owed her something all his life. It must have been stolen money, too.

The last piece of paper was a recent receipt from April 12. The day I sat in her office and saw her hold this folder.

We have evaluated your double rose-cut yellow diamond ring and can offer you payment by Friday for $12,900.

Not enough money. She would want more.

I reached my hand down into the hanging file to see if anything else was there. The file was empty, but it was slightly raised. It looked like something was underneath.

A dark blue box. I pulled it out. I opened the little gold clasp.

Edith's watch. The remains of it, empty flower shapes that had been pried open, gnarled, and ruined—all the stones had been removed.

I picked it up and turned it over. The back read: THE GRAYSON JEWELRY COMPANY, NEW YORK, NEW YORK.

I glanced at the clock. "Let's get going soon in case she comes back early."

I moved toward the couch to sit down and look at the file

and jewelry box more closely. I sat down on top of the piles of laundry and blankets.

Underneath me, the laundry moved. It groaned.

I screamed.

thirty-four

LAUNDRY HORROR SHOW

Dyna stood in place, stunned.

Blankets and socks and washcloths kept moving, falling on the floor.

Someone emerged from under the heap of cloth. My palms watered, an ocean rising.

Ms. Leery.

Dyna screamed. Uriah ran in. He saw Ms. Leery and backed away, slowly.

Ms. Leery blinked in the light. She looked groggy, her eyes bloodshot, unfocused. "What's happening?"

My legs wouldn't move, stuck in place.

"What is the meaning of this?" Her voice was raspy. She

kept blinking, as if she couldn't quite figure out if we were real.

She looked so different than I remembered. Was she always that frail? In my memory she'd been gigantic, looming, and terrifying. Now she seemed like a wounded animal, her shoulders hunched, her thin arms brittle. Her beige suit was faded and wrinkled. She held on to the arm of the couch, as if she was steadying herself on the deck of a ship. She stood up.

As she rose, her muscles stiffened and she began to return to her old self. My heart sped. Her features twisted with anger. She stepped toward us. Her face darkened, the volcano rumbling, ash about to burst.

Dyna said matter-of-factly: *"Run."*

I grabbed the "Willa Thornton History" file, my artwork, and the jewelry box, and Dyna, Uriah, and I took off as fast as we could.

"Stop!" she yelled behind us. Her voice was pure rage.

Her words grew fainter as we rushed down the hall and out of the building—she hollered at us out the window now, from her office—and we raced back to the kitchen, next to the parking lot.

Flo met us there. "What happened? I heard her yelling—I didn't even see her come back!"

"She was in the room the whole time!" Dyna said.

"We need to get out of here," I said.

"Hop in my car—I'll drive you." Flo reached for her purse.

"No, you can't," I said. "If she finds out you helped us, you'll lose your job. We'll run on foot."

Flo shook her head. "You can't—she'll catch you."

Uriah held his car keys up—the keys to his grandfather's car, Mr. Fell's black hearse-like sedan.

"Are you sure you can drive us?" Dyna asked.

He nodded.

"They'll punish you," Dyna said, but he was already running out the back door, toward his grandfather's car in the parking lot, and waving at us to follow.

"Go with him," Flo said. "I'll keep tabs on what's happening here. I'll give Ms. Leery a false lead—I'll say you're driving to Houston or driving back to New York. In the meantime, here's my address—please come stay with me till you figure out your next step."

We hugged her and thanked her, grabbed our things, and ran to Uriah's car. We jumped in and sped away, and the gates of Thornton Academy disappeared behind us.

thirty-five
A NARROW ESCAPE

" I think we should go straight to the airport," Dyna said. "Flo's house will be the first place Leery looks for us. We can't get Flo in trouble." She sat in the front seat beside Uriah, who made a turn at the stoplight and headed toward the airport.

"You're right." We needed to get back to New York as fast as we could. I held the file on my lap. Here was the proof we needed. Finally, the police had to believe us.

Uriah kept driving to the airport. On the way, we called Mimsy and put her on speakerphone. I quickly told her what had happened, and that we needed to fly back now.

"I'm so glad you're okay," she said. She turned on her computer, and I heard keys tapping in the background. "Here you go—you'll have to have a layover, and the connecting flight is a red-eye, but this will get you out of there now. Let me see if I can switch your tickets."

We pulled into the airport, and Uriah followed the signs to long-term parking.

Mimsy said, "You're in luck! There are a bunch of seats left."

Uriah parked, took out his notepad, and scribbled:

I'm coming with you

"Are you sure?" I asked him.

He nodded.

"He can't stay behind," Dyna said. "They'll kill him when they realize how he's helped us."

Uriah nodded forcefully. He picked up the pen again and scribbled:

It's not the same without you here
And I want to help you
Please
I'll buy my ticket

He took his wallet out of his back pocket and handed it to me. I stared at his big eyes and thought about when I'd left Thornton weeks ago, and he gave me the copy of *Jane Eyre*—how everything felt so uncertain. Everything still felt uncertain, except for one thing: I was relieved to never go back to Thornton again.

I explained to Mimsy that we were going to need three tickets, and she booked seats for Uriah next to ours on the same flights. "I knew it was Clifford all along," she said. "All he ever wanted was Edith's money. He and Beverly must've planned this together. I bet he pushed Cyrus when Cyrus began to find out too much."

I touched the file on my lap. "I think Leery had Clifford put copies of my file from the Incident under Nanette's door so I'd take the blame for the attempts on Edith's life, and on Cyrus's."

"I think you're right," Mimsy said.

"What's Peter's connection, then?" I asked.

"I think he was in the wrong place at the wrong time. Maybe he bought Edith's diary from Cyrus because he sincerely wanted to help find her," Mimsy said.

"I think we need to confront Clifford as soon as we get back," I said.

"How will we get him to confess?" Dyna asked.

Mimsy said, "I'm not sure." She hesitated. "I'll meet you at the airport when you land. We'll make a plan as soon as we're all together again—there are three of us—four of us, counting your gentleman friend. We'll confront Clifford. Now that you have the file, I think the police will finally believe us." Her voice was strong and steady. "It's time to do it. To get our Edith back. Now hurry and get on that plane. In the meantime, I'll see if I can make sure Clifford stays put and doesn't escape, if Beverly tells him that we're on to him. Let me see what I can do."

I thanked her, and we said goodbye. We grabbed our bags

and headed into the airport.

As we waited in line to get through security, I started to get scared, worried that they'd issued an Amber Alert or something—but we were able to go through just fine.

We passed through security and reached our gate. Before our flight was called to board, Uriah answered his grandparents' texts—he told them that he'd taken his grandfather's car to go off on a hike alone in Balcones Woods, and he'd be back soon. His grandmother, Mrs. Fell, my old art teacher, said, "Wonderful, dear," and his grandfather said, "Stay out of trouble."

Apparently Ms. Leery hadn't told them what had happened. Uriah looked scared, but excited, too. Then he turned his phone off.

"Maybe there's no Amber Alert for us because she doesn't want to involve the police," Dyna said.

"Maybe," I said. "I hope that we can get out of here." I checked the time—ten minutes till boarding.

I took a deep breath—I had one more message to send, though the thought of it terrified me. I typed a text, my fingers trembling:

This is Lucy—I'm on a phone that Mimsy gave me.
I want to tell you the truth.
You might be receiving a call from Ms. Leery any moment.
Or maybe you already did. I hope that for the first time, you'll believe me instead of her. We have proof that she was trying to hurt Edith, with her son Clifford's help.

Here are other true things, too: since coming to NYC, I've felt like myself for the first time in years—my real self. I've always felt so scared of not measuring up to the bar you set for me. Not meeting your standards. Disappointing you.

I just want you to accept me for who I am.

I haven't been following your prompts for the diary. I haven't been following your food plan.

I want to come see the pink room. But only if you'll stop trying to change me or set goals for me or always put your own needs first. I want to set all the goals for myself. I want to feel that I matter to you.

I pressed send.

They called our flight to board. I shifted in my seat. I kept checking my phone to see if they'd texted back. Right before we took off, they did.

Thank you for telling the Truth. This is hard for us to process, but we will try. It is hard for us to understand why Beverly would do that. But we are on your side. It's time for us to be together as a Family. What we want most of all is to know you are safe. We love you—that is what most matters.

Love, Dad and Mom

I read those sentences again. And again.

Our plane took off.

thirty-six
INVISIBLE ARMOR

Mimsy met us at the airport in the morning. We'd all slept a little bit on the flight, but we were mostly coasting on adrenaline.

The closer we got to confronting Clifford, the more my heart echoed inside me.

"What's our plan?" Dyna asked.

"I'll call Edith's housekeeper, Cora, now—I asked her earlier to keep track of Clifford's whereabouts for us, to make sure Clifford's home," Mimsy said. "She said he's been acting normally, with no plans to leave." She thought for a moment. "This is the plan. We just do it. Without a plan. Sometimes you have to jump off a cliff and risk it. That's another Mimsy's Rule."

She dialed Cora, who said Clifford was upstairs in bed, still asleep. It was Trish's day off, and he didn't have another nurse scheduled that day, so he planned to stay home. Mimsy told her not to wake him, and not to tell him that she'd called, but that we'd be over as soon as we could.

She hung up the phone and took a deep breath. "If he's asleep, that's a good time to catch him off guard. Let's go over there and wake him up. Everybody ready?"

"I'm bringing this," Dyna said, hugging her viola to her chest like a security blanket. It *was* her security blanket. Mimsy had put it in the car for her.

"I knew you wouldn't want to be away from Rosie for too long," Mimsy said.

"I kind of feel like we need armor or a weapon, or something," I said. "You probably don't want to bonk him on the head with your viola."

"I could play screechy music till he cracks," Dyna said.

Uriah picked up a book from the back seat—one of Mimsy's books about numerology—and waved it in the air like a sword and a shield.

"That's a good weapon," I said. "Could do worse. What's my weapon and armor?" I picked up my bag with my diary inside it. "I could take out my pen and scribble about him till he cowers in fear. I'm sure he'll be terrified." I turned to Mimsy. "We could stop and grab you a costume on the way."

She touched the fabric of her muumuu. "We don't have time. This is my costume. I'm dressed as a crazy old actor lady."

"Crazy in a good way. In the best of ways," I said.

It took over an hour to get to Manhattan with the traffic. We approached the Village. Mimsy parked on Summer Street, and we steeled ourselves as we walked to the door. I tried to summon all my strength, my superpowers, whatever they were. I glanced at the little plot of earth Jack's mother had planted, where the ferns grew. Maybe I should grab a fern to battle Clifford with.

A man walked down Summer Street, and I did a double take—it was the hairy man from weeks ago. "Hey hey! My girlfriend—long time no see! Love that tushy!" he said.

"I know!" I said back to him. "I have an amazing butt!" I was clearly starting to lose it a little.

"It is amazing," Mimsy said.

"Completely," Dyna said.

"Thank you," I said, unsure of how this incredibly weird conversation about my butt had happened. "Since that's settled, let's do this."

We stood before the front door. Mimsy pressed the bell.

thirty-seven

A FOX'S RULES TO STAY ALIVE

Cora buzzed us in.

We rode the elevator, and Cora met us in the hallway. "He left ten minutes ago! You just missed him—he woke up and came downstairs, then he was sitting at the coffee table and said he was going to search for Edith—I tried to stop him, but he wouldn't listen."

"He left by himself?" Mimsy asked.

Cora nodded.

"Did he say where he went to look for her?" Dyna asked her.

Cora shook her head. "He seemed agitated." She picked up some papers off the coffee table and gave them to me. "Also, Jack stopped by this morning—he'd gone to Mimsy's house to see if you were there, but no one was home, so he checked here. I told him I expected you back later, so he asked if I could give this to you."

It was a handwritten card and three large photos. I looked through the photos first—they were of Mandragora. A close-up of a bee on a flower. The ferns in the Ruin. And the cut flower garden, more lush and fully planted since we'd been there.

I opened the card.

Lucy—

I apologize for the way I spoke to you in the folly, and the way I showed you that file. It was insensitive and I'm so sorry.

I trust you and I believe you. Sometimes I act like my dad—critical and judgmental—and I'm trying to change that part of myself. I don't want to be like him. I'm not him. But it still feels hard sometimes.

I went to Mandragora yesterday to be close to my mom. So much more is blooming now. Here are a few pictures—I took the one of the flower beds by the pond yesterday. The fairy-tale flowers made me think of you.

I'm not sure where you are, but please call me as soon as you return.

Jack

I touched the photos—real photos that you could hold in your hand, not just scroll through on a screen. I felt a warmth under my skin—Jack wasn't the policeman in Austin. He wasn't his father. In the photos, the flower beds by the pond looked so lush and full—it was an explosion of colors, with yellows and oranges like sunshine, and deep blues and purples. Petunias, poppies, sunflowers, and pansies. I felt a pang, aching to have Edith back.

"If we could find out where Clifford went, that might lead us to Edith," Dyna said. "Do you think there could be a clue in his apartment?"

"Let's check," Mimsy said. We went up the stairs and knocked on the door. No answer. She took her keys out—she still had the key to his apartment—and unlocked it. Uriah offered to stand guard outside, in case Clifford returned.

Inside, it was perfectly tidy, as it had been before. We walked down the narrow hallway. The coat closet was ajar—I looked inside. A short black coat—that had been there last time. And something in a garment bag. I unzipped it. My stomach dropped.

A gray hooded coat, just like the one Edith had described on the person who'd followed her. A coat that smelled faintly of that familiar cologne.

"It would be the perfect coat to wear if you wanted to follow someone—it would cover all of you and still look stylish, not out of place," Dyna said.

"He must've taken it from Cyrus, when Cyrus left it in the library. Maybe Cyrus found out too much about Clifford, and that's why Clifford pushed him," Mimsy said. "Let's keep looking—there has to be something here that will tell us where Clifford went."

We searched the apartment. In Trish's room, her craft table was neatly arranged, her baby penguin pictures in a tidy stack. The Levion notebook was open: *150 mg. Side effects too extreme. 125 mg. 100 mg. 50 mg. Side effects lessening but still present.*

Then we went into the kitchen.

On the table was a copy of a Fox's Rules column from April 1956—the one that Edith had left for us when she disappeared. This one had been torn out from the magazine.

Trust. Dormancy Is Not Death. Record Everything. We All Stand on a Precipice.

This month, design a bed of annuals in a perfect rainbow to shock the neighbors: red petunias, orange poppies, yellow pansies, blue ageratum, and violet snapdragons.

I still held Jack's photos from Mandragora in my hand. Red petunias, orange poppies, yellow pansies, blue ageratum, purple snapdragons. Sunflowers, too. It was the flower bed where the violas had been planted when Jack and I talked to Peter—that bare patch of earth that was filled with annuals now. I looked at the photo, then back at Edith's column.

At the Mandragora party, Peter had said, *I think she's sending a message to me in these flowers.* And I thought of Edith's diary, how her mother had sent her a message in flowers, too. *I love you.*

I felt a chill. "Someone planted all these flowers recently—they weren't there at the Mandragora party. All annuals arranged in this order. Not a coincidence," I said.

Edith had planted them.

She was at Mandragora. She was sending a message to us that she was alive.

"Maybe that's why she chose this column to leave. This column didn't have a clue to where the diary was—it had a message to us to not lose hope. To know where to find her," Mimsy said. She paused. "She's also in danger. If Clifford saw the photo from Jack, maybe he realized this, too. He's on his way to get to her first."

We left for Mandragora as fast as we could.

thirty-eight
MANDRAGORA'S MYSTERIES

We got in Mimsy's car and drove to Mandragora. We sped through the city, and the buildings gave way to trees and bushes and farmland. I sat in the front passenger seat, and Dyna and Uriah sat in the back. On the way, we called the local police, and told them we believed Edith was at Mandragora and in danger. They said they'd search the property and call us as soon as they found her.

An hour later, while we were still driving, the police called back—they'd finished searching the property but found no sign of her.

"How long did they search? Police are worthless. Mandragora is filled with secret hidden spots in its sixty acres. They didn't look hard enough," Mimsy said.

"I'm going to text Jack, just in case. Maybe he can help us have some kind of police backup. If he really does believe us now." I sent the text just as we arrived at Mandragora's front gate.

The gate was open. There was no sign of the police; they'd come and gone. Mimsy parked the car. "I hope we're not too late," she said.

I kept my backpack on, wanting my inhaler inside it—my chest tightened as we approached the stone mansion first. The front door was locked. We walked around to the back. There was no sign of anyone. We stepped out onto the main path.

"They could be anywhere," I said.

Mimsy spoke calmly. "Here's what I think we should do. To cover all sixty acres, Uriah and I will take the northern path, past the willows and the gravel garden, and you and Dyna check the southern route, along the woods, the big pond, and the Ruin. We'll scour as many acres as we can, as fast as we can, till we find them, and until more police get here—hopefully Jack will call in backup for us. Be careful, and if you see any sign of Clifford or Edith or anything off at all, call right away." She held up her phone.

"Is splitting up a good idea?" Dyna asked. "In thrillers and horror movies that never goes well."

"We won't be alone, and we have our phones, so we can keep track of each other all the time," Mimsy said.

My phone buzzed. A text from Jack. "He said he's sorry the

local police were no help. He's on his way with a friend from the New York City police. He said to wait till they get here."

We looked at each other. We were not going to wait. Not if Edith was in danger.

"We can do this," Dyna said.

Uriah nodded; he was fine with the plan. He stood next to Mimsy. Dyna and I said goodbye to them and walked down our separate paths. I kept my phone out, ready to call Mimsy in a second.

Dyna and I made our way through the forest, past the winding stream and the flower beds by the pond. There was no sign of Clifford or Edith. And then we came to the back of the Ruin, to the private, shaded area enclosed by ferns and the hemlock tree, and the small locked room with the green roof. I heard a faint, soft voice.

Dyna and I tiptoed. Who was it? The voice wasn't Clifford's— it was higher, whispery. Edith's?

My skin prickled.

It took a second to recognize her—her white hair wild and free, no navy uniform or headband.

Trish. I felt relieved for a moment—she must be here looking for Clifford, too. I held up my phone to call Mimsy. In a flash, Trish moved in front of me.

She pointed something in my face. My eyes focused.

She gripped a gun.

This can't be real, it can't be happening, it can't be her. That can't be a real gun. She'd never do that.

She swiped my phone and threw it against the Ruin's rock wall. It shattered. She grabbed Dyna's phone and smashed it, too.

She opened the door to the small once-locked room attached to the Ruin and gestured to us to go inside.

There were Edith and Peter, alive. Their hands were tied with rope, and their mouths bound with black cloth.

I couldn't move. My heart stopped.

"Sit down." She ordered us beside them and gathered more rope with her free hand.

Everything around me swirled. I turned to Dyna and put three fingers to my lips. Her mother's gesture of *I love you*.

Trish tied the rope to our wrists. She had a set of leaves arranged on a plate—they looked like *Brugmansia*.

Connections bloomed in my mind, like links in a chain locking into place.

"You planned this with Beverly and Clifford," I said. "We have proof—"

She made a scoffing noise. "Clifford is innocent. Everything I've done is to help him."

My wrists burned as she tightened the rope.

"We know Clifford is Beverly Leery's baby," Dyna said.

"We found a birth certificate. It said, 'B. Leery.' They faked the DNA test with her DNA," I said.

Trish smiled, the smile that once seemed kindly. "You don't know anything." She tore a section off a roll of weed cloth.

"We found a photo of Beverly Leery's mother in Edith's

diary. We know she planned this with Clifford. Her son," I said.

Trish flinched, then shook her head. "You're wrong. Clifford has nothing to do with this. All I've ever done is help him. To give him everything I could." She worked methodically. "Beverly likes to seem in charge. My sister isn't Clifford's mother. So much for your proof."

I couldn't absorb what she was saying, what she meant.

"Clifford is mine. *I'm* his mother. He's always been mine." She said it with pride and a glance at Edith, envious and punishing.

Images and words flashed through my mind.

My sister, Bea, Ms. Leery had said. B. Bea. Beatrice. *Trish*.

The kestrel paintings in her office. *My sister, Bea, painted that when she was your age*, Ms. Leery had said. I pictured Trish at her craft table. Her paints.

Hovering over Clifford. Getting trained in physical therapy to help him. Her selfless, lifelong devotion to him. Her son.

Her knowledge of medical conditions, of Edith's heart condition, and digoxin. She knew about plants because Edith had taught that to her here, almost sixty years ago. She knew the paraquat was in the shed because she'd seen it there herself.

When they explored Mandragora, Clifford knew the secret spots—the hollowed-out cottonwood tree—because Trish had known them well, too. When Trish seemed scared of Clifford after Edith disappeared, she wasn't scared of him harming her—she must have been scared for herself.

"You're Kestrel," I said.

She stepped back and pointed the gun at me.

"I told Jack everything we know. The police are on their way now," I said. My voice sounded hoarse. I tried to keep it level and calm. It will be okay, I told myself. You can do this. I needed to keep her talking, to buy time until Mimsy and Uriah found us, or Jack and the police arrived. "They'll be here any moment."

She kept pointing the gun at me. Where were Mimsy and Uriah? Had they noticed our phone signals disappearing? Had they called the local police to come back?

I couldn't breathe. She took another piece of black cloth and wrapped it around my mouth.

My chest closed up. I stopped breathing. I closed my eyes.

"Stop!" My father's voice, faint and faraway.

I was imagining it again, like after the air conditioner fell and I was recovering, picturing my parents rescuing me— another fantasy, an impossible dream. I kept my eyes closed, waiting for the end.

thirty-nine
TRUTH

heard my father's voice, and my mother's. I opened my eyes. I didn't imagine it. They were real.

It happened quickly—my father grabbing the gun, my mother beside him, her face pale—a blur of bodies holding Trish to the ground.

I couldn't breathe.

"Get her inhaler!" my mother said. She got my inhaler out of my backpack and gave it to me.

"We're here now. You're safe," she said.

My mother untied me, and I took two puffs and began to feel better. Then the two of us untied Dyna, Edith, and Peter.

Peter helped my father keep Trish restrained. We called the

local police. Mimsy and Uriah found us, and we hugged each other, relieved.

My parents put their arms around me and asked to speak to me alone. We walked over to the side of the Ruin where the hemlock tree was and waited for the local police to arrive.

"I can't believe you're here," I said.

"When we got your text, we were in Los Angeles meeting with our producers. We told them our daughter needed our help, and they put us on a private plane to New York. We went straight to the apartment on Summer Street, and the housekeeper told us you'd already left, and we raced here," my father said.

"You believed me."

"We didn't know Beverly had anything to do with this. At the end of March, when Beverly suggested she had a perfect apartment for Nanette, I thought it was Beverly's good intentions. She always had such good intentions."

"The intention was to help herself," I said.

"The past is done. What matters is now, and we want to bring you home with us," my mother said. "All that matters is we love you."

All that matters is we love you. They had said that all my life, again and again.

"Did you really think you were doing what was best for me?" I asked. "Sending me to Thornton all those years? Believing Ms. Leery's word over mine?"

"What's in the Past is gone now. It's time for the present. We sent you the photo of your room—" my father said.

Something twisted inside me. I could live with them, finally—I saw the pink room in my mind. Except I didn't even like pink.

"In the fall, we'll register you for the local school," my mother said. "It's very good. I know you'll be happy there. We've waited so long for this. The TV show—this is big news that we couldn't wait to tell you—the producers want another season. They want you to be in it. On the show."

A television show. That's why they were here, that's why they'd rushed from meeting producers in LA to New York, to see me. I had the weirdest feeling, as if my organs were rearranging themselves, my skin itself, around this new information. A missing puzzle piece.

"The police will come and arrest Trish. You're a hero now. We're all heroes," my father said. "We're trying to help you. But you need to help us help you."

I always felt this fear around them—what was I so afraid of? It was part old humiliations, part longing, and part never knowing when that curtain would come down again.

"We'll get through this. We will. We're doing this because we love you," my mother said.

We love you. I'd clung to those three words for so long.

Except now it felt like a mask had fallen off the world, and it revealed that I hadn't been imagining how horrible Ms. Leery was—she was even worse than I ever could've imagined. The world had worse parts to it than I'd ever thought.

And I realized that I was lucky that my parents didn't raise me. It seemed a crazy thing to think, and it went against everything society said. Yet it was true. Nana wasn't second best. She'd given me one thing my parents never could: actual unconditional love.

I thought of all the people who lacked it, who withered from the lack of it, or who'd gotten a twisted version of love—Beverly and Trish, my father and mother—how that shaped them forever, their own inability to love.

And I thought of how, after reading about the intense love Edith felt for Clifford, I realized my parents had never felt that for me. It had been easy for them to have Nana raise me instead. That felt so disturbing, deep inside me—that disturbed feeling I'd felt since Nana died—maybe that was the core of it, the heart of it.

That was the truth, wasn't it? All these years. Thing One was right when she said the truth was too painful to see. I hadn't been able to hear it.

"We love you, Cricket. That's all that matters," my father said.

I thought of how "I love you" could be an excuse, or a promise, a pull, or a reward.

"Come back with us now. This will be in all the magazines. On TV. How you solved this case. How all of us did," he said. "We told the producers about your life in New York, and they were thrilled."

I paused and leveled my voice. Their words felt like pinpricks on my skin. "That's not why I did this—not for approval. Not to be on TV. I did it because I love Edith."

"Of course you do, Cricket," my father said. "What a wonderful woman."

"I can't go back with you. It was a lie really, that you couldn't raise me, that Nana had to. There could've been a way if you'd really loved me. You would've found a way."

"We do love you. How dare you say that? Of course we love you. You're our daughter. Our only child," he said.

I thought of the dictionary in Edith's library, looking up love. All those pages and pages of definitions for something that was such a mystery. And yet right now not a mystery at all—because deep inside you, you knew when it was real and when it wasn't.

I'd felt real love with Nana, Dyna, Gertrude, Flo, Edith, Mimsy, and maybe even Jack. That was a lot of love.

"Love isn't a transaction or something you toss around like a ball—it's not only a feeling—it's closeness and warmth and tenderness and giving, it's pages and pages in the dictionary. What we have is only one line of it. I had a full page of it with my cat. I spent more time with my cat. I had more love with my cat." My voice was calm and clear. I hadn't realized I'd thought that until the words were out of me, but it was true.

They looked like I'd slapped them.

"Lucy. Apologize right now. That's cruel," my mother said.

"No."

"Apologize," my father said. "This second."

I'd never really showed them my true self. I was always

339

scared to because my deepest, darkest fear was that they would see that person and not love me, not accept me.

"All this time, through all those mistakes you made—sending me to Thornton, not listening to me about Ms. Leery—you've never apologized," I said.

They didn't now, either.

"You're being unfair. And ungrateful. We always did our best," my father said.

"We've never lost faith in you. In who you can become. We know that you can be your best self, achieve so much, meet your dreams—" my mother said.

I said, "I'm not going back with you. I'm not going to be on the TV show. It's not about what I want to achieve or become. It's about who I am right now. That I have value and worth as a person just being who I am. I don't have to do things or achieve something for approval, for love. For you to love me."

They didn't respond.

"You don't even know me," I said. "The name Cricket was from before I could speak. I think you liked it better when I couldn't speak."

"Lucy," my mother warned. "Don't talk to us that way."

"You never loved me. Not in a true way."

"Enough." My father moved toward me. "The showrunner loved the idea of a family season. You've been under a lot of stress. We will take you back, and then things will be different—"

"No," I said. "*No.*"

I leaned against the hemlock tree. *I feel like myself here*, Jack had said here at Mandragora, in the tree. *I am myself here.*

"I'm not something you fix like a broken plate or revise like a term paper. I'm a person. You love a person by accepting who they are, not constantly fixing them or trying to shape or change or teach them."

They gave me that concerned look that people loved in their videos, faux understanding and faux compassion and faux sympathy. It seemed sincere through a screen. Not in real life.

For so long, I believed in the fantasy that they loved me because it felt good to believe it. It felt better than the truth.

And I realized that all along the world had lied—those Hallmark movies and greeting cards and glossy ads of families, and *honor thy mother and father*, as if they were infallible beings.

Real love was being there for you, day after day, adopting a cat together, watching hours of *I Love Lucy* together, teaching you how to tuck baby plants into the soil, inviting you into a home with tea and food when you had nowhere else to go. That was family. That was real love.

"I'm not going to apologize for who I am," I told them. "There's nothing wrong with me. I didn't do anything wrong. I was unlucky that Nana died—that's all."

I remembered how after my parents dropped me off at Thornton for the first time, I couldn't stop shaking. I snuck out the next day after lunch and walked to the edge of the school property, around the fence, to try to calm myself, and I wandered into a playground across the street. It was a Sunday; nobody was there. I sat on a blue plastic swing seat, alone, and watched droplets fall from my eyes onto my jeans, making widening dark circles. I thought, sitting there: This is how it will be?

After I returned to my dorm room that day, the droplets kept falling, a stream. I couldn't stop them. I lied and said I had an upset stomach and couldn't come to dinner. That was before my body became clogged, before I learned to stop crying, before the years of mud and debris.

The droplets came now, again, first one, then another—it felt awful and like a relief all at once.

My parents tried to wait for the tears to subside. They never had patience for crying. "Everything we did was for you. To help you," my mother said quietly. "To secure your future. Come with us. Now. We'll forgive everything once you come with us." She reached her hand toward me.

"No." I shook my head.

"You're coming with us." My father grabbed my wrist.

"*No.*"

His grip was tight. I wrenched myself away as strongly as I could, and I fell backward and hit the stone ground.

My head pounded. Everything went black.

part vi

HOW TO STAY SANE AND HAPPY
IN A DARK, DARK WORLD

To be nobody-but-yourself—in a world which is doing its best, night and day, to make you everybody else—means to fight the hardest battle which any human being can fight; and never stop fighting.
—*E.E. Cummings*

forty

blinked. My eyes slowly focused. I looked around. "Where
am I?"

"Lucy." Dyna's voice. She leaned in toward the bed and
squeezed my hand. "You're awake."

Flowers filled the room, on every shelf and surface. Clouds
of hydrangea, tulips, peonies, purple alliums, a whole blossom-
ing field inside.

"You're at Mimsy's house," Dyna said. "You had a head
injury. You spent one day in the hospital. You were awake, and
the doctors seemed sure you'd be fine, though they said your
memory might be hazy for a little while. Everyone's felt so
worried. You've been mostly sleeping since they released you.

Edith, Mimsy—everyone's okay. We've been staying here, taking shifts. We didn't want you to be alone when you woke up again." She had a book in her lap—*Jane Eyre*. "Your parents stayed in New York while you were in the hospital, but they had to get back or their show would be canceled. They left you several voice messages—they said to tell you to listen to the messages when you were feeling better."

Voice messages. Not enough. I remembered everything until the hospital. "Where is everyone?"

"Asleep." She pointed to the clock on the wall. "It's one o'clock in the morning." Her eyes searched mine. "Trish is in jail. Ms. Leery is, too. The board of directors is talking about shutting down Thornton."

I tried to let it all sink in.

"Here." She unfolded a blanket from the foot of the bed and put it around me.

"I'm so sorry." She pressed her lips together. "That your parents treated you that way."

"Humans. Not the best species in the world," I said.

"A Mimsy's Rule." She smiled. We were quiet for a while, and then she said, "I just heard from my dad yesterday."

"How is the Hairy Tomato?"

"He remarried last weekend. The not-so-surprise wedding in Bora Bora. I actually told him the truth—I told him how I got off the ship and I was here in New York City living in the West Village and he said, 'Wonderful!' I think he was drunk. The wedding had a theme—even though it was only the two of them and a couple of guests at their over-water bungalow hotel."

"What was the theme?"

"Being a dick," she said.

I laughed even though it made my head hurt. "That's a perfect wedding theme. He should write a self-help book."

"How to Be a True Dick and Find Your Own Dickish Path."

"How to Be a Dick to Your Children."

"Raising Perfect Kids the Dickish Way."

There was a knock on the door.

"Come in," Dyna said.

"Is she awake?" It was Jack. "I couldn't sleep—I thought I heard voices in here."

"She is." Dyna hugged me. "I'll be right back. I'm going to get you something to eat. The doctor said you'd be starving when you woke up."

"I am. Thank you."

She put three fingers to her lips.

I put three fingers to mine.

She smiled and closed the door.

Jack sat down by the bed. "What a relief. You gave us a scare there." He paused, and then looked me in the eyes. "I'm sorry I ever doubted you and Edith." He smoothed the corner of my blanket. "Trish confessed everything."

"What did she say?"

"She'd fixated on Edith ever since their days at the maternity home—she believed Edith represented everything she lacked in her life—advantages, privileges, wealth. Love."

"Love?"

"I think she envied the sense of security Edith had, even sixty years ago, because Edith's mother had loved her deeply. A sense of poise Edith had—still has. Even though Edith's mother was gone, that kind of deep love leaves its mark. The jewelry from Edith's parents was a symbol of that."

He hesitated. "Trish gave birth to Clifford just twelve hours after Edith gave birth to her baby—Edith's baby also caught the polio virus in the newborn ward—there was an outbreak. Unfortunately, Edith's baby died three days after birth."

"Oh no." My chest felt hollow, thinking of Edith hearing that news. I hugged my elbows. "Why didn't Trish ever tell Clifford that she was his real mother?"

"Trish's entire life was built on a false story, like a house of cards—she did everything she could to keep the house from falling. It was a closed adoption, and she became a nurse and physical therapist to care for him—she started as his caregiver when he was tiny—and she didn't think he'd ever forgive her if he knew the truth."

"So she hatched the plan to get more of Edith's money," I said.

He nodded. "While Trish was at the maternity home, Beverly had a job cleaning rooms in the local hospital. That was how she was able to steal Edith's watch when Edith went into labor. And when Edith left the maternity home, Edith gave the fox necklace to the woman in charge to give to her baby, but the woman threw it away after Edith's baby died. Trish took it out of the trash, thinking it might be valuable, too, like the watch. Beverly saved it."

"In her file room, of course."

"Yes." Jack picked at the blanket's unraveling edge. "Fast-forward to years later. Clifford's condition is worsening. His adoptive parents have died and his money is running out. An experimental drug will help, but it costs tens of thousands of dollars. Beverly has sold off nearly all the jewels from Edith's watch—that source of the sisters' wealth has almost run dry. If Trish doesn't act, Clifford won't have the treatment he needs. He might also lose his health insurance, and they'd be separated permanently." He pulled a thread out of the blanket's fringe. "Over the years, Trish had followed Edith's career, and saw her online posts trying to track down her baby. So the sisters developed their plan. Trish hasn't aged well—she looks nothing like she did sixty years ago. She's gained over fifty pounds. Her thick, long, dark hair is now sparse, short, and gray. Trish was certain that Clifford would share his inheritance with her—and she promised her sister she'd share it with her as well, if Beverly helped her."

"The last jewel from Edith's watch was the one in Ms. Leery's wedding ring, wasn't it?"

"Exactly. Beverly never even married—she had the wedding ring made because she thought it gave her an air of respectability and prevented anyone from questioning where her wealth came from. She told people she was a widow."

I shook my head. "Why did they decide to send *me* here?"

"When Mimsy suspected Clifford, Trish needed to take the suspicion off him and herself. Beverly figured out the perfect person to take the blame."

I pulled the covers up around me.

"*You.* Beverly suggested to your father that Nanette move into one of the vacant apartments in Edith's building, which Edith had mentioned in one of her letters to Clifford—and Beverly concocted a way to send you to New York. They sped up their plan to send you after Mimsy questioned Clifford, and Trish worried even more that Clifford was a suspect. Beverly and Trish never expected that you'd bond with Edith and help her. Trish also didn't expect Clifford to bond with Edith. Trish confessed that she was adjusting Clifford's Levion dose to a lower level, because she was worried it was working so well that he'd no longer need her at all."

"That's so awful." I shook my head and adjusted the covers. "Your father finally believes us?"

Jack tried to put the pulled-out thread back into the blanket's fringe. "Trish was the 'medical professional' who convinced him that Edith had dementia in the first place. I asked him why he doubted Edith for so long—we finally talked it over. He's embarrassed that he didn't realize how much Edith's close friendship with my mom made him distrust Edith. Edith helped my mom when she left my dad—she offered her the affordable apartment and helped her with me—I never understood before how deep my dad's resentment and distrust of Edith was. It colored his view of her always." He stared down at his feet. "He apologized to Edith."

He touched a peony on my bedside table. "You solved an attempted murder case and a sixty-year-old theft. You're a much better detective than I am."

We heard voices outside the door, and Mimsy came in carrying a tray of soup and tea, with Dyna and Edith behind her. Mimsy whooped when she saw me awake.

Edith held both my hands. "I'm so glad you're okay."

She told us how she'd first had the idea of running away on our Sea Change Day, on the ferry. She was scared that the person going after her was Clifford. She felt responsible, and that she'd put him through enough. She'd put everyone through enough—people were in danger because of her. After the attempt at the Mandragora party, she decided to act, to take control and to write her own ending. She snuck out at night, changed into an old costume—Mimsy had given it to her years ago—in the ferry bathroom, threw off her coat into the sea, and took a car to Mandragora. She hid out in the old stone mansion on the property.

"Why the note, and leaving the columns?" I asked.

"I needed to leave a message for you, but if I'd told you exactly what I was doing, it would be hard for you to lie to the police—I didn't want to put you in that position. I knew from the paraquat poisoning attempt that the person after me had a connection to my past, and it scared me. Peter suspected that Cyrus was stealing books from my library, and Peter was so determined to find the diary for me that he paid Cyrus an enormous sum to buy the book back."

"What happened to Cyrus and Nanette?" I asked.

"He's out of the hospital, and they're investigating him for the stolen books," Mimsy said. "He found Trish's cold frame—a mini greenhouse—on the roof, where she was raising the poisonous seedlings she stole. He confronted her and said he was going to tell the police unless she paid him off. He also found that she'd 'borrowed' his gray coat, after he left it in Edith's library one night—that explains the cologne. So she pushed him. Nanette decided to move into a new apartment uptown. Clifford is still working at the florist shop. He's going to keep living here in the city."

I tried to take it all in.

"You look tired," Edith said. "I think we should let you get some rest."

"Thank you," I said. "It feels good to be home." And I slept and slept.

part vii

BELONGING

If you look the right way,
you can see that the whole world is a garden.
—*Frances Hodgson Burnett*

forty-one
A BIRTHDAY GIFT

RECIPE:
HOW TO MAKE A WHOLE NEW
LIFE FROM SCRATCH

1 serenade of viola music composed by Dyna
1 book, The Wisdom of Tree Energies, *from Mimsy*
1 vintage book, Green Thoughts, *from Uriah*
200 dahlias
21 weeks therapy with Dr. Jane Rosenbaum
1 new diary from Edith
1 set of drawing pens from Mimsy and Dyna

The forecasters predicted snow tonight, on November first, the first frost of the season, so we cut every flower in Mimsy's garden to enjoy before they died in the freeze. It was the night before my birthday.

Dahlias overflowed from every corner of Edith's apartment. The Poohs exploded like sunshine, with cherry-red petals and yellow tips. The Fuzzy Wuzzys had notched white ends on each pink petal, like frosted cupcakes baked by nature. The Mandragora Moons were white ball-shaped flowers, like tiny planets. Each with its own personality, its own sense of humor.

Edith was right: flowers that you grew yourself felt different. You'd tended them, cared for them, raised them, poured your time and love into each plant.

I could see why Edith fell madly in love with dahlias, why they were her favorite flowers. They were out singing when everything in the world around them seemed to be dying. Some had fluffy centers like powder puffs, and others were bigger than my head, with floppy faces like Muppets. Flamboyant, defiant, triumphant.

Tonight, as the sun set, we all sat in the library. Dyna played Rosie—she'd been accepted into the pre-college program at Juilliard. She'd started composing music on Mimsy's piano, too, and learned to play Edith's old theremin that Uriah had excavated from the unused room. She still played in the subway with Julius and Ramona, and a video someone made of one of their songs went viral. Yesterday, a producer for an off-off-Broadway theater contacted them about hiring their band for a show.

I'd gotten into a small humanities public high school out in Queens, which had a school garden and even a flock of chickens. Every morning, Dyna and I took the 1 train uptown together, and I hugged her goodbye before I switched for the 7 train to my school.

Uriah cataloged Edith's books and papers, holding each one like a treasure. He'd been working at it for months.

Mimsy read a book Uriah found in Edith's unused room, called *The Ancient Art of Tea Leaf Reading*, and examined her empty teacup. "A rabbit! That means success! This seems quite accurate, really." Underneath her cup was a script for a new production of an Agatha Christie play that she'd gotten a part in. The director had said she was a natural.

After Uriah cleaned out Edith's unused room, she invited Dyna and me to move in. Uriah was living in Clifford's old apartment upstairs and had gotten an internship at the Greenwich University library. After school and on weekends, I worked as Edith's official assistant horticulturist in caring for Mimsy's garden.

Jack was traveling—he said he was researching a top-secret case for his father—but he promised he'd be back for my birthday the next day. He said this would be the last task he did for his dad, before he devoted himself to his ecology degree.

I'd made some progress with making sense of everything that had happened with my parents. Dr. Rosenbaum said it was going to take a long time, probably my whole life, to accept it.

I kept thinking of what Edith had said months ago. *Stories can seem like tragedies, depending where they stopped. Now, taking the long view, all those things were sort of rough turns along the way, detours to get here.* Where I was now.

There was a knock on the door. Mimsy went to open it.

It was Jack. He stood at the door to the library, holding a gigantic white cardboard box. He came over to me. "I have your birthday gift. I know it's not till tomorrow, but—well."

"Thank you," I said. "You didn't need to—"

He placed the box on the floor in front of me.

"What is it?" I asked.

"Open it."

I knelt down, took off the lid, and out came a flash of gray fur—and a fluffy face and a pink nose. She nestled into my neck. Her little white paws. The three-quarter moon on her back.

I buried my face in her fur. My eyes stung.

Gertrude Badass.

Dyna squealed and rushed over.

"How did you find her?" My throat dried up.

"I've spent the last four days working on this—I figured if you could solve an almost sixty-year-old theft, I could find a missing cat. I contacted every shelter in Austin and the surrounding towns. I befriended about ten different cat ladies."

"That must've been fun," Dyna said.

"It is the right cat, isn't it?" he asked.

Dyna and I both smiled. "Yes," we said, and we nuzzled her.

"Thank god. Your friend Flo and her brother-in-law the

veterinarian helped—they put me in touch with a woman named Myrtle who had twenty cats in Pflugerville. The cats were perched on the rafters. One peed on my coat. Myrtle put me in touch with another rescue person out in Cedar Park, and that's where I found Gertrude."

I picked her up and held her close. She slowly blinked at me, then touched her nose to mine.

She'd been raised from the dead. I'd grieved her. And here she was.

"Can you stay for cake?" Dyna asked him. "We're going to eat it at midnight."

"I'd love to," he said.

I walked out into the hall, still holding Gertrude, to show Jack the birthday cake Dyna had made.

"Thank you," I said to him, "for finding her."

"I had to. I needed to make it up to you, for acting like my father. For not believing you when you were telling the truth." In the kitchen, he stared at the cake on the counter—a layer of chocolate and a layer of vanilla, and an entire layer of chocolate caramels on top, all in the shape of a hedgehog.

"It took so much strength to do what you did," he said. "To accept the truth about your parents."

"Did I accept it? Dr. Rosenbaum says that will probably take my whole life."

"You made a choice in that moment not to go with them."

"It didn't feel like a choice—"

"That's it. You had the strength to do what you knew inside

you was right. To break free, for real." His voice was the gentle, soft one from in the hemlock tree, his words slow and measured, each carrying his thoughts, considered, like a weight on a limb.

The refrigerator hummed and Gertrude meowed. He leaned down and scratched her head, his face an inch from mine. He whispered to her, "You're home."

I kissed him.

His lips felt soft and he kissed me gently, then strongly. I touched his hair, realizing how much I'd wanted to for months.

He caught his breath. He held me to him and kissed my forehead, and then kissed my lips again. "This is against New York State law," he said.

"What?"

"The age of consent in New York is seventeen."

"Consent for kissing? Is that part of the law?"

"I think so," he said.

"Then I give you my consent now and at midnight when I'm seventeen."

"Look. We're in a dahlia patch," he said, looking around us at the buckets and mason jars and vases filled with dozens of flowers.

He held my hand. I ran my fingers across his palm, the roughness and crevices, his thousand-year-old hands. Those withered and scarred hands, which were around me now, holding me to him like a whole secret world, a gentle castle.

forty-two
HOME

W e ate dinner, built a fire in the fireplace, and stayed up till midnight, till my official birthday.

Edith sat at her desk in the corner, typing on an antique red typewriter that Uriah had unearthed from the unused room. She'd given Peter the first draft of her memoir to read when they finally took their honeymoon trip together, and was working on the second draft now. They were still married, and still lived in their own separate apartments, which was the way she liked it.

Dyna played Rosie, and the notes floated through the room.

Jack read *Ferns of North America* across from me on the window seat.

The fire murmured and crackled, and Gertrude lay on my lap, curled into a ball. Wiggy was enjoying a big pile of roast chicken in Jack's apartment, happily alone.

Out the window, the snow started in soft, giant flakes.

I opened the new diary that Edith had given me. I drew a cross-hatched picture of Gertrude and her adventures while we were apart—she flew through a lava sea, defeating warthogs and blobfishes, and now here she was.

I wrote:

Lucy's Rules for Living

1. Life is strange and messy and you are strange and messy. Strange and messy is beautiful.
2. We all stand on a precipice. Choose.
3. You'll always find your way home.
4. There are no rules. And if you think there are any, break them.

I leaned back into the library's window seat and gazed at the street below, at the snow sugaring the parked cars and the tiny patch of earth that held the ferns and the fairy-like flowers that had died back months ago. I knew that underneath, those flowers weren't dead at all. They were quietly gathering their strength to bloom again in the spring.

acknowledgments

This book would not exist without the faith and support of my extraordinary editor, Alexandra Cooper, who nurtured it since it was a quirky idea about a mystery and a garden—thank you for believing in this book.

I'm grateful to the fantastic team at HarperCollins, especially Rosemary Brosnan, Jacquelynn Burke, Lisa Calcasola, Aubrey Churchward, Shannon Cox, Audrey Diestelkamp, Katie Dutton, Lisa Lester Kelly, Ebony LaDelle, Lauren Levite, Alexandra Rakaczki, Mimi Rankin, Patty Rosati, and Allison Weintraub.

Thank you to Lisa Perrin for the beautiful cover art, and to Laura Mock and Joe Tippie for the gorgeous design, and for bringing Lucy's world of flowers and gardens to life.

Thank you to my agent, Emily van Beek, for your exceptional kindness and magical matchmaking. Many thanks to the wonderful team at Folio: Elissa Alves, Madeline Froyd, and Melissa Sarver White.

I'm grateful to the readers of various drafts of this novel for their wisdom and advice: Allison Amend, Dalia Azim, Judy Blundell, Kristin Cashore, Marthe Jocelyn, Dika Lam, April Lurie, Mariah Schug, and Rebecca Stead.

Thank you to my friends for cheering me on throughout my long writing process: Edward Carey, Elizabeth Everett, Carrie Fountain, Marissa Golden, Liz Gordon, Deborah Heiligman, Devon Holmes, Rose Isard, Saba Khan, Barb Kerley, Colleen Law, Amanda Levinson, Daniel Loayza, Elizabeth McCracken, Madeline Miller, Alexandra and David Nickerson, Mila Dever Ohlstein, Betsy Partridge, Sharmila Rudrappa, Delphine Salkin, Judy Schachner, Natalie Standiford, Sarah Squire, Nicole Valentine, Lara Wilson, Julien Yoo, Melissa Zexter, and Jennifer Ziegler. Thank you also to my local book tribe: Heather Hebert and all the staff at Children's Book World; Ellen Trachtenberg and everyone at the Narberth Bookshop; Wendy Dyer-Avis, Marnie Ray, and the staff at Character Development; and Brad and Andrew at the Narberth Public Library.

Thank you to my family for their support and encouragement: Jackie Rabb and Robert Meyer; Laura, Dusan, Mila, Iva, and Ana Knezevic; Andrea, Phil, Olivia, and Jack Dickey; Jeff,

Pam, and Aaron Silber; and Barbara and Michael Silber.

I'm grateful to Leif Richardson for taking the time to talk to me about bumblebees, and for his excellent book, *Bumble Bees of North America*, cowritten with Robbin Thorp, Paul Williams, and Sheila Colla. Thank you to Dave Kahn for the insights on heart conditions, to Anne Maloney for answering my questions about auction houses, and to Nina Brown Theis for advice on poisonous plants. I'm grateful for the books *The Healing Energies of Trees* by Patrice Bouchardon, *Molecules of Murder* by John Emsley, *The Girls Who Went Away* by Ann Fessler, *The Gastronomical Me* by M. F. K. Fisher, *Oaxaca Journal* by Oliver Sacks, and *The Gardener's Bed-Book* by Richardson Wright.

The food in this novel was inspired by Buvette and Little Owl in the West Village, Ladurée in SoHo, and an unforgettable experience at Curtis Duffy's Grace in Chicago. The allium flower dessert was inspired by Grant Achatz's allium creation at Chicago's Alinea (I haven't been lucky enough to eat there, but I hope to someday).

Thank you to Allison Amend for taking me to a secret garden in the West Village on a spring day, which inspired Mimsy's garden.

This book would not be the same without Chanticleer Garden in Wayne, Pennsylvania, where I wrote many of these pages; I'm especially grateful to Chris Fehlhaber for the many conversations at Chanticleer about the philosophy and meaning of gardens, which inspired so much of this book. Mimsy's garden and Mandragora are both based on Chanticleer, with its

Ruin, stone library, and magical designs. Thank you to all the staff at Chanticleer past and present, especially Erin Dougherty, Joe Henderson, Lisa Roper, Anne Sims, Bill Thomas, Chris Woods, and Jonathan Wright.

I revised the final drafts of this book during the pandemic, and I'm grateful to Dika Lam for the daily talks and laughs, and to my writing group, the Misanthropic Stabbers, for refilling the well during our many Zooms.

Thank you, especially, to Delphine, Leo, and Marshall, with all my love.